"Did I frighten you?" Jack asked gently, cursing himself and his odd, compelling need to be near her.

"It's okay." She touched his arm—a quick, light touch, but it was enough to send a jolt through him. Just like before.

Staring at her, he wondered if she'd felt it, too.

"I saw you were out for a walk. Since I am, too, I thought I'd ask if you minded if I joined you." He smiled at her, wondering why she didn't smile back. They'd agreed to be friends, after all.

"We can't hold hands," she blurted, her face turning a becoming shade of pink. "I have to apologize for that before. I don't know what I was thinking. I never should have..."

"It's okay." Interrupting her before he did something even worse, like kiss her, he hid his smile. "You're a good person, Sophia Hannah. You didn't do anything wrong."

If anything, his praise made her blush even harder.

She muttered something under her breath that sounded like "If you only knew."

* * *

If you're on Twitter, tell us what you think of Harlequin Romantic Suspense! #harlequinromsuspense

Dear Reader,

For whatever reason, I've always been fascinated by cults. And one day, as writers do, I got to thinking, "What if?" What if a woman had been raised in a cult and knew nothing else? To her, that would be her reality, her life, her world. And then to have that world turned upside down, both by actions inside the only home she'd ever known, as well as by a handsome outsider...

The story was fun to write. I grew to love the characters, too, and exploring the various pathways to logic. When I'd finished writing the story, I wanted to go back in a year or two and see how the people of the cult were, what choices they'd made and how they'd continued on with their lives. Yes, I'd grown attached to many of them. But the one thing I know beyond a shadow of a doubt was that Jack and Sophia had found true love in each other. I'm quite confident the others would have found their own paths to happiness, as well.

I hope you enjoy this unusual story!

Happy reading!

Karen Whiddon

WYOMING UNDERCOVER

Karen Whiddon

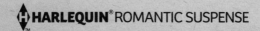
HARLEQUIN® ROMANTIC SUSPENSE

Recycling programs
for this product may
not exist in your area.

ISBN-13: 978-0-373-40238-0

Wyoming Undercover

Copyright © 2017 by Karen Whiddon

All rights reserved. Except for use in any review, the reproduction or
utilization of this work in whole or in part in any form by any electronic,
mechanical or other means, now known or hereinafter invented, including
xerography, photocopying and recording, or in any information storage
or retrieval system, is forbidden without the written permission of the
publisher, Harlequin Enterprises Limited, 225 Duncan Mill Road,
Don Mills, Ontario M3B 3K9, Canada.

This is a work of fiction. Names, characters, places and incidents are
either the product of the author's imagination or are used fictitiously,
and any resemblance to actual persons, living or dead, business
establishments, events or locales is entirely coincidental.

This edition published by arrangement with Harlequin Books S.A.

For questions and comments about the quality of this book,
please contact us at CustomerService@Harlequin.com.

® and ™ are trademarks of Harlequin Enterprises Limited or its
corporate affiliates. Trademarks indicated with ® are registered in the
United States Patent and Trademark Office, the Canadian Intellectual
Property Office and in other countries.

Printed in U.S.A.

Karen Whiddon started weaving fanciful tales for her younger brothers at the age of eleven. Amid the gorgeous Catskill Mountains, then the majestic Rocky Mountains, she fueled her imagination with the natural beauty surrounding her. Karen now lives in north Texas, writes full-time and volunteers for a boxer dog rescue. She shares her life with her hero of a husband and four to five dogs, depending on if she is fostering. You can email Karen at kwhiddon1@aol.com. Fans can also check out her website, karenwhiddon.com.

Harlequin Romantic Suspense

The Texan's Return
Wyoming Undercover
The CEO's Secret Baby
The Cop's Missing Child
The Millionaire Cowboy's Secret
Texas Secrets, Lovers' Lies
The Rancher's Return

The Coltons of Texas

Runaway Colton

The Coltons of Oklahoma

The Temptation of Dr. Colton

The Coltons: Return to Wyoming

A Secret Colton Baby

Silhouette Romantic Suspense

The Princess's Secret Scandal
Bulletproof Marriage

The Cordiasic Legacy

Black Sheep P.I.
The Perfect Soldier
Profile for Seduction

Visit the Author Profile page at Harlequin.com for more titles.

As always, to my family and friends.
Love you all so much!

Chapter 1

Sophia Hannah loved her job working as an assistant in the Children of Eternity, or COE, medical clinic. They worked hard at matching their young adults with the perfect job. Sometimes there were false starts, but not in Sophia's case. She'd truly found her niche assisting Dr. Drew, its main physician.

As COE grew, the medical needs of its members multiplied, and a few years ago Dr. Drew had finally brought in someone else to help Sophia. An older woman named Ana. She didn't like to work too hard, using her age as an excuse to sit back and watch while Sophia bustled around. But Sophia didn't really mind. Staying busy made the day go by fast. And since she hadn't yet married or started a family, she wasn't in a huge hurry to go home after the clinic closed, so she used that time to catch up.

Right now, Ana had disappeared again. A few times

Sophia had seen her outside chatting with one of her friends. She figured Ana's lack of a strong work ethic, something highly prized within COE, might be the reason why she kept getting moved between jobs. Ana had once boasted that she'd worked at ten different things.

The front door opened and Ana came in. Her normally pale skin looked pink and her faded blue eyes sparkled.

"Sophia, you're not going to believe this! I have great news!" she exclaimed. Though she kept her wiry gray hair pulled back in a bun, some pieces had escaped here and there, giving her a slightly disheveled appearance. She wore COE's typical golden band around her throat, a choker-like piece of jewelry that indicated she was married. Here in the COE compound, these necklaces were preferred over a wedding ring. Sometimes late at night, Sophia ached with the desire to wear one. But so far, no man had even showed interest in her, never mind claiming her as his wife.

"Sophia?" Ana prodded. "Don't you want to know?"

Ana had clearly been gossiping, an activity that was frowned upon.

"Aren't you even curious?" Ana asked. "You should be, because this concerns you."

For whatever reason, possibly her innate stubbornness, Sophia didn't want to give Ana the satisfaction of showing interest. Instead she tilted her head, eyed the other woman and waited.

"You've been claimed!" Ana exclaimed. "Great honor and prestige has been heaped upon you, lucky girl."

"Claimed?" All Sophia could do was repeat the word. "But I haven't even been courted by anyone."

"Pfffft." Ana waved away her concern. "This situation is different. You'll need to begin preparations immediately, as your new husband-to-be is impatient. I was told that your wedding is to be in one month."

One month? Sophia stared, her heart racing. "Are you playing a joke on me?" she asked. "Because if you are, this isn't the slightest bit funny."

"I'm not, I swear," Ana said.

"Where did you get this information?" Sophia asked as she tried to figure out who among the many unmarried young men might have claimed her. The situation seemed strange, wrong somehow. She wanted to be courted, to fall in love. But this…

"Well?" Ana demanded, clearly annoyed at Sophia's lack of outward reaction. "Aren't you curious? Along with excited, ecstatic, thrilled? All perfectly reasonable reactions to news such as this."

"Of course I am." Sophia kept her voice calm as she spoke the lie. Truth be told, her insides were now a twisted mess of nerves. While she had been impatiently waiting to be claimed for six years, ever since she'd turned eighteen, the way it was happening had her sick with dread.

This was not routine or normal. COE was all about both of those things.

"Girl, you sure don't act like it," Ana grumbled. "You haven't even asked who he is."

Mentally, Sophia listed and discarded the names of any man who might be about to become her new husband, and came up empty. She'd rarely dated, and she couldn't imagine anyone having the gall to announce a marriage that she hadn't even agreed to.

"Tell me," she demanded, partly ashamed and partly worried. "Who is he?"

"Okay, okay." Grinning, Ana actually made a show

of looking around as if to ensure no one else might be listening. "You've somehow managed to catch the eye of our leader, Ezekiel. That's why the announcement is being made without your consent. You're lucky, because you will be honored above all other women." Her smile turned a touch malicious. "Well, except for all his other wives."

Ezekiel. Dumbfounded, Sophia stared, hoping against hope that the other woman would poke her and admit she had only been joking. Ezekiel must be at least eighty years old and she'd never even met him. Alone among the people he led, he was permitted to marry more than once. Many of his wives were old enough to be Sophia's grandmother.

Instead, Ana cocked her head. "You should be celebrating," she prompted. "Yet you don't even look happy, never mind thrilled."

"Thrilled? But I don't want to marry him!" Sophia heard herself protest, shocked that she'd even dared.

Ana reared back, her eyes wide. "Don't say that," she admonished. "You know him choosing you is the highest honor."

She shuddered. "I just can't do it." This protest came out weaker. They both knew she had no choice whatsoever. Not in this. And after her wedding, not in anything.

Hurriedly, Sophia dropped into a chair before her legs gave out. "When did he even see me?" she wondered. "I assume he must have. Otherwise why would he have singled me out? I'm just one of many."

Making a face at her, Ana shook her head. "I'm sure he must have caught a glimpse of you somewhere. I know you don't realize it, but you're actually really pretty."

"Right." If she truly had real beauty, the other young men would have been vying to become her husband the instant she'd turned eighteen. Instead she'd turned twenty-four, still single, without ever truly being courted.

"You should get ready for when they send someone for you," Ana said.

Sophia winced, smoothing her hands down her long, cotton skirt nervously. Part of her still balked, though pragmatically she knew she had no choice. The people of COE knew to bow to the wise and gifted will of their leader. And if Ezekiel, a man so powerful he'd been chosen to be the mouthpiece of the Cosmos, wanted her for one of his wives, then she had no place wishing otherwise.

Except she did. She really, really did.

Jack Moreno sauntered into the dimly lit room. Without making eye contact with anyone, he chose a folding metal chair close to the back—and the door, which meant he could beat a quick exit once the meeting had ended. Since he'd only arrived in Wyoming yesterday, all the people inside were strangers, but they shared one thing in common. They might come from vastly different backgrounds and their ages varied from teenager to elderly, but they'd all once been addicted to some sort of narcotic. Meetings like this had probably saved more than one of them from dying.

For him, he believed this to be an unavoidable truth. The first time he'd walked into a Narcotics Anonymous meeting, having no real hope of it helping, he'd felt welcomed and, more important, accepted. Now, no matter where he went or how rough his life might become, he actively sought out the local chapter of NA. And even though it made him a bit nervous, he'd left his wallet with his ID, cash and credit cards back in the safe in his hotel room. His phone, too. More than once he'd been hit up by an addict more interested in scoring than recovering.

Funny thing about life. Each time he'd been actually convinced he'd hit rock bottom, something happened to turn his life around.

Like the job that had brought him to this little town in the middle-of-nowhere Wyoming. Since he'd started his own private investigation firm, any kind of work had been few and far between. He'd begun to despair, wondering how he was going to pay his rent, when the Bartlett family had showed up on his doorstep wanting to hire him.

Wanting, hell. They'd *begged* him to take their case.

After listening to their story, Jack had agreed to help. Even if he'd been drowning in work—which he definitely wasn't—their case had intrigued him. Of course, anything involving a missing child and a huge cult called the Children of Eternity would. Their compound was located about ten miles from the town of Landon, Wyoming, which was why he'd traveled here.

The first thing he'd done was locate the local NA chapter.

Now that he was seated, Jack allowed himself to check out the others in the room. The group was small, which was to be expected due to the size of the town. But wherever he was, addiction didn't discriminate. Young and old, several races and all types of people were represented here. He counted maybe twenty-five souls in various stages of recovery.

Good. Maybe here, someone would let down their guard enough to talk to him about COE. So far, despite numerous inquiries around town, he'd learned exactly zero about the cult. Wait, scratch that. He'd learned the good townspeople of Landon distrusted and disliked the cult members. Despite that, they weren't willing to discuss their reasons why. Of course, it didn't help that they were suspicious of any outsiders.

A tall, heavyset woman went to the podium at the front of the room. It appeared the meeting was about to start.

She cleared her throat and waited for the cluster of stragglers hanging out at the coffeepot to disperse and take their seats. While they shuffled into chairs, the back door opened and another man hurried in. Head down, he had the furtive sort of movements Jack so well remembered from the first days' attempt at getting clean. He knew desperation and despair would be in the man's face, if he would lift his gaze from the floor.

Since all of the chairs in Jack's row were unoccupied, the new arrival sat in the one next to Jack.

"Hey," Jack said quietly. "Welcome."

Though the man nodded in response, he didn't look up.

As usual, Jack barely heard the speaker's first words. Though there was no set speech, the message would be one of welcome, encouraging people to share and offer each other support. Accountability played a big role in the journey toward recovery and that was the reason they advised attending meetings as often as possible.

Though Jack had been clean six months, he still feared a relapse. Especially when his leg and back injuries started hurting and he found himself craving relief with the pain meds that had gotten him hooked in the first place. Prescribed by his doctor, he'd initially begun taking them to help with the loss of his leg and then later while he'd healed. But he'd quickly built a tolerance and had to take more and more to get any sort of relief. Soon, he'd found himself taking them like candy. In NA, he'd learned his story was an all too familiar one.

The man next to him shifted in his chair. When he eventually raised his head, he focused all his attention on the speaker. The tense line of his shoulders and the way he kept jiggling his left leg spoke of his nervousness.

When the call went out for people to come up and share their stories, Jack thought the newcomer might bolt.

"Don't worry," he said, touching the man's arm and keeping his voice low. "No one will make you do anything you don't want to do."

"Thanks," the guy muttered. After a moment, he stuck out his hand. "I'm Thomas."

"Jack." It was common at these kinds of meetings to only use first names.

One at a time, a few different people went to the front and told their stories. Thomas listened intently. Jack did, too, but since he had no intention of sharing anything personal at the first meeting, he felt relaxed.

Finally, after the last person had gone up and talked— and there were many who, like Jack and Thomas, did not—the meeting was adjourned. Coffee and refreshments were in the back.

Thomas eyed the group once again congregating near the coffeepot and remained seated. Since Jack figured he had a few minutes before he'd head back that way to try got get information from one or two of the others, he did, also.

"Are you from around here?" Thomas asked, putting his arm along the back of the metal chair.

"Nope." Eyeing the other man, Jack gave a casual shrug. "Just passing through. I always try to make an NA meeting if I can. It really helps."

"Any family in the area?"

Jack shook his head. "I lost all my family and close friends while I was battling my addiction. I've tried to reach out and make amends, but none of them want anything to do with me."

"That's a shame." Thomas sounded sincere. "Have you heard anything about the Children of Eternity?"

Just like that, every nerve ending went on full alert. "I have heard they're nearby," Jack said carefully. "I find the concept fascinating, to be honest. But when I asked around town, no one would tell me anything about them."

Thomas regarded him curiously. "What do you want to know?"

"Quite honestly? I'm thinking their way of life might be exactly what I need." Jack swallowed hard, glad he'd rehearsed this speech on the off chance someone connected would talk to him. "Simple and clean. Letting someone else call all the shots."

Bracing himself for the other man's reaction, Jack was surprised when Thomas flashed an approving smile. "Really?" Thomas shrugged. "That's refreshing and unusual. As it happens, I know quite a bit about COE. But if you want to discuss them, we'll need to go outside. I won't talk about them here."

Which sounded both perfectly reasonable and a little bit suspicious. Still, Thomas was offering more than Jack had been able to glean from multiple queries around town.

"Sure." Jack pushed to his feet. "Lead the way."

He followed Thomas outside. The sun had set, but

full darkness had not yet fallen. "I'm parked over there." Thomas pointed to a mostly empty lot behind a deserted building. "We can sit in my car and talk."

Instinct urged Jack to decline. Instead he heard himself agree.

As they approached Thomas's car—an older, nondescript black vehicle that seemed almost government-issue—Jack had second thoughts. "Hey, wait." He grabbed the other man's arm. "How about we just talk here, outside? It's a nice night and I really enjoy the fresh air."

Thomas gave him a look full of disgust. "I'm not going to come on to you or assault you, if that's what you think. Never mind. I'll just leave. I really thought you were interested in learning about COE." He shook his head and strode for his car, using the key fob to unlock the doors.

Damn. "Wait." Jack hurried to catch up. "I'm sorry. I didn't mean to give that impression. But you know, strange things have happened. One can't be too careful."

"I agree." Opening the driver's-side door, Thomas got in. "Are you coming or not?"

Taking a deep breath and hoping he wasn't making a colossal mistake, Jack got in on the passenger side. Turning to face Thomas, he opened his mouth to speak. Before he could say a single word, someone clubbed him hard in the back of the head.

For the rest of the day Ana left Sophia alone. Each worked independent of the other, taking turns assisting as their doctor saw patients. All were for routine things—a pregnancy check, a sore throat and someone who'd pulled a muscle while working in the fields. Every time Sophia thought about her impending marriage, tears threatened, so she decided it would be easier to push it to the back of her mind.

But that didn't mean she could make it go away.

Ezekiel. The Anointed One. Since she'd never even spoken to him, Sophia wondered if she'd be considered out of line if she asked for a face-to-face meeting, just to see if they'd be even remotely compatible. Unfortunately, she already knew the answer to that. Ezekiel got what Ezekiel wanted. Her feelings would have no effect on the outcome.

"Sophia! Ana!" Dr. Drew hurried into the workroom, calling their names as he came. "We have an injured man coming in."

The two women exchanged a glance. "From where?" Sophia asked, hoping it wasn't the husband of one of her friends. "Was he hurt farming or in the repair shop?"

"Neither," the doctor answered. "All I know is that Thomas is bringing this man in himself. Our patient has a head injury and is currently unconscious. Get a bed prepared in the infirmary. I'll let you know once he arrives."

Immediately, Sophia hurried off to do as her boss ordered. For once, Ana was right on her heels.

"Don't you think it's weird that Thomas himself is bringing him in?" Ana asked, wide-eyed. She had a valid point. After all, Thomas was Ezekiel's right-hand man and, as such, the second most powerful person in COE. If he himself was delivering the injured patient, the man must be someone very important indeed.

Barely twenty minutes passed before Dr. Drew hurried back, leading the way for two workers carrying a clearly unconscious man on a stretcher. Thomas followed along behind, his expression revealing absolutely nothing. If the patient was someone close to him or Ezekiel, they had no way of knowing.

Dr. Drew began barking out orders. As the more experienced nurse, Sophia fulfilled them, relegating Ana to handing over necessary instruments. Meanwhile, Thomas remained in the corner of the room, watching them all.

A large bloody gash at the back of the patient's head told them why he was in such condition. While Ana hooked him up to an IV, as well as the blood pressure cuff and the finger heartbeat monitor, Sophia cleaned the wound. "This will need stitches," she said, getting everything ready.

Dr. Drew took care of the stitching quickly, his movements competent and efficient. Once he'd finished, Sophia dressed and bandaged it. Despite being unconscious, with his dark shaggy hair and rugged features, the patient looked handsome. Sexy even. To her surprise, she felt an immediate visceral tug of attraction. This was so incredibly rare, she nearly gasped out loud. Wrong place, wrong time and definitely the wrong person. She wondered what was wrong with her. It had to be shock due to her impending wedding.

"His vitals are good," she announced.

Dr. Drew nodded. "He's taken a nasty blow on the head. We'll keep him under observation until he wakes. Once he does, Thomas wants to be notified immediately."

Again Sophia eyed Ezekiel's top assistant. Did Thomas know she was to become his boss's newest bride? "Of course," she murmured.

"Sophia, I don't want you to leave his side," the doctor ordered. "Ana, you can assist me in seeing the remainder of the patients. Sophia, beep me the instant this man opens his eyes." He pointed to the buzzer on the wall. It corresponded to the walkie-talkie he wore on his belt. "Understood?"

Both women nodded.

"Good. Ana, come with me," he barked, turning to hurry away. As Sophia watched them go, she realized Thomas and his two assistants had already disappeared.

Aware she might be stuck here awhile, even after her shift had technically ended, she pulled up the visitor's chair and planted herself in it. While she wasn't allowed any reading material at work, she did keep a pad of paper and a good pen. Sometimes she drew, sometimes she wrote poetry or amusing short stories. When she'd finished, she always destroyed whatever she'd created, fearful that someone would see.

The stranger in the bed stirred. Not a full move, just a jerky shifting of his position and a hitch in his breath. She put her untouched paper and pen aside to study him. His thick, dark hair was nearly black. Wondering if it would feel as silky as it looked, she glanced around once before she reached out and drew a few strands of it through her fingers. Yep. Exactly as she'd thought.

Her touch apparently made the man restless. He began tossing his head from side to side, muttering under his breath. When he gave a loud groan, she stood, eyeing the machines that monitored his heartbeat and blood pressure. While they'd climbed a little, the numbers remained well within the realm of normal.

When, after a moment, he didn't move again, she sat back down. She felt confident he'd wake soon and, when he did, no doubt he'd have a lot of questions. She suspected this was why Dr. Drew had requested immediate notification. He wanted to be the one to give the answers.

But she wouldn't press that buzzer until the patient had regained full consciousness. She'd learned the hard way that one of the worst things she could do was waste the doctor's precious time.

Sighing, she debated reaching for her pad of paper again. Her fingers itched to sketch the chiseled planes of this man's face. But such a drawing would take time and she didn't want to be caught with it, so she remained empty-handed, simply watching. And waiting.

When he opened his eyes and focused on her, she caught her breath. They were blue, a peculiar light shade that almost appeared gray.

"Where am I?" he rasped, wincing as he tried to lift his head.

Now she knew she had to call the doctor. "Just a minute," she told him, trying to sound soothing. "I need to—" Her words cut off as he shot out his hand and gripped her wrist. Hard.

"Don't lie. Tell me where in the hell I am."

Shocked, she tried to pull free. His grip was surprisingly strong for one so recently injured. Finally she succeeded in yanking out of his grasp and rushed to press the buzzer. Once she'd accomplished this, she spun around, chest heaving. "The doctor will be right in." Of course, she was short of breath.

He didn't respond. With his eyes narrowed and his jaw hardened, he looked dangerous. A jagged thrill shot through her, again making her question her sanity.

Then Dr. Drew arrived, Ana close on his heel.

"Here's our patient," the doc exclaimed. His tone and expression both were far too jovial—completely unlike him. Sophia and Ana exchanged a quick glance. More proof that this patient, whoever he might be, had some stature.

"You have quite the nasty wound on the back of your head, but we've got you fixed up. You'll soon be as good as new."

"Thomas has been notified," Ana put in. "He is on his way here."

At her words, the patient swung his head toward her. "Thomas?" The name came out a snarl. "That's exactly who I want to see. He's sure as hell got some explaining to do." Crossing his muscular arms, he glared at Ana, then Sophia and lastly Dr. Drew.

No one said anything. Even Dr. Drew didn't dare cross someone who mattered to Thomas and, by extension, Ezekiel.

The silence felt incredibly awkward. To everyone except, apparently, the patient.

"Well?" he demanded. "What's the holdup? Where's Thomas? One minute I'm getting into his car and the next—"

"You're here. Very good." Thomas strode into the room, cutting him off. "I'll need a few moments alone with Jack," he said. "Everyone clear out."

Of course they did exactly that, without hesitation or question. Prompt adherence to rules was one of the reasons COE ran so smoothly. No petty differences or spite or hate. Everyone knew their place and what they had to do and they did it. Sophia had always found that very comforting.

Until now, she realized. Now that she was facing a forced marriage to a powerful but elderly man, she felt a seed of resentment sprouting.

As she exited the room, she noted that Thomas's two bodyguards had remained. For protection? Or assistance?

One thing was for sure, she'd never know. She wasn't

at a high enough level. Yet. She couldn't help but wonder if that would change once she was married. No doubt it probably would. Even the lowest of Ezekiel's numerous wives had a more elevated status than everyone else. One of the few benefits, as far as Sophia could tell.

Chapter 2

"Well?" Head throbbing, Jack glared at Thomas. "You need to explain. Immediately. And whatever reason you have for what you did damn well better be a good one."

Thomas smiled coldly. "It's actually quite simple. You wanted to join COE. Now you can."

At first Jack didn't understand. "What?"

"Children of Eternity. COE. I apologize for knocking you out, but it was necessary."

"You hit me in the head so I could join a cult?" The instant he finished speaking, he realized his mistake.

"We are not a cult." Thomas eyed Jack with the same type of expression one might use to pick up a dead slug. "Perhaps I was too hasty bringing you inside."

Inside? Damn. Now he had to backpedal. By a strange quirk of fate, he'd somehow landed exactly where he'd wanted to be. Inside the compound. Remembering Thomas's earlier questions, he thought he understood.

Of course they'd want someone with little or no ties to the outside world. Jack fit that criteria perfectly.

"Sorry." Still frowning, Jack made a show of rubbing his temples. "My head hurts, so it's hard to think clearly. I'm not sure what exactly you prefer to be called. Why don't you fill me in?"

The answer came instantly. "We call ourselves The Chosen. All Children of Eternity are so blessed."

Of course. Jack nodded, as if he completely understood. Unfortunately the movement made his head pound even worse, making him wince. "Explain again why you had to knock me unconscious?"

"So you would awaken in your new life. Consider yourself privileged. Outsiders are rarely allowed here. You have truly been chosen."

"Sounds good," he allowed, even though privately he thought it was one of the craziest things he'd ever heard. "But what if I decide not to stay?"

At the question, the other man's expression hardened. "No one does that. You see, it's simply not possible. No one ever leaves. No one wants to."

The phrase reminded Jack of the old Eagles' song "Hotel California." The sinister implication behind Thomas's words didn't escape him. What the hell did they do if someone decided he wanted out? Kill them?

"I get it." Jack forced a smile. "Why would anyone want to leave paradise, right?"

"Exactly." Sounding pleased, Thomas walked to the window and peered out.

"But why did you have to slam me in the back of the head?" Jack persisted. "I would have gone willingly if you'd only asked."

"Because," Thomas answered without turning around.

"There is a certain ceremony to everything. This was how I wanted you to enter your new life."

Crazy. Were all the cult members this nuts? Jack knew he had to go along, at least until he found out what he needed to know. Chiefly, whether or not the Bartletts' son had been abducted by COE five years ago.

When Jack didn't respond, Thomas turned and studied him. "I'll let you get some rest. Once the doctor has released you, we'll talk about where you will be assigned." He turned and gestured to his guards to follow as he walked out.

Assigned. Sounded like a prison detail, actually. Oh, well. None of that mattered. He was on the inside, where he needed to be. He simply had to keep his head down and do as he was told. At least until he could gather some information on whether or not COE abducted children as well as adults. After what Thomas had done to him, he wouldn't be at all surprised to learn they did.

Head still aching, he closed his eyes and willed himself to sleep.

When he woke, the small room seemed flooded with light. Stretching, he gingerly moved his head. Good, the pain had gone. He pushed himself up on his elbows, looking around. The IV had been taken out and he was no longer hooked up to any machines. That must mean they felt he'd recovered enough to be sent to his assignment, whatever that might be.

A strange sensation filled him. Anticipation, something he hadn't felt in a really long time. This job had not only saved his business, but was proving to be a hundred times more interesting than anything he could ever have imagined.

Someone entered the room. Slowly he turned his head and met the wary brown eyes of one of the most beautiful women he'd ever seen. He'd noticed her before, but in his confused and painful state, he'd figured she might have been only a figment of his imagination.

"Hello," she said softly. "I'm glad you're finally awake. How are you feeling?"

"Confused," he answered honestly. "Just trying to figure out my place in all of this."

The strangest expression crossed her face. Only for a second and then the placid calmness came back. "You'll be fine," she said, her tone full of certainty. "What happened to you before? I saw your scars."

Shocked, he didn't bother to hide his surprise. "How do you...?"

"I work here as a medical assistant." Her simple answer came without pretense. "I assisted when the doctor examined you."

He decided he might as well be blunt. "Does that matter?"

"I don't understand. Does what matter?"

"My scars. Does the fact that I have a disfigured body impact my ability to join COE?"

Her lovely brown eyes were clear and guileless. "No. Why would it?"

This time, he had to work to keep his shrug casual. "I wasn't sure if you allowed people to join who weren't whole."

Instead of answering, she continued to regard him, her perfectly arched brows slightly lowered. He actually began to feel foolish, as if his statement had been ridiculous.

But it wasn't. He'd been rebuffed by enough women who'd been put off by either the fact that he was missing a limb or that the limb had been replaced by a manmade one.

And then she smiled. He felt the sensual power of that smile like a slow flame igniting his gut. "To be honest with you, I have no idea about that. It's very rare we even bring anyone in from outside. Thomas must think you very special indeed to have allowed you to join us."

Managing to smile back, he refrained from letting her know just how wrong he found her statement. After answering a few pointed questions at a Narcotics Anonymous meeting and following Thomas to his car, Jack had apparently qualified.

When she turned as if to leave, Jack asked her to wait. "Where are you going?" he asked.

"I have to let our doctor know you're awake again."

"First, tell me your name."

His question appeared to startle her. "I'm Sophia Hannah," she said. He found the way her full lips quirked as if on the verge of a smile unbelievably sexy. His entire body stirred. Of course, he ignored this. The last thing he needed right now was to get his insides all tangled up because of a woman.

And then, before he could ask her anything else, she spun on her heel and left.

Part of him wanted to go after her. Instead he hunted around for his clothes. Might as well get dressed while he waited to see what would happen next.

He located his shirt and jeans in a beige metal locker. They were neatly folded, with his briefs tucked in between. His socks and boots had been placed on a shelf nearby. Everything appeared to be in good condition, which meant whoever had undressed him had done so carefully. He wondered if the pretty little nurse had helped.

Glancing back once at the doorway, he dressed hurriedly, using the hospital gown as a sort of impromptu curtain. Just seconds after he'd finished, he heard voices coming closer. Male voices, so most likely the doctor or maybe Thomas and his bodyguards.

Three men stepped into the room. They all had a wholesome sort of look. Short hair cut the same way— one light, two dark—and identical expressions of earnest friendliness on their clean-scrubbed faces. Jack didn't recognize any of them. But then, why would he?

"Welcome," one of them said, stepping forward and offering his hand. He stood at least six-four, with an impressive girth. When they shook, Jack took note of the rough calluses on his fingers.

"I'm Phillip." He smiled, less of an *aw-shucks* grin than Jack had expected. "You'll be staying with me. We single guys all room together. Also, you can tag along with me when I go to work tomorrow. I'll keep you busy, at least until they assign you to your job."

"Assign?" That word again. Asking might be the wrong move, but Jack did anyway. "I don't get to choose?"

All three of the men exchanged glances before breaking out into laughter. Though Jack listened, he couldn't detect anything but humor in the sound. No uneasiness or fear.

"Nope," one of the other men answered easily. "I'm Randy and this is my brother, Jeff. In case you can't tell, we're twins. Not identical, though. But I think we still look a lot alike."

Glancing from Randy to Jeff, Jack had to wonder how he'd missed the resemblance. Same eyes, chin, skin tone and nose. There were a few differences—all minor—but enough to be the difference that would enable anyone to tell them apart.

"We work with Phillip," Jeff chimed in. He smiled

with the same open friendliness as the other two men. "If you're lucky, maybe you'll get to work with us. Ever done any carpentry work?"

Regretfully, Jack shook his head.

"Ah, well." Phillip clapped Jack on the shoulder. "I'm sure you have your own set of skills. Come on. We'll show you where you're going to be living."

After the three men had shepherded the handsome newcomer out of the medical facility, Sophia sat and tried to catch her breath. She wasn't sure what it was about the man, but she'd felt the strangest sort of anticipation whenever she'd been anywhere near him. A kind of thrumming in her veins that made it difficult to think straight never mind breathe. Though she recognized her attraction to him, she didn't pretend to understand why. Most likely because she'd just become newly engaged to a man she hadn't even met.

As if she'd read Sophia's thoughts, Ana hurried into the room. "Here," she said, shoving a sealed white envelope at Sophia. "Thomas left this for you on the front desk. It's probably the official notification of your engagement."

Accepting it, Sophia turned the envelope over and over in her hand. Part of her didn't want to open it, as if by not doing so, she could wish away her new future.

"Read it," Ana demanded. "If you're not going to, I'll be happy to do it for you."

"No." Using her fingernail, Sophia slit the seal. Inside she found an embossed white card. The front read *Congratulations!* Inside, the specifics of her upcoming nuptials were spelled out. *Upcoming wedding between Ezekiel and Sophia Hannah*, and then the date and time and place.

"That's it?" Sophia said. "Nothing more? I find this cold and rude and, quite frankly, insulting." Her anger surprised her. And Ana, too, whose eyes had gone huge and round.

"Well, at least it's official." Briskly, Ana changed the subject. "What's the story on him? The guy who just left?"

Sophia considered. "He's new," she said carefully. "Apparently, Thomas brought him in from the outside. I have no idea why."

Pursing her lips, Ana swallowed as she digested Sophia's words. Though Sophia could tell the older woman wasn't enamored of the possibility, she also knew Ana would never dare express disapproval about anything Thomas did. After all, Thomas only acted at their leader's discretion. And everyone knew that everything Ezekiel did was always, without question, for the best of his Chosen children.

"Well—" Ana dusted her hands on the front of her shift "—we've got more important things to worry about. We have a wedding to plan."

Sophia stared. While she didn't want to hurt Ana's feelings, she had always figured she and her best girl-friends would plan her wedding. After all, she'd certainly helped with all of theirs. Sophia knew they'd all be over-the-top excited once she gave them the news. Until they found out her intended husband was an old, old man.

She sighed. "Of course we do," she said softly. "But first I have to let my friends and the rest of the family in on the news. I'm pretty sure I'll have lots of help getting everything set up."

Narrowing her eyes, Ana nodded. "You do understand that this can't be just any wedding, right? You're going to be marrying our leader. Think back to his last wedding, if you're old enough to remember. Now *that* was a spectacle. You've got to think big, flashy and showy. You know Ezekiel will finance whatever you want."

All three of the adjectives Ana had just used were the antithesis of what Sophia had wanted. When she'd dreamed of her wedding, she'd planned more along the lines of classic, understated elegance. A quiet ceremony and later a joyous celebration of the love she and her new husband shared.

She didn't have that, either. There would be no love, no joy and certainly no celebration. At least on her part, though she knew she'd have to put on a show.

Did Ezekiel still even celebrate? After at least twenty-five or thirty marriages, she figured this would be old hat to him now. Since she didn't know him, she had no idea how Ezekiel felt. Though as far as she and everyone else was concerned, his feelings were everything. All that mattered was keeping Ezekiel happy.

What Ezekiel wanted, he got. And right now, he apparently wanted her.

Later, after arriving home to the house she shared with her best friend Rachel and two other single girls, she tried to summon up the appropriate excitement to deliver the news. Luckily, all the others were younger than her and had enough abundant glee to cover her lack.

"You've been chosen by our leader?" Rachel squealed, wrapping Sophia in a tight hug before spinning her around the room. "What an honor! I can say I knew you before!"

Her best friend's unbridled happiness finally coaxed a smile from Sophia. "It's kind of weird, though. He's never even spoken to me. I don't even know how he came to know of me."

One of the other girls, a quiet, mousy brunette named Cheryl, snorted. "Have you looked in the mirror lately?"

The others giggled.

"I'm sure he must have seen you somewhere." Heather, who shared a room with Cheryl, smiled. "He probably took one look at you and knew you were the one he wanted for his next wife. You're so lucky."

She did look in the mirror—every single morning when she got ready for her shift at the medical clinic. She knew some might consider her features pleasing if not ordinary. Brown hair, brown eyes. Definitely nothing extraordinary enough to draw any man's attention—witness her lack of marriage offers. And really, if one considered the fact that the only man even remotely interested in becoming her husband was nearly four times her age, the "struck by her beauty" explanation didn't work.

Cheryl, who was always up for a good party—hurried into the kitchen and returned with a bottle of homemade red wine. "We need to have a toast!"

"Yes, we do," Rachel agreed, going for the juice glasses. She brought six—all mismatched—out on a round tray. "I hope it turned out good."

Heather, who made the wine in secret, grinned. "Oh, it's good. Believe me. I tried some last weekend. Even Danny liked it." As usual, she blushed after saying her boyfriend's name. Everyone knew it was only a matter of time before Danny petitioned to become her husband. Some girls got lucky that way.

In fact, every single one of Sophia's married friends had been ecstatic over the man they'd been joined with in matrimony. Leave it to Sophia to be the lone exception.

"Hey." Rachel sidled up to her, handing her half a juice glass of wine. "You seem lost in thought. What's wrong?"

Sophia blinked, suddenly aware that everyone had stopped talking and now watched her intently.

"Are you all right?" Rachel asked, her low voice radiating genuine concern.

Wondering what would happen if she blurted out the truth, Sophia swallowed hard and tried to summon up a smile. She didn't know how they'd react if she shared with them her concerns. Later, she knew she could confide in Rachel. And she would, as soon as the opportunity presented itself.

For now, she needed to laugh and pretend to celebrate with her roommates.

Of course everyone wanted to offer their ideas on decorating for the wedding. Sophia made a face and relayed to them what Ana had said.

"You know what? She's right," Rachel said thoughtfully. "This won't be an ordinary wedding."

"I wonder if Ezekiel will assign some of his staff to plan the ceremony. Provide the decorations and everything?" Heather put in.

The other women murmured their agreement. None of them had ever been a part of something so big before. Speculations ranged from the outlandish to the ridiculously expensive.

"I'm thinking Sophia will want classic elegance," Rachel insisted. Since she knew Sophia better than anyone else, no one argued.

Classic elegance. Sophia wasn't even sure if such a thing could be applied in this situation. Glumly, she realized she didn't even care. For most of her life, she'd spent a lot of time imagining how her wedding would be. The colors, the dresses, the flowers. Where, when and the poignant reactions of the guests to her and her groom's individual, self-written vows.

None of that mattered now. She wished she could find something positive in all of this, but she only felt numb. And she tried hard not to picture her wedding night.

After the entire bottle of homemade wine had been emptied, everyone drifted to separate parts of the house. Relieved, Sophia escaped to her bedroom and plopped down on her bed. Earlier she'd thought she would welcome a good cry, but the initial numbness had seeped through her veins and now all she could do was stare up at the ceiling, dry-eyed and sick to her stomach.

Rachel came in quietly. Since they shared the room, she didn't knock. She sat next to Sophia on the edge of the bed and waited, aware her silence was its own form of support.

"I don't know what I'm going to do," Sophia finally blurted out. "I had so many hopes, so many dreams. Now they're nothing. How can I marry him? I just can't, Rachel."

Instead of overreacting to her desperate plea, Rachel simply nodded. "You don't care that it's a great honor, do you? Of course not," she answered her own question. "You've always been a romantic. This development calls for you to become a realist."

The words calmed Sophia, exactly as Rachel had known they would. In reality, there was nothing Sophia could do about her impending marriage, so she might as well resign herself to it.

"Status," Rachel said, poking her. "I know you're

looking for something good and right now that's the only thing I can think of. Right now, you're just a regular person. Sure, you're one of the Chosen, but so is everyone else. Once you're married to Ezekiel, you won't be regular any longer. Your status will be hugely elevated."

"As if I care about that." Sophia's laugh verged on the edge of hysterical. "All I ever wanted was someone to love who would love me back."

"Well, maybe Ezekiel will love you. And you never know, you might come to grow fond of him, too."

Sophia stared at her friend in disbelief. "Talk about rose-colored glasses," she said.

This made Rachel laugh. "I learned from the best, you know. You can't let your shock kill your positive outlook. After all, it isn't like you have a choice."

While her words might be harsh, she was right. Again. Because Sophia had no choice. She needed to figure out a way to come to grips with the turn her life had taken.

"I just need time," she said, her tone firm as her confidence returned. "Time to get used to the idea."

Rachel nodded and hugged her. "That's the spirit. Now, come help prepare dinner. You know it's our turn to cook."

Sophia jumped to her feet. "Good. That's exactly what I need. Busywork, to keep from dwelling on this mess."

"That's the spirit." Rachel grinned. "Much more like the Sophia I know." She linked her arm through Sophia's. "Come on. Let's make something delicious for our dinner."

Sophia let Rachel drag her to the kitchen. Reminding herself that she had time made it much easier to breathe.

Maybe she could even figure out a way to extend the time and make her upcoming wedding date even further away than the one month Ana had mentioned earlier.

She couldn't help but hope she'd have some wiggle room on the date.

Chapter 3

Following his new pals outside, Jack looked around carefully, squinting in the bright daylight. The sun, warm for spring, sat high in a bright, blue, cloudless sky. It wasn't humid, though, but a dry heat, and not nearly as hard to take as spring in Texas. The air felt different here, purer somehow. Must be the higher altitude. Surrounding the compound as well as within, there were lots of trees, evergreens along with hardwoods. His first impression was wilderness. The cult's encampment appeared to be in an isolated area, far from any other dwellings, towns or people. All around the settlement he saw nothing but undeveloped terrain.

The building they'd left, the hospital, looked identical to several other cinder-block buildings loosely grouped around what appeared to be some sort of central square. Everything had been painted a pale shade of dried mud. Boring, yet soothing, too. There didn't appear to be any external individualization—no colors or decorative accents adorned anything. He couldn't even tell which structures were residences and which were businesses—assuming they had any. He'd venture a guess that any type of monetary capitalization was frowned upon here—no doubt the leadership dispensed what was needed to the residents. That way they were dependent on the organization for everything in every aspect of their lives.

It definitely seemed slower paced, more evenly regulated than the competitive world he was used to. And as far as he could tell, none of his companions seemed to be suffering. As they walked, the other men joked with each other, jostling elbows and laughing easily in a way that reminded Jack of college kids. He supposed these guys weren't much older than that, which made him feel sort of ancient. But, no matter. He hadn't come here to make friends. Though being pleasant wouldn't hurt. More flies with honey and all that.

The paths were all gravel or cobblestone; nothing as efficient or modern as pavement.

His companions stopped in front of a single-story, unassuming building, one of many in a neat row. These were slightly smaller than some of the others, their rectangular shapes and placement reminiscent of row houses.

"Here we are," Phillip said, beaming with pride. "Home. Thomas wants you to room with me. Here, single people all live together, two to a bedroom. I have an empty bed since Prescott got married."

Jack nodded. "Sounds good."

Phillip opened the front door with a flourish. "Come on in. I'll show you where you'll be living."

Stepping inside, Jack looked around. After the outside, he'd expected a seriously Spartan interior, with scant decoration and functional furniture. He saw he'd been correct about the furniture—the small living room contained a boxy, two-cushion couch, one chair, a plain, rectangular coffee table and a matching end table. But the real surprise hung on the walls.

Paintings—splashes of lush color—hung on the walls. A landscape here, a floral there. An abstract, and a portrait. All of those in one room. Intrigued, Jack strolled over to inspect the landscape, which appeared to be inspired by the local forests surrounding the compound.

Now, Jack was no judge of art, but he knew what he liked and this—clean lines, bold brushstrokes of color—was it. "That's amazing," he said. "Who's the artist?"

"Me," Phillip responded, pleasure warming his voice. Jack turned to see his new roommate beaming with pride. "When I was in school, I demonstrated this talent, so I was permitted to keep it as my hobby."

"Permitted?" The word slipped out, but Jack felt it was reasonable.

"Everyone is allowed to have one hobby, as long as it doesn't interfere with their work and study of the *Volumes of Choice*."

Though Jack hadn't heard of the *Volumes of Choice*, it seemed pretty self-explanatory. It must be COE's religious tenet.

Instead of commenting, he moved on to inspect the next painting. A single flower, painted in five different shades of the same color. Beautiful, in a completely different way than the first painting, though the artist's style remained the same.

He moved onto the third and then the fourth. "You're really talented, Phillip."

Clearly pleased, the other man ducked his head. Eyeing him, with his large, beefy frame and thick, callused hands, Jack couldn't picture his fingers holding a paintbrush. Just goes to show, once again, Jack thought, that one couldn't judge people by their exterior.

"Come on," Phillip said. "Let me show you the rest of the place."

In addition to a cozy kitchenette, there were two small, identical bedrooms and one bathroom. If not for the brightness of the paintings hung everywhere, it would have been a very dull, even depressing, place.

"I sure am glad you paint," Jack said as he inspected his bedroom. A huge painting of a lake under a full moon hung at the head of the twin bed.

"Are you?" Phillip chuckled. "I was about to ask you if you wanted me to remove that painting."

"No. Please don't. I really like it."

"Great." Phillip backed out of the room. "Listen, Thomas wants you to go to work with me tomorrow. I start work at eight, so please be ready to leave by around seven thirty or so."

Surprised, Jack nodded. "Sure. Can I ask what I'll be doing?"

"Whatever I need you to." Phillip's easy smile seemed reassuring. "I work in construction, doing mostly interior finishing work on new buildings. You'll tag along with me and we'll see what you might be good at. Does that sound okay to you?"

Wondering what the other man would do if he said no, Jack nodded.

"Great. We eat supper at six. I'll cook tonight and then we'll work out a schedule for chores."

Before Jack could respond, Phillip closed the door and left him alone with his thoughts.

The next day Sophia reported to work, unable to keep from wishing her handsome former patient was still there. She needed a distraction, and she told herself it was only because she liked having someone to look after. The clinic had no current patients at all, and she didn't expect any to show up today. Dr. Drew spent one day every two or three weeks visiting each family groups' assortment of children and this was that day.

Often, Sophia went along with him. She had fond memories of her childhood family group and of all her parents. In COE the close connection between mother and child was severed once the child was a week or two old, when the infant was passed among a small group of nursing mothers so the child didn't bond to any one in particular. Despite this, Sophia often dreamed of the day when she, too, would have her own baby. The thought had always filled her with so much longing and joy. Of course, that dream, like so many others, didn't seem destined to come to fruition now.

For the first time she wondered about Ezekiel's children. He had many, she knew. Grandchildren, too. He paraded them all in front of everyone when the Chosen had celebrations. Ezekiel took pride in his offspring, along with his numerous wives. Of course, some of his children were actually twice as many years older than Sophia, of an age to be her own birth parents. And while she knew Ezekiel had a lot of wives, she knew nothing about them as he tended to keep them hidden away from the general populace.

While she loved the way her COE family raised children as a group rather than with only a small, singular couple, she wasn't sure how she felt about being one of many women married to one man.

Check that. Okay, she knew how she felt. She didn't like it. At all. Or wouldn't have, had her new spouse been anyone other than Ezekiel. On the plus side, maybe being one of many would mean once the newness wore off, he would let her disappear into the crowd and forget she existed.

The prospect of a loveless, unfulfilled life made her feel even worse. Tears pricked the backs of her eyes and she let herself wallow in self-pity.

"Girl, you're not going to believe this!" Ana rushed into the room, waving her arms in excitement. She skidded to a stop, eyeing Sophia askance. "Are you *crying*?"

"No," Sophia lied, wiping at her eyes. "My allergies are bad today."

"Oh." Ana accepted her explanation with a shrug. "Listen. Deirdre has asked to see you." Ana spoke the words as if giving Sophia a great and unexpected gift. "You've got to get yourself cleaned up pronto. She wants you at the main house in thirty minutes and you know it's at least a five-minute walk."

The main house. Sophia swallowed hard. Deirdre was Ezekiel's first wife. As the first and the eldest, she was in charge of all the others. Sophia had never met her, though she'd certainly heard of her and seen her at her husband's side.

Generally, Deirdre was regarded as a woman of importance, second only to her husband, Ezekiel, and his assistants.

Though she suspected she knew, Sophia asked anyway. "Why?"

Ana frowned. "No doubt to give you all the rules

you'll have to follow once you're a member of the Anointed One's household."

Rules. Sophia winced. When she'd dreamed of her life as a married woman, not once had she thought it would be upended so completely. Usually, the married couple chose which household to join—some became part of the wife's and others chose the husband's. Clearly, wedding someone of Ezekiel's stature meant Sophia would move into the big house and become part of what she'd always privately thought of as the harem.

"Sophia?" Ana's voice cut into her thoughts. "Are you there?"

"Yes. Sorry, I was just thinking."

"Well, you can think later. Right now, you'd better run home and change," Ana urged. "You can't go meet Deirdre dressed like that."

Sophia looked down at her work dress. "Since she sent for me while I'm at work, I'm thinking she probably knows what I do. I think this will be just fine."

Though Ana actually gasped, she didn't argue. "At least wash your face and take your hair down."

Actually, Sophia thought the opposite. The less attractive she could make herself look, the better. If she looked at things from an aging first wife's viewpoint, she imagined the older woman would be extremely tired of dealing with an influx of younger women. Therefore, Sophia wanted to appear as insignificant as she could possibly make herself.

Once in the clinic's small bathroom, she splashed water on her face and redid her bun, making it as tight and severe as possible.

Glad she'd chosen to wear the dull gray work dress that morning, she took a deep breath, squared her shoul-

ders and marched back into the clinic area to let Ana
know she was leaving.

But someone sick had come in and Ana was doing
her best to tend to him without Dr. Drew on staff, so
Sophia slipped out without saying goodbye.

She took her time on the walk to the big house, nervous despite her resolution not to be. She hadn't asked
for any of this, so perhaps Deirdre would cut her a
break.

All of the dwellings inside the encampment were the
same, except for Ezekiel's home, a structure befitting
that of the leader, which had been built with an outer
courtyard and a tall, stucco wall surrounding that, and
the homes for his entourage. Native landscape—firs and
oaks—had either been brought in or left in place when
the structure had been built years before Sophia's time.

The wrought-iron gate was locked. Heart pounding,
Sophia pressed the call button, giving her name to the
man who answered. With a buzz and a click, the gate
was unlocked.

Hoping someone would show up to direct her, Sophia stepped inside. She clasped her hands together to
keep the trembling from being noticeable. She wasn't
afraid, not exactly. More like uncertain and uncomfortable. She hated being put in a situation where she didn't
know what was expected of her.

She let the gate clang closed behind her, not surprised
when it locked. Standing just inside the courtyard, she
took in the stone bench and the large water fountain
crowned with a massive cement angel.

And still no one came to fetch her. She had to stifle
the urge to shake her head. Seriously, she really wanted
to turn around and go back home. And she would have,

except one did not ignore a summons from someone like Deirdre.

Fine. Following the stone path, she made her way toward an elaborate wood-and-iron door. First she knocked and, after waiting for a response, she tried the handle. Not sure if she should be surprised to find it unlocked, she pulled the heavy door open and entered.

Just inside, she found herself in a large, two-story foyer. Her shoes squeaked a bit on the glossy marble floor. Turning slowly, she took in the luxurious surroundings—so unlike those she knew.

She cleared her throat loudly and waited. While she could see how someone might expect her to find her way through the gate to the front door and even inside, no way in heck did she intend to start wandering around the house alone. As a matter of fact, if someone didn't come for her soon, she planned to take it as bad-mannered rudeness and go back home.

"There you are!" a cultured, feminine voice exclaimed. "I apologize for not being there to greet you, but I had to discipline one of the younger women. Welcome, darling."

Registering the word *discipline*, Sophia looked up. The white-haired woman making her way down the stairs so gracefully she appeared to float smiled warmly.

Automatically, Sophia held out her hand. "I'm Sophia Hannah," she began.

"We're not formal here," Deirdre said, ignoring the outstretched fingers and going in for a hug instead. She wrapped her surprisingly sturdy arms around Sophia and held on. Sophia tried to hug back, but Deirdre had pinned her arms at her sides. Her perfume—some floral mishmash with heavy musky undertones—had been liberally applied. Sophia couldn't help herself; though she ducked her head and tried to be as quiet as possible. She sneezed.

Immediately, Deirdre released Sophia and stepped back. "You're not sick, are you?" she asked, narrowing her eyes.

"No, ma'am. Just allergies."

"Don't call me ma'am," Deirdre snapped. Then, as Sophia tensed, her expression softened. "Sorry. That's just one of my pet peeves."

Sophia nodded as if she understood and waited to hear why Deirdre wanted to see her.

"Follow me," the older woman abruptly declared, turning on her heel and marching off. Her long gown trailed behind her like a frothy cape.

Reluctantly, Sophia followed. To her surprise, Deirdre led her into a sunny and bright kitchen. Shiny stainless-steel appliances reflected the light. The counters were made of some sort of natural rock and the oak cabinets appeared sturdy and well made. The entire effect was modern and pleasing. And surprising, when Sophia considered what her kitchen looked like.

"Sit." Deirdre indicated a chair at the round table.

She waited until Sophia had taken a seat before speaking. "You're about to become a member of my household, and as such there are a few things we need to discuss."

Sophia nodded. She figured she had a pretty good idea of what was coming. Rules and regulations, and words to make sure she understood how lowly her place would be in this home. Sadly, she couldn't really blame Deirdre. She could only imagine how much it would hurt to be the first wife forced to watch while your husband took younger and younger women and made them somewhat equal.

Watching her, Deirdre's hard expression softened. "You have no idea what you're in for, do you?"

"No." Sophia decided to be blunt. "I've never even met your husband. I have no idea why he chose me."

Deidre gave a snort. "Child, have you looked at yourself? Ezekiel has never been able to resist a pretty face."

Sophia wasn't sure how to respond to that, so she said nothing.

After a moment Deidre continued, "Things here are going to be a lot different from what you're used to. How many people are in your family group?"

"Thirty-three total," Sophia answered proudly, feeling a rush of love when she thought of them. "Twenty-four adults besides me, and eight children, though most of them live at the school now."

Deidre raised her brows. "All paired adults, except for you?"

"Yes."

"Well, that's about to change," Deirdre said, her tone brisk. "Here, you will be one of many, but that can be a good thing. At first, Ezekiel is always obsessed with his latest woman, but eventually he'll get distracted by someone else and will leave you alone."

The words and their meaning made an involuntary shudder snake up Sophia's spine. While objectively she knew she'd have to let her husband touch her, the actual thought made her want to gag.

Deirdre's sharp gaze missed nothing. "It won't be so bad," she said. "We can give you a pill or drinks beforehand to blunt the experience. Are you untouched?"

"If I say no, will he call off the wedding?" Sophia couldn't keep the hope from her voice.

"I doubt you'll get out of this that easily." Deidre chuckled. "Do you know how many new wives-to-be

I've had to have this discussion with?" Without waiting for an answer, she continued, "Too many to count. In the early days, when Ezekiel was young, they were eager. Bent on becoming his favorite, thinking they could wrest my power from me."

Her laugh relayed how impossible she believed such a thing to be. "Over the years, despite his penchant for taking more and more wives, things have changed. The women have gone from eager and calculating to resigned and terrified."

Terrified? Sophia struggled to process that.

"Lately," Deirdre continued, "the last few have been like you. Frightened, maybe even repulsed."

Aware that Deirdre might be testing her, Sophia hurriedly shook her head. "Oh, not repulsed," she said. "Never that. How could one be, when such a great honor has been bestowed?"

A hint of wickedness flashed in Deidre's gray eyes. "Honor, eh? Maybe so, since he is the Anointed One who will lead us into eternity. But as far as the earthier things, well… We'll talk again on the morning after your wedding night."

Oh, no. Again, Sophia shuddered.

"At least you don't have to worry about getting pregnant," Deirdre continued thoughtfully. "His seed are too old now to be fertile. Though if you could manage to get with child somehow, your status would instantly be elevated."

Then, while Sophia pondered a statement that on the surface made no sense, Deirdre winked. "I tell you this just in case you're one of those women who've always wanted children. The time to do that is before you marry."

Embarrassment warred with horror as Sophia realized what Deirdre meant. She mumbled some sort of response, hoping it didn't sound too much like agreement. Was this some sort of test? It had to be, because there was no way Deirdre could be serious.

Something of her thoughts must have showed on her face. Deirdre chuckled again before patting her on the head the way one would a wayward child. "Go on back home now," Deirdre said. "We'll talk again closer to the ceremony."

Sophia felt another flash of panic. "About that..." she began.

"You don't need to even worry about that," Deirdre said. "It will all be handled by our staff, including our dress. All you have to do is show up."

One more dream dashed. Of course everything about this marriage-to-be was the opposite of her hopes and expectations.

Somehow she managed to respond with a thank-you before turning and heading back the way she'd come.

Chapter 4

Jack couldn't stop thinking about the beautiful nurse. He knew he needed to focus. A feminine distraction could only be potentially catastrophic. So he went to work with his roommate Phillip, who seemed hopeful he could teach Jack how to become a skilled carpenter. While Jack had his doubts, he was game. Anything to help him blend in with the group. At least being new, he could ask a lot of questions. And despite his resolve, he lasted three days before he found himself casually asking about the nurse he'd briefly met in the medical clinic.

"Sophia Hannah?" Phillip's incredulous expression was comical. "You don't want a woman like her."

"'A woman like her'?" Repeating the words, Jack waited for the other man to elaborate. "What do you mean?"

"Clearly you've seen her."

Jack nodded. "Yes. She's gorgeous."

"Oh, stunning. And that's the problem. Everyone knows women who look like her are nothing but trouble."

Unsure how to respond to that, Jack simply shrugged. Maybe it was a cult thing.

"Anyway," Phillip continued, "it doesn't matter. Sophia is claimed already. And by none other than our illustrious leader. A man as powerful as him is the only one who could handle a woman like that."

"Ezekiel?" Jack had done his research. The cult leader was at least eighty. "Isn't he a little…old for her?"

"He's Chosen," Phillip said, as if that explained everything. "He has more wives than I can count. And some of them are younger than his own children—heck, his own grandchildren." And then he laughed, as if that was the greatest thing he'd ever heard.

Nothing new there. Men in power often went in search of women many years younger. But Jack would bet Sophia was in her mid- to late twenties or, at most, early thirties. That would make Ezekiel forty or fifty years too old for her. He couldn't help but wonder how she felt about that.

"So." Phillip clapped him on the back, still grinning. "She's off-limits. But I know plenty of other girls still looking for a husband or fun. Once you get settled in here, I'll take you around to meet some of them."

Though Jack wasn't even the slightest bit interested— he hoped he wasn't around long enough to have to deal with any of that—he nodded. "Sounds good. Now, how about you show me what you want me to do with those cinder blocks?"

They were building more dwellings. Phillip had explained that all residence buildings were built from the exact same blueprints. No one's home was better than any other's. The only ones that were different were those built to house Ezekiel's family members.

While Jack had never worked on a construction job site before, this one ran like clockwork. Everyone went about their chores with dedicated efficiency if not out-right happiness. Lots of whistling and good-natured joking.

"All the workers seem to really enjoy their jobs," Jack commented. "I haven't heard a single complaint. Observing, they all seem focused."

"Oh, they are," Phillip said confidently. "Since child-hood, we know we have to find what we do best, so by the time we're adults, we can excel."

"I'm guessing everyone is well paid."

"Paid?" Phillip laughed. "Oh, we're paid, all right. We have a roof over our heads, food in our bellies and direction to help us strive to reach a higher level of consciousness."

Jack stared. On the surface, everything inside the compound seemed ordinary. But he sensed there was more, lurking.

"The system here is simple," Phillip continued, the earnestness in his expression letting Jack know this was important. "If you do well, you're rewarded. If you don't…"

Jack waited for his new friend to finish.

Instead, Phillip shook his head and asked a question, "You say you've been in the military, correct?"

"Yes." Jack nodded. "The army. Afghanistan." Which had also been where he'd suffered his injuries and nearly lost his life, though he didn't say that out loud.

Again he thought back to the pretty little nurse. So-phia Hannah, promised to a man old enough to be her grandfather. He gave a mental shrug, aware he didn't need to be thinking about her.

Suddenly aware Phillip watched him, he grimaced. "Why? What does my having been in the service have to do with any of this?"

"I just figured you'd understand our system more quickly, that's all." Phillip shrugged. "From what I understand, they use a similar system of punishment and reward. Helps you become the best soldier. Here, we think it assists you in becoming the best you can be."

Jack nodded. "I understand." Even though he really didn't.

Phillip smiled and they went back to work.

The next day, Phillip told Jack he planned to train him on a new task. Jack was agreeable since, as of yet, he hadn't seemed to be a good fit for any of the others he'd tried. Though he kind of sucked as a construction worker, now that he had the routine down, Jack thought he might improve with practice.

After he'd been injured and once he'd gotten out of the hospital and dealt with his addiction, he'd been adrift.

He'd tried to work as a police officer in a small town southwest of Fort Worth, but soon realized he was too jumpy. PTSD, they'd called it, but he'd never actually bought into the idea. For one thing, most of the time he'd felt fine. Sure, the occasional loud noise had him throwing himself to the ground, but that was to be expected of a man who'd nearly lost his life in an IED explosion. He'd been damn lucky to come out of it with only the scars.

He knew his refusal to get treatment had been part of the reason they'd politely asked him to leave. The other part? He didn't like to think too much about that. He'd pulled over a robbery suspect and the guy had jumped out of the car and taken off. Jack had given chase and adrenaline—along with maybe something else—had kicked in. The backup officer who'd arrived had pulled Jack off the other man before he'd hurt him, sat him down in the back of his squad car and called their superior officer.

Ultimately, Jack had reluctantly agreed it'd be better for everyone if he left law enforcement.

Since then, he'd been drifting, working odd jobs to stay afloat until he figured out what to do. He'd decided to start up his own private investigation firm. The few small jobs that had come his way hadn't been nearly enough to keep him afloat, and he'd begun to contemplate doing something else.

Until the Bartlett family came along, desperate to find someone—anyone—who'd listen to them and help them. They'd exhausted every other avenue and claimed the authorities had grown tired of hearing them ask questions.

They didn't know it, but when they'd hired him, they'd given him a chance to make a go of the PI business. Plus, he liked them. They were genuinely nice people. If anyone deserved to find their son, they did.

So lost in thought was he, that he accidentally continued using the nail gun on a section of beam that didn't need it, nearly getting his own hand in the process. Luckily, he jumped back in time.

Taking a deep breath, he stopped and looked up, only to find Phillip and one of the other workers eyeing him. Since he routinely made weird mistakes like this, he supposed they weren't really surprised, but he found it embarrassing just the same. Some people just weren't cut out for this kind of work. Apparently he was one of them. He wondered what the process would be to ask if he could switch jobs.

"Hey, you got a minute?" Phillip asked. "We need to talk."

Here it came. Jack nodded. He followed his room-mate over to the road, away from everyone else.

"It's not working out." Phillip sounded both nervous and regretful. "I just don't think you're cut out for this type of work."

In all fairness, Jack had to agree. He could do the work, but he made mistakes, mostly because he found it boring. Yet being fired yet again rankled.

"I agree," he said. "I was just wondering what the process would be to ask to be assigned somewhere else."

"We don't have a process like that." Phillip's tone came out flat.

"So, what now?" Jack asked, keeping his voice light. Part of him actually wondered if there would be some sort of punishment, since that had been brought up earlier.

"You tried but didn't excel." Now Phillip appeared miserable. "I really like you, Jack, and I'm sorry but I had to report this. Thomas has requested you be sent to him immediately."

"Immediately? When exactly did you make your report?"

"A few minutes ago. Things like poor job performance are taken very seriously. That's why Thomas wants to see you."

Concerned, Jack nodded. "Friend to friend, Phillip. Tell me. You speak of punishment. What's he going to do to me?"

"Probably nothing." But Phillip's answer came too

quickly. "You'd better hurry and get up there. He doesn't like to be kept waiting."

Jack didn't move. "Up where? I have no idea where I need to go."

Eyes wide, Phillip shook his head. "Come on, I'll show you." He took off at a jog without looking back to see if Jack followed.

Of course, Jack did. Phillip led him past the residential area and into what Jack privately thought of as the upscale part of the compound. The houses were larger, more ornate. And the closer they got to the massive structure where Ezekiel dwelled, the more elaborate they became.

"Here we are." Phillip stopped in front of a huge place right next to Ezekiel's walled-in fortress. "Good luck. I'll hopefully see you later on tonight."

And he took off.

Hopefully, huh? Jack took a deep breath and pushed the buzzer. After he gave his name, the person on the other end remotely unlocked the door and let him inside.

Security measures, eh? Maybe things weren't always so great here in paradise.

He barely had time to process the thought when Thomas strode into the large, octagon-shaped foyer. "Greetings," he said, sounding neither angry nor friendly.

Considering what he'd said earlier about punishment and rewards, Jack braced himself.

"I understand you've been struggling with construction."

Slowly, Jack nodded, resisting the urge to defend himself.

"That's okay," Thomas continued, surprising him. "You're new here. With the others, we've had years to discover where their aptitude lies. So I've decided I'm going to reassign you."

Surprised, Jack thanked him. Then mentally berated himself for allowing the other man to make him feel as if he'd been given a gift. Though in the end, maybe he had.

"Have you ever worked in the medical field?" Thomas asked. "Maybe when you were in the service?" He eyed Jack expectantly.

Though the closest Jack had come to anything even remotely medically related had been when he'd briefly dated one of the military doctors, he nodded. "A little bit," he allowed, hoping he wasn't making a mistake. "Nothing major. More like an aide or a therapist than anything else."

"Perfect." Thomas beamed. "Right now we only have two women to assist our doctor at the clinic. We've been thinking about having someone stronger to do the heavy lifting and whatever else is needed. I think this might be a good fit for you."

The clinic. Where the nurse with the amazing caramel eyes worked. Maybe working there wouldn't be as boring as construction work. Swallowing, he gave a slow nod. "Thank you."

"Report to work there at seven tomorrow morning." Waving his hand, Thomas dismissed him.

Jack half expected a couple of goons in suits to appear to escort him from the premises. When they didn't, he turned and went back the way he'd come.

Only when he once again stood outside the gates did he allow himself to think—really think—about what had just happened. For whatever reason, Thomas had decided to show him leniency, at least if the punishment/reward system was to be believed. This time, at least.

Surely he could manage to do okay working as an orderly in the medical clinic. Lifting boxes and mattresses, maybe helping to move supplies. He'd done similar work before in the military.

However, he'd have to be careful. Considering the strength of the attraction he felt for Sophia Hannah, he'd need to take care to keep his distance. Especially since she was promised to the head of the entire organization. Even the most casual flirting could be misconstrued and the last thing he needed was to get that kind of reprimand.

Thoughtful, he headed back to the house he shared with Phillip.

After meeting with Deirdre, Sophia found herself a mess of nerves with what felt like a forty-pound weight nestled snuggly around her shoulders. She went back to work, but Ana had surprisingly already done everything needed to close out their shift, so she went on home.

Rachel was already there when Sophia arrived. She'd started the evening meal—chicken, rice and vegetables—which smelled heavenly. Sophia stood for a moment in the doorway to their small kitchen, breathing in the scent of curry, and tried to regain her feeling of normalcy.

"Oh, good!" Rachel exclaimed, looking up from the pot she'd been stirring. "I was hoping you'd get done early. Once we eat, do you want to sit down and start planning your wedding? I brought home one of the sketch pads from work." Rachel taught art and music to the children.

Shaking her head, Sophia relayed what Deirdre had told her. "Basically, everything is being handled by Ezekiel's people."

"You don't get to have a say in anything?" Clearly disbelieving, Rachel's eyes narrowed. "Anyone who knows you is aware of how long you've waited to get to plan your wedding. This is every young woman's dream and right. Why are they taking that away from you?"

All Sophia could do was shrug. She knew if she spoke, she'd break down crying. The last thing she wanted to do was to reveal the depths of her unhappiness. That wouldn't be worthy of a Child of Eternity. Not in the slightest.

The other two girls had met friends for a picnic, so it was just the two of them. Rachel continued to pepper her with questions all through dinner, most of which Sophia was glad to answer. She described what little she'd seen of Ezekiel's house, the outside gardens and what Deirdre had been wearing. Whenever Rachel circled around to the wedding, Sophia changed the subject. Finally, Rachel appeared to get the hint and began chattering away about things her students had done that day at school.

Listening to her friend, Sophia reflected on Deirdre's words. Unless she did something dishonorable and completely contrary to the laws of COE, Sophia would never have children of her own. Never have the experience of carrying a child inside her body for nine months or holding her son or daughter close to her breast for the first time.

Part of her—the rebellious, secretive part she'd long kept deeply buried—wanted to go find a man, someone like the mysterious stranger Thomas had brought from outside, and have wild sex with him. Enough times as it took to make a baby.

The other part of her—the rule-abiding, good Child of Eternity—was appalled. Ezekiel had been Anointed and he'd chosen his Children. He only did what was best for each and every one of them. If he wanted Sophia to be his wife and remain childless, who was she to question?

She went to sleep that night with her heart heavy and her throat aching from unshed tears.

The next morning, though the sun had not yet risen, the overcast sky and warmish temperatures promised thunderstorms. After her shower and breakfast, she walked to work like she always did, arriving early. She liked to get to the clinic first and turn on the lights, get a pot of coffee going and have everything in order and ready so the doctor could start the day off right. Ana always wandered in right before her assigned start time, acting surprised and grateful at all the work Sophia had already done.

And Sophia found the familiar routine calming. She'd begun to discover that if she kept busy, she could forget about the wedding looming in one month.

As she approached the medical clinic, a figure detached itself from the wall. She jumped back, startled, glad the sky had lightened enough so the man, whoever he might be, wasn't hidden in complete shadows.

Assuming he was either sick or injured, she hurried over. Then she realized he was the handsome man from outside. Jack. Despite herself, her heart skipped a beat.

"Good morning," he said, smiling at her. "I'm here to report for work."

"What?" All she could do was stare at him.

"Yes. I've been reassigned to the clinic. I'm to be an aide or intern or something. Thomas said you need someone to do the heavy lifting."

Her flush heated her entire body. "I apologize for my surprise. No one told me," she said quietly. Digging her keys from her pocket, she unlocked the back door. "Follow me inside. There's a lot to do before this place is ready to open in the morning."

Though he did exactly as she'd asked, staying close behind her, his silence and size made her very conscious of his presence. And she was unsettled. She and Ana had gotten along fine for years. As far as Sophia knew, Dr. Drew had never complained.

Of course, being second in command under Ezekiel, Thomas's orders were law. What he wanted, he got. If he said Jack was to work in the medical clinic, then they'd make room for him no matter what they had to do.

It seemed, once again, she wouldn't be given a choice. Again, she had to struggle with resentment, which wasn't at all like her.

Putting her mood down to stress about her upcoming life change, she summoned up a smile as she showed Jack around the clinic.

"Funny, I was a patient here first and now I'll be working here," he mused. "This place was the first part of the compound I ever saw."

"It's a good place to start." While her reply might not be as certain as usual, it would have to suffice. "Dr. Drew is the physician on call."

He nodded, giving her a curious glance. "Is the other woman who works with you very strong?"

Strange question, but okay. "She and I are about the same, though she's a bit taller. Why?"

"I was told that I'm needed to help lift patients and heavy supplies. I guess I assumed she was doing that previously since you're so tiny."

His comment made her smile. "I might be small, but I'm pretty strong. And anyway, together Ana and I manage. We always have."

"How long have you worked here?"

She actually had to think. "Since I was eighteen. So that would make it six years now."

His gaze darkened. "That would make you twenty-four."

"Great math skills," she shot back. "How old are you?"

"Older than that." And then he laughed, the masculine sound making her mouth curl up in response.

Something about this man… Just being around him for a few minutes made her feel energized. Exhilarated. She took another look at him, with his dark hair and startling blue eyes, trying to decide what it was about him that drew her. Handsome, true. But there were many good-looking men here at COE and none of them had made her wonder how it would feel if he put his mouth on hers.

Heat suffused her. That thought had come out of nowhere. Luckily, she was saved from making a fool of herself by Ana arriving.

"Hi, Sophia." Ana's gaze slid past her to Jack. "Hi, uh…?"

"Jack," he said, stepping forward and holding out his hand. "Jack Moreno."

Gingerly, Ana shook it. "You look familiar. Weren't you a patient?"

"No," Sophia answered for him. "Jack's been assigned to work with us here."

Ana choked. "What? Why? Who assigned him? Dr. Drew?"

"Thomas," Jack said smoothly. "You seem surprised. Why?"

"I, uh…" Ana looked at Sophia for help.

"We're just not that hectic here," Sophia said. "But

I'm sure we can find enough work to keep you busy." She pretended to think, snapping her fingers as if the idea had just come to her. "As a matter of fact, we've been talking about reorganizing the storeroom. How about I show you where that is and you can get started on that?"

Though she tried for a calm, unruffled exterior, inside Sophia was a quivering mess of nerves. Around him, she felt a mishmash of unfamiliar sensations. She felt overly sensitive to his every movement, so much so that she could swear she heard every breath he took. Her pulse jumped, making her wonder if even her heart beat in time with his. Foolish, she knew. But something about this man lured her, as powerful as the spring sunshine guided a field flower to open toward it.

She'd need to be careful around him. Just his presence could turn out to be dangerous to her peace of mind.

Chapter 5

After the beautiful Sophia left him alone in a cavernous storeroom that appeared to have been stocked with no discernable method of organization, Jack knew he needed to come up with a plan. He knew virtually nothing about his new position, including how long he'd work each day. All Thomas had told him was to be at the clinic at 7:00 a.m.

In order to find out if the Bartletts' son was here, Jack had to figure out a way to be around the children without appearing to be creepy. If he'd been asked what he'd like to do, he would have volunteered to help at their learning center, or whatever they called a school here. Since he hadn't been given a choice—apparently, no one was—he was stuck at the medical clinic. Which, considering the strength of his attraction to Sophia, could cause trouble.

No, he needed to get his information and get out, as

quickly as possible. Without being discovered. Maybe he could offer to do volunteer work, such as tutoring. Except he didn't have any idea if things like that were done here.

He already was an outsider, working his best to fit in. Unfortunately that took time. And patience had never been his strong suit. Not only that, but the Bartlett family seemed almost at the end of their rope. The faith they'd put in him made him even more determined to get them answers.

Right now, he'd have no choice but to take things as they came. Since he was assigned here, he needed to get to know the rest of the staff so they'd feel comfortable answering questions. Therefore, the sooner he got the storeroom cleaned up, the better.

He worked hard, tackling the task with single-minded intent. Around noon, his stomach growled and he realized not only had no one come to check on him, but he had no idea what time he should go to lunch.

Deciding now sounded like a good time, he straightened and walked out of the storeroom into the main part of the clinic. He'd find Sophia and see if she'd be open to having a bite to eat with him.

The clinic appeared strangely empty, making him think they must close it for lunch. If there was a break room or kitchen, he hadn't yet seen it, so he took himself on a quick tour hoping to find it. When he'd worked construction with Phillip, they'd all gone home to eat lunch at the same time every day. Most likely that was the routine here, as well, but then again, how could they close down for an hour? What would happen if there was a medical emergency during lunchtime? He had to think they'd leave someone with medical expertise on the premises.

As he walked down a hallway, past three empty exam rooms, he came to a set of double doors with a sign marked Private. He didn't remember seeing this before when Sophia had given him the short version of a tour.

Assuming Private meant people who didn't work there, he pushed through. From a room around the corner, he heard the sound of a man's voice, which could only be the doctor. Since he hadn't met him yet, he figured now would be as good a time as any.

But as he drew closer, something the man was saying stopped him in his tracks.

"Thomas, I understand, believe me. But they're traumatized. You can't just uproot them, take them away from everyone and everything they love and expect there not to be consequences."

Silence followed this statement, making Jack think the other man might be talking on a phone. Which would be really unusual since Jack hadn't seen a single phone, whether cell or landline, since arriving here. Maybe doctors got special privileges.

Not only that, but it sounded as if the conversation might be about abducting children and bringing them inside the compound.

Shamelessly eavesdropping, Jack waited to see what the man would say next.

"I'm not a psychiatrist. I told you that. I'm a medical doctor. I have zero experience in dealing with the kind of emotional trauma we're dealing with here." Frustration rang in his voice. "And yes, while it does sometimes manifest shortly after arrival, the repercussions can last for years."

Jack struggled to contain his mounting excitement. Finally a possible lead. Of course, he'd need more than a single overheard conversation that notably lacked specifics.

"Then you'd better find a shrink or, at the very least, a therapist, and bring him here." With that, the man slammed down the phone.

Which was Jack's cue to back away. Because he'd just had an idea. Sure, he'd have to do some fast talking, if not outright lying. But what better way to find out if the COE was kidnapping children than to be their therapist?

After going home for a quick lunch with Phillip, who genuinely appeared happy to see him, Jack hurried back to the clinic. Walking there, he struggled to calm his jangling nerves. This could be huge or it might be only nothing. He wouldn't know until he tried.

Reaching the front door, he saw the sign now read Open. He'd only been gone thirty minutes, just to be on the safe side. Next up, he'd need to figure out a way to meet the doctor who'd been talking on the phone.

Sophia greeted him the instant he walked in the door. "I'm sorry I forgot to come get you to let you know we were closing for lunch." She flashed a quick smile, which lit up her eyes, changing the velvety brown to a deep, captivating amber. "But I see you figured it out anyway. I was just about to go check on your progress."

He gave a mock bow. "I'd be delighted to show you what I've accomplished. I'm thinking I can finish by the end of the day."

"Great."

As he turned to head back toward the storeroom, a large man in a white coat entered the reception area. Frowning, he glanced from Sophia to Jack. "Who's this?" he asked, annoyance echoing in his tone.

Yep, the same man he'd heard earlier. "I'm Jack

Moreno," he said, holding out his hand. "Your newest employee."

"Dr. Drew." After the handshake, the doctor's frown cleared. "I do remember Thomas telling me something about you. You're the man he brought in the other day."

Jack nodded, and realizing it was now or never, he gave a self-deprecating shrug. "I used to be a therapist once, so in a way a medical clinic is right up my ally."

Though he registered Sophia's surprise, he kept his attention on the doctor.

"A therapist?" Dr. Drew's brows rose. "Thomas didn't mention that."

Jack shrugged, as if it was no big deal. "Probably because I didn't tell him. It was a long time ago and all very informal. I apprenticed under the military psychologist, but I was never actually licensed to practice."

"Interesting." Turning to Sophia, the doctor dismissed him. "Do we have any patients scheduled for this afternoon?"

Sophia shook her head. "None scheduled. Probably just the usual walk-ins."

"Good. I'll be back in my office. I've got quite a bit of paperwork to catch up on. Let me know if there's something you and Ana can't handle."

Jack watched as the other man took off down the same hallway and pushed through the double doors marked Private.

Now all he needed to do was wait to see if his carefully placed offhanded comment would work.

Sophia couldn't believe the amount of work Jack had been able to accomplish in one day. The storeroom looked nothing like it had before, when supplies had been heaped upon each other with no discernable method of organization. Now, every single shelf was neat and organized with like items grouped together. "You're definitely a hard worker," she said, turning so she could take in both him and the now extremely well-organized storeroom. When she met his blue gaze, her breath caught in her throat. "This is amazing."

"Thank you." He beamed at her praise, causing warmth to uncurl low in her belly. "I made a data sheet showing where everything is and how much of it we have in stock."

"You took inventory, too?" She couldn't contain her disbelief. "Wow. Just wow."

He glanced at his watch, drawing her attention to his muscular arms. "If there's nothing else I need to attend to today, is it okay if I head home?"

Though she didn't wear a watch, the time showing on wall clock revealed it was well after quitting time. "Of course," she said. "As a matter of fact, if you'll wait a minute, we can go out together."

He nodded. "Where's Ana and Dr. Drew?"

Hurrying around to turn out lights, she barely glanced at him. "Ana already left. And Dr. Drew might still be in his office. I'm not sure. But he always goes out the back door. He expects me to make sure everything up front is off and locked up."

"I'm surprised you lock up here," he commented. "Have you ever had a problem with crime?"

"No. At least, not that I'm aware of. But Dr. Drew keeps a minimal supply of drugs here and he says it's better not to tempt anyone." The second she spoke, she remembered what she'd been told of his background. "I'm sorry," she muttered. "I know you're a recovering addict."

A mixture of surprise, anger and resignation flashed

across his face. "I am," he answered easily. "Though I wonder why they—I'm guessing Thomas—felt compelled to tell you."

Now she'd really done it. Still, she owed this man the truth. "He didn't, actually," she admitted. "I read it in your file. Dr. Drew left it out on his desk and I had to file it. I was curious, so I peeked." She could feel her face blaze with heat as she admitted she'd been a snoop.

To her surprise, he chuckled. "Okay, that makes more sense. I wasn't aware I had a file."

"Oh, everyone does. I imagine it's the same outside, isn't it? Personnel files and all that."

"True." He didn't seem curious about what else might be in the file. She might have been, but then again, maybe not. Especially if he didn't have anything to hide.

Walking home after work with Jack by her side, Sophia couldn't shake the feeling that her life was about to change. Well, of course, it was. She'd be getting married in less than a month.

As usual, her stomach turned at the thought. Then she glanced at the tall man next to her and everything seemed to come into focus.

She knew she ought to be worried, but how could she be? No matter what emotions Jack might stir in her, nothing would change. She'd still be married off to Ezekiel, and she'd try to do her best to achieve the destiny she'd been born to fulfill.

Still, this was…nice. With another man, she might have felt the urge to chatter, to fill the silence with sound so her nervousness didn't strengthen. With him, she felt calm, at peace, relaxed.

"I'm just learning my way around here," he finally said. "And I don't know a lot of people yet. Since I sort of know you, I thought I'd ask if you'd mind giving me a tour."

She eyed him, hoping her expression didn't reveal the way her heart skipped a beat. "I'd heard you were living with Phillip," she teased. "Why haven't you asked him?"

"Ouch." He put his hand to his heart, as if her words had physically wounded him, which made her smile. "He's been really helpful—over and above, actually. He tried to teach me how to do carpentry work, even though I wasn't all that good at it. I thought I'd give him a break."

Continuing to hold his gaze, she nodded. "That makes sense. But you worked really hard today. Do you want to wait until you're more rested?"

"No," he answered. "Unless you're too tired."

Again she found herself suppressing a grin. "Come with me. I'll give you the grand tour." And then, despite shock at her own daring, she held out her hand, aware she might be making a huge mistake. Oddly enough, she didn't care. She felt brave and bold and hopeful. And more alive than she had in months, maybe years.

After one quick, startled glance, he took it, his large hand completely engulfing her small fingers. The simple, friendly gesture felt more intimate than it should. So much so that she almost jerked her hand away.

She wondered if he thought her so innocent that she believed holding hands meant nothing. But since he continued to hold on, she had to believe that he liked it, too.

His fingers were rough, the skin newly callused. A testament to the hours he'd spent learning his new trade before being reassigned to the medical clinic. She knew, even if he didn't, that everyone had been furtively watching him, and the gossip had flowed as the women wondered how long before he sought a mate.

It wasn't often that someone from the outside joined their group. The mere fact that Thomas had brought him inside meant Jack had been specifically chosen.

His handsome features, broad shoulders and muscular arms hadn't gone unnoticed, either. And Sophia hadn't been able to figure out why she felt a tiny little pang of possessiveness every time someone mentioned him with longing. As if he were hers.

Which he never would be.

They walked that way silently for a few minutes. If she'd thought about this beforehand, she'd have thought one of them would grow uncomfortable. After all, they barely knew each other.

Yet the quiet they shared felt like contentment. She was sensible enough to recognize that this could be dangerous. "We can't let this become a habit," she said.

"Really?" he teased. "Why not? Are there rules about two friends walking together?"

The reasons all stuck in her throat. Not only did she already understand she couldn't think of him as much more than a friend, but she was engaged, about to be married. She was so lost in thought, she didn't respond.

"Is there any reason why two friends aren't allowed to exercise together?" he persisted. "I know I'm male and you're female, but it isn't like we're lovers or anything."

Lovers. An electric shock went through her. He had no idea she was a virgin, still untouched and unwanted at the ripe old age of twenty-four.

And she suspected lovemaking with Jack would definitely be something amazing and wonderful. Again, she thought of Deirdre's words and her own longing for a child. Still, not only would that not be fair to Ezekiel, but what about Jack? She could never use him to father a child he wouldn't even know he had.

She wasn't that type of person. Yet her fingers were still intertwined with his. Slowly, she pulled her hand free.

"What?" he asked, giving her a sideways glance. "Are you all right?"

She nodded, wishing she could stop blushing around him. "I'm fine."

"Then let's keep going. Walking in the fresh air will be good for us. Don't read more into it than it actually is."

"Yes," she said, surprising herself. "You're right. Let's go for a walk."

This time, she kept her hands close to her sides so she didn't do something foolish, like reach for him. Under any other circumstances, she would have given him enough hints to let him know that, if he wanted to court her, she'd welcome his advances.

Imagining Jack as her beau filled her with a mixture of savage joy and sorrow.

She had a little time left until her marriage. What would be the harm in pretending, just to herself? She'd just need to make sure Jack never caught on. Or anyone else, for that matter.

They began their stroll as she always did, heading toward the barn so she could see the livestock.

"You know," Jack said, looking around. "Where are all the children? I never see any running around or playing."

"They have organized playtimes," she told him. "Once during the school day and for one hour after. My roommate Rachel is one of the teachers."

Silently, he considered her words. "Interesting," he replied.

In response, she only nodded.

"So how did you and Ezekiel meet and fall in love?" he asked.

"What?" She glanced at him to make sure he wasn't teasing. But no, his expression appeared to be serious. Then she realized he truly didn't know.

"I haven't ever met Ezekiel," she responded, and then waited for the questions that were sure to come.

"You're joking, right?" His expression darkened.

"Nope."

He stared at her, frowning. "Then how did you become engaged? Don't tell me it's one of those arranged-marriage type things, where your parents promised you to him at birth. It isn't, is it?"

She wasn't entirely sure how to answer that. With the truth, she supposed. "Not exactly. Apparently, Ezekiel saw me and decided he wanted me for his next wife. And what Ezekiel wants, he gets." Her words sounded bleak. But, truthfully, in her darkest of hearts, she felt that way. "I'll be the newest of his many wives."

"Wives?" he asked. "How many does he have, exactly? And how does he get away with that?"

She sighed. "I forget sometimes you came from outside. I have no idea how many women he has, but I think there are at least twenty, maybe more. And since Ezekiel is the Anointed One and is our leader, he is able to make his own rules."

Still, Jack appeared thoughtful. "Is every man in COE allowed to have more than one wife?"

"Of course not," she scoffed, even though she realized his question made sense. "At first, I think Ezekiel took several wives as a way to spread his seed. He has children and grandchildren and even a great-grandchild or two."

"At first. But now? The man must be eighty if he's a day."

"I don't know." This time, she couldn't keep the misery from her tone. Luckily, they'd reached the barn. She tugged at the heavy door and began sliding it aside. Jack reached around her and moved it for her.

"Sophia," he began, touching her upper arm. "I think—"

"No." She cut him off with a single word and a wave of her hand. "I don't want to talk about this. It is what it is. Neither you nor I can do anything to change it."

"I wouldn't be too sure about that," he muttered behind her. "I wouldn't be too sure about that at all."

She decided to pretend she hadn't heard him. "This is where we keep our livestock. I come here when I'm done my shift and visit the animals. We're not allowed to have personal pets."

He frowned. "But I've seen dogs and cats running around here. What's up with that?"

"Just like everything else here, the dogs and cats, even the cows and horses, belong to everyone and to no one. We're all responsible for their care, though some people are actually assigned work taking care of the livestock."

"I would have liked that job," he said, surprising her.

"Me, too," she admitted softly, feeling as if she could melt into the kindness in his blue eyes. Eventually, she forced herself to look away. "But I work with helping people heal, so that's better anyway. Still, I love animals and I have my favorites. There's a mama cat who hunts mice in the barn. I've been feeding her scraps I save from my noon meal. She knows me now and will run over as soon as she hears my voice."

"You've really never had a pet? Not even one of the community dogs or cats that you might have secretly adopted as your own?"

She hoped her casual shrug hid the longing in her heart. "Not personally. That really isn't the way things are done around here." Then, to her disbelief at her boldness, she patted his arm. "You'll see. Once you learn how we live, everything will make more sense to you."

"Will it?"

"Hopefully," she answered, gently pulling her hand free. "Everything takes time."

Though he nodded, his expression appeared skeptical. She was okay with that because she knew he'd eventually come to see the benefits of becoming one of the Chosen.

After that, she went from stall to stall, greeting each of the animals by name. The horses reached out their long necks for her to scratch them; the cows ambled over to have a sniff just in case she'd brought a treat. The goats all rushed to the stall door, jostling each other in an attempt to be the first she petted. Even in the last stall, where they kept two young pigs they'd recently acquired, though they didn't yet come to her, she could have sworn they raised their heads in recognition when she called their names. She dropped two small pieces of cut-up apple in the space between them and the door, smiling as they went over to investigate the treat. "Soon, they'll know my voice and that I bring them a snack. Once they figure that out, I trust that they'll come to greet me, too."

He nodded. "You really do have a way with animals." This time she didn't bother to try to hide the pleasure she found in his words. "I do, don't I?" she said happily. "I really enjoy interacting with them."

Before she left, she went back to the huge gray horse she considered her favorite. He nickered softly, wanting a little extra attention. Grinning, she walked back down the aisle. "This is Smokey," she said, scratching the big head right behind the ears. "He's my favorite gelding."

Once they'd left the barn, she took him toward the two huge greenhouses that housed their crops in the winter. "They're empty now," she said. "Because since it's spring, we've planted the crops in the fields."

He nodded, his distracted expression letting her know his thoughts were elsewhere. She wondered if he thought of his former life, the one he'd left behind. Had there been someone special he missed now? Taking a deep breath, she tried to work up the courage to ask him.

Instead she picked up the pace, giving him no choice but to hurry if he wanted to keep up.

"What's the rush?" he asked.

"We've still got a lot of ground to cover if you want to see everything. You asked for a tour, and that's what you shall have."

For the next twenty minutes she kept to business, leading him around and pointing out each of the different buildings and their use.

Earlier, she didn't know what impulse had made her reach for his hand to begin with, but once she'd made the gesture, it had felt right and she couldn't exactly change her mind. The instant his big paw had engulfed hers, she realized she liked the way it felt, probably more than she should have. Time to take a deep breath, and get back to reality.

After all, she didn't know this man, not really. They

worked together, true, but that was it. Yet, sadly, already she knew him better than the man she was to marry in less than a month's time.

"I feel like I've known you a long time," he mused, echoing her thoughts. "Do you feel the same?"

She flushed but managed to keep her tone light. "No." But despite her denial, there was truth in what he said. Or maybe it was just because that's how she wanted it to be. Holding hands with him and walking aimlessly around had felt like something she'd ached to have for so long. As if they were courting.

The instant the thought occurred to her, she felt the wrongness of it. She was promised now, soon to be the wife of the most powerful man in COE. "I'm glad you feel that way. We can be friends, I think. But nothing more." Her bluntness, though necessary, had her blushing again.

He gave her a startled look. "Of course."

If anything, his easy acquiescence made her blush even worse. "Great," she replied.

She left him at his lodgings and continued on toward home. Weird how being around him made her every nerve ending sing inside her. Not good; in fact, she'd only be asking for trouble. Yet Deirdre's words from earlier kept running through her head. If she wanted a child…

No. Though she wouldn't deny the temptation was strong. Almost overwhelmingly so.

Chapter 6

Pushing the dangerous thoughts from her mind, Sophia went inside her house and headed straight to the kitchen to see if Rachel needed help. This week Rachel and Sophia cooked, then their other two roommates would rotate the chore.

Instead of at the stove, she found Rachel at the kitchen table, head down and shoulders shaking. When Rachel heard her come in, she raised her face, held out her arms and let out a loud wail. Sophia hurried over, wrapping her friend up in a hug and holding her while she wept as if her heart had broken.

The front of Sophia's shirt was soaked by the time Rachel got herself under control and stepped back. "I'm sorry," she sniffed. "But it was a rough, rough day at work."

Careful not to show her relief, Sophia nodded. "I

thought maybe something had happened in your family group," she said.

"Oh, no." Rachel shook her head. "Everyone is fine, as far as I know. But my class… One of the boys is attempting to work through something. Whatever it is, it's awful. He keeps trying to run away. Escape, he calls it. Says he wants his mom." Her eyes filled with tears again, though she angrily tried to wipe them away. "He'll bolt right in the middle of a lesson. The first time I was so startled he got outside the building before someone stopped him." She took a deep, shuddery breath. "No matter how much I or anyone else tries to soothe him, he isn't having it. He knows he's got a bunch of loving parents in his family group, but says he doesn't care."

Sophia pulled out a chair and took a seat across from her roommate. "It might be something medical? If so, have him brought to the clinic and Dr. Drew will take a look at him."

Though Rachel nodded and attempted to look upbeat, the misery in her expression told another story. "They called. Dr. Drew believes it's his mind," she said. "The kid is absolutely convinced he doesn't belong here, even though I've known him since he was a toddler."

COE children were kept in their family group's nursery along with all their other children, until old enough to go to school at age five. The nursery did all the early training.

"Did he have the same problem in the nursery? It had to start somewhere."

"I know, but other than being a very quiet child, none of this started until he moved up to my class." Rachel taught kindergarten through fourth grade.

"Poor child." One of the things Sophia loved about

Rachel was how much she cared. "What are you going to do about him?"

"I don't know. He needs a therapist, that's what Thomas said. Dr. Drew contacted him personally, because things have gotten so bad." Rachel's eyes filled again. "That child is on the verge of causing serious harm to himself or to others. It's scary."

Sophia remembered what Jack had told Dr. Drew earlier. "The new guy at the clinic—Jack—says he used to be a therapist. Maybe he can help. He told Dr. Drew, so if he feels like Jack can help, maybe he'll have him do so."

"Really? Oh, that would be amazing." Relief shone in Rachel's face. "At least maybe that one boy can get help. I wish they all could."

"All?" Confused, Sophia eyed her. "What do you mean?"

"There are others. Two more, potentially three. This last group of young kids seems to have more problems than normal. I'm not sure why—they all come from different family groupings."

"That's weird. I don't remember anything like that happening when we were children."

"Me neither." The glumness in Rachel's voice matched her expression. "I wish I knew what was going on."

Sophia took a deep breath. "Maybe we need to try to find out."

"Maybe. But how?"

She had a point. Since questioning was frowned upon, there weren't that many options.

That night, she tossed and turned, troubled.

The next morning, Sophia followed her normal routine, taking comfort in the familiar. Ana had the day off, which meant Sophia should have been busy. But Jack had organized everything and had also given the clinic a thorough cleaning, something she'd always counted on for busywork during the slow times.

She'd actually both looked forward to and dreaded spending a slow day with Jack, but Dr. Drew had given him a list and sent him out to procure some ingredients from the herb growers. Which meant Sophia again found herself left to her own devices, with nothing left to do but think.

Dr. Drew had closed himself in his office with stern instructions not to be disturbed unless there was an emergency.

Never had Sophia checked the clock so many times. The minutes crawled as she waited for the day to be over so she could go home. Her stomach grumbled, making her realize she was hungry way in advance of her scheduled dinnertime.

Desperate for distraction, she began to try to hunt down a snack. Sometimes patients brought baked goods or sweets, but there hadn't been any lately. What she'd give for a few pieces of dark chocolate. Her mouth watered at the thought.

Thinking of chocolate made her realize it had been a long time since she'd been rewarded or even complimented. In years previously, Dr. Drew had presented her with a certificate and a reward for work well done. Once it had been dark chocolate, her favorite and a delicacy unobtainable on a regular basis.

Frowning, she realized that had been well over a year ago. Of course, it was possible he didn't think she'd done anything wonderful lately. She tried to think, aware nothing had changed in her habits. She knew she hadn't missed a single day of work in over a year. She'd trudged in, even on days when she felt too ill to have a coherent thought, and managed to do her job competently. She kept Ana working, and dealt with patients cheerfully, doing whatever Dr. Drew needed.

Yet clearly that hadn't been enough, since Thomas had brought in Jack and Dr. Drew had added him to the staff, even though there was barely enough work for Sophia and Ana combined. Did Dr. Drew believe she'd somehow failed? Of course, without any kind of review, she had no way of knowing.

As if her thinking had conjured him, the doctor opened his door and emerged from his office. Spying her, he cleared his throat. "Could you get me a cup of coffee?" he asked.

"Of course." She hurried off to do just that. While the coffee brewed, she brooded. Though questioning was frowned upon, she decided she'd go ahead and ask her boss when she could expect her review. After all, it was entirely possible that he'd forgotten. No matter how slow the clinic might get, he stayed busy. She could certainly understand how such a trivial milestone might have slipped his mind. Though, of course, to Sophia, a review and potential reward would never be trivial or unimportant.

Nor should it be to any of the Chosen. Sophia, like everyone else she knew, lived to excel. After all, they were aware excellence led them further up the path toward enlightenment. From early childhood on, they were all taught to strive to do above and beyond, with the promise of a reward. Until recently, that promise had been as certain as breathing.

Once the coffee had brewed, she carried it to him in his office. She waited until he'd sipped some before taking a step closer to his desk. "Doctor?" she asked, keeping her tone low and pleasant. "Might I ask a question?"

He squinted at her, disapproval plain on his aristocratic features. "What?" he grumbled.

Heart pounding, she swallowed. "I'm just wondering, sir, if my work lately has been…satisfactory?"

Was that impatience curling the corner of his lip? Or disgust? She took a step back, suddenly ashamed, although she didn't understand why.

"Your work has been…satisfactory," the doctor said. "Though this—" he waved his hand toward her "—is a bit out of line."

Pretending not to realize he chided her, she nodded. "Well, then, I wanted to point out that I haven't missed a single day in the entire past year. This will be my fifth year without a single absence." Now that she'd had enough courage to blurt out the words, she waited for his expression to clear. Surely now he'd realize he'd completely forgotten her review.

"That's what this is all about?" Anger flashed in his gaze. "Because you didn't get your chocolate?"

Put like that, in the particular tone he used, it did sound petty. And stupid.

A low burn of anger simmered in her belly. Dangerous, so she kept it banked and gritted her teeth.

"It's not just about the chocolate," she said, hoping she'd succeeded in keeping her voice level. "Though I do enjoy that." As if on cue, her stomach rumbled. She ignored it and continued. "But about what I strive for. The recognition of my excellence. Going without any sort of feedback is…distressing."

"Well, maybe you'd better get used to it." Dr. Drew's thunderous expression matched the bluntness of his words. "Your life is about to completely change. You'll soon be moving into an entirely different stratosphere. Things aren't even close to the same in the big house."

"I don't understand," she replied before she thought better. "You're saying once I marry, I'll no longer be able to strive for excellence?"

Indulgent now, Dr. Drew actually reached across the desk and patted her on the head, as if she was a small child in need of appeasement. "Our leader's excellence will convey to you as one of his wives. In his shadow, all you will strive for is to please him."

Staring, she tried to process what he was saying. Did he truly mean she would no longer be her own person? No more an individual, but simply one of Ezekiel's shadows, existing only at his whim?

Suddenly more terrified than she'd ever been, she managed to nod in what she hoped was a docile manner and slowly backed out of his office. "Thank you for your words of wisdom," she murmured when she really wanted to shriek and scream and throw things, which would be decidedly un-Chosen-like.

When Jack returned from getting the herbs—a large, zip-locked bag full of who-knew-what that made him feel like he was couriering illicit drugs, the clinic seemed strangely empty. He knew Ana had the day off, but neither the doctor nor Sophia was anywhere in sight.

Maybe they were with patients. If so, then what to do with the herbs? Maybe he should take them to the doctor's office.

Jack had barely walked down the hallway when Dr. Drew appeared and snatched the bag from him. "Thanks," he said. "Please get us both a cup of coffee and come back to my office," he ordered, striding away.

This could be a good thing or a bad. Hope flooding him that it would be about his alleged therapy experience, Jack kept his expression neutral as he poured two cups and then returned to the office. He still saw no sign of Sophia. If she was intentionally making herself scarce, she was doing a good job. He pushed away his disappointment, aware he needed to focus.

The doctor's office, though small, had been richly furnished. An ornate, dark mahogany desk dominated the small room. A high-quality leather chair sat behind it. Two richly upholstered chairs faced the desk and, after placing the coffee mugs on the desk, Jack took a seat in one of them.

The leather chair squeaked as Dr. Drew lowered his bulk into it. After taking a long drink of his coffee, he used his hands to make a steeple on his desk. Silently, he eyed Jack.

"When we spoke earlier, you mentioned you'd been a therapist," the doctor finally said. "May I ask where you received your training?"

Jack pretended to be confused. "I haven't had any formal training. I acted as an apprentice for the army psychologist in my unit. There were too many soldiers who needed help for him to handle. So he taught me, showed me what to do and I helped him out. Why do you ask?"

Instead of answering, Dr. Drew stood abruptly and walked to the door, opening it. "Thank you. That'll be all. I'll let you know if there's anything else."

Damn. Struggling to contain his disappointment, Jack pushed to his feet and left. He hunted down Sophia. Pushing away the instant pang of attraction that made him want to linger in her proximity, he kept his demeanor professional and asked her what she needed him to do.

Her smile turned his insides to mush, but he thought he managed to keep his expression blank. He didn't react, even when their fingers brushed as she handed him a list of chores, which sent a jolt straight to his groin.

The rest of the day passed with busywork. He hardly saw Sophia at all, which was probably a good thing considering the strength of his attraction to her. She and the doctor appeared to stay busy with patients, although it had been quiet when Jack had returned.

He completed everything on the list and found himself searching for more work.

At last, Dr. Drew came through, clearly on his way out. Noticing him straightening up the reception area, he grunted. "You can go now," he said.

Jack nodded. He almost said he'd be staying, longing for one last glimpse of Sophia, but in the end, decided to head on home. He needed to stop thinking about a woman he couldn't have and do some more scouting around the compound to see if he could find out where they were keeping the children.

Since he knew Phillip—and his former construction crew coworkers—would still be hard at work and he didn't want to fend off their questions, he headed in the opposite direction. By his calculations, he had another hour before most of the adults finished their workday and headed home. In the outside world, the kids would already be out of school and running around, but as usual, he didn't see a single youngster. He couldn't help but wonder why no one else seemed to find this odd.

He walked in a direction he hadn't previously gone, wanting to check out the perimeter. Since apparently no one ever left, he had to wonder if COE had installed some sort of electric fence as a deterrent.

When he reached a wooden pole fence that he thought must be the extreme edge of the compound, he stopped.

On the other side, the clearing continued for maybe ten or fifteen feet before the forest had been allowed to grow wild again. He inspected the fence, finding no electrical wires. As far as he could see, there was nothing to keep anyone from climbing over or going under and disappearing into the woods.

After a quick glance around to make sure he hadn't been observed, he decided to try. Bracing himself for the unexpected, he climbed the first pole and swung his leg over the second.

Nothing happened.

Mildly disappointed, he let himself drop to the ground on the other side and began walking toward the forest.

Once he'd gotten deep enough inside the undergrowth that the fence was no longer visible, he stopped. As far as he could tell, he could continue hiking in any direction, even though he had no idea which way the road might be.

Good to know. Which also must mean that the members of COE didn't want to go anywhere. Were they truly that brainwashed or was it possible they were simply happy?

Something to ponder. In the meantime, he need to figure out where they hid the children.

He'd gotten this far. He was here for a reason and he didn't need to allow philosophical musings or anything else distract him. Especially not a gorgeous young woman who happened to be engaged to the cult's leader.

Which was why, as he walked back toward the compound after his brief stint of freedom and caught sight of Sophia Hannah, he told himself not to go after her.

Of course, he did anyway, feeling the pull of her as if she'd tethered herself to him. Since she was clear on the other side of the communal garden, he jogged in that direction.

"Mind if I join you?" Though he slowed when he reached her, he made no effort to hide the fact that he'd had to hurry to catch her.

She started, swinging herself around to face him. She'd clenched her hands into fists and, judging from her tense expression and narrow-eyed glare, she felt combative or defensive.

"Did I frighten you?" he asked gently, cursing himself and his odd, compelling need to be near her.

Slowly, she relaxed, shaking her head. "No. Just startled me. When you came running over here, I thought you were about to tell me I was needed back at the infirmary."

He felt like a heel. He hadn't even thought of that.

Some of his consternation must have showed in his face.

"It's okay." She touched his arm—a quick, light touch—but enough to send a jolt through him. Just like before.

Staring at her, he wondered if she'd felt it, too.

"I saw you were out for a walk. Since I am, too, I thought I'd ask you if you minded if I joined you." He smiled at her, wondering why she didn't smile back. They'd agreed to be friends, after all.

"We can't hold hands," she blurted, her face turning a becoming shade of pink. "I have to apologize for that before. I don't know what I was thinking. I never should have—"

"It's okay." Interrupting her before he did something even worse, like kiss her, he hid his smile. "You're a good person, Sophia Hannah. You didn't do anything wrong."

If anything, his praise made her blush even harder.

She muttered something under her breath that sounded like, "If you only knew." This intrigued him, but since his goal was to make her feel comfortable, he didn't pursue it.

"Are you going to the barn?" he asked, surprising himself with his eagerness to share the experience with her again.

Instantly she shook her head. "Not today. Right now is about the time when the animals are being fed and I don't want to interfere with that. I'm just stretching my legs and getting some air."

With that, she began walking away. Without asking permission, he fell into place with her.

"Busy day at work today," he commented, more to break the silence than anything else.

"It was, after a quiet morning." The look she directed his way seemed cool. "You certainly made yourself scarce today."

He grinned. "Correction. Dr. Drew made me scarce. I had to get everything on that list he gave me."

"Did you?"

"I did."

One of her brows rose as if she didn't believe him. "Is that why you left early? Because you figured if you were finished with Dr. Drew's list, you didn't have to do anything else?"

Maybe that explained her aloofness.

"Dr. Drew told me to go ahead and leave," he explained. "He said you all were done for the day."

"Oh." She inhaled sharply. "I didn't know."

"Was that wrong? Should I have stayed?"

"No, that's fine. He's the boss, after all." She made

a dismissive gesture. "I'm sorry. I'm just having a bad day."

The urge to take her in his arms and somehow make everything better was way stronger than it should have been. So intense, in fact, he stepped back.

And stopped, stunned by the quick look of hurt that flashed across her mobile, expressive face.

"Sorry," he said quickly. "I've had a bad day, too."

She accepted his words with a quick jerk of her head. "Walks sometimes make everything better."

"Have you ever gone into the woods on the other side of the fence?" he asked. "I went out there earlier today and it really seems peaceful. And beautiful, in a pristine sort of way."

When she didn't immediately respond, he wondered if her next words would be taking him to task for going outside the confines of the compound.

Instead she stopped and turned to face him. "Yes, I have. I often do. But it's not something you should speak about out loud."

"Why not?" This time, he had to push. He truly wanted to understand if she, along with all the others who lived here, truly understood how restrictive the authorities of COE had made their lives.

"I don't know. But it's kind of a guilty pleasure most of us indulge in, especially once we reach adulthood. Until we finish school, our lives are so regulated, going over that fence is a heady breath of freedom. We don't discuss it, mainly because if the others realize how much it means to us, it can be restricted as a form of punishment."

The matter-of-factness in her tone astounded him. "You don't find that…odd?"

"It's just the way it is." She wrinkled her nose, the

gesture so cute he found himself leaning in for a kiss. Of course the instant he realized that, he kept himself still.

"That doesn't mean it's right." Inwardly he winced, wishing instantly he could call back the words. He wasn't there to start an insurrection.

Clearly not caring, she shrugged. "To be honest, I have much worse things to worry about."

"Your upcoming marriage?"

"That, too." Her deep breath sounded shaky. "I was talking to Rachel and she was telling me about something that's been happening with some children in her class."

"Rachel?"

"My roommate. She's one of the teachers here. She was very upset yesterday because a few of her students are having serious issues. Apparently they're pretty severe." She looked down. "She's been a teacher for a long time and says she's never seen anything like this before. Worse, she doesn't know why."

When she raised her face to his, the hope blazing from her eyes made his heart catch. "Earlier I heard you say something about being a therapist before. Do you think maybe you could help them?"

Chapter 7

As Sophia gazed up at Jack, her heart pounding in her ears, she thought for one breathless second he was about to kiss her. But then, just as she'd begun leaning in, he took a step back. Hopefully her expression masked her disappointment.

"I'll do the best I can," he said. "If they'll let me. Dr. Drew asked about my experience again today, but didn't ask for my assistance. I get the impression I can't simply show up at the school and offer to help."

He had a point. "True."

"I have to say," he continued. "I feel bad for the children. I wonder if the way they're kept under such strict control has anything to do with the emotional problems beginning to surface now."

Puzzled, she frowned. "I'm not sure I follow. All the children are given appropriate levels of freedom for their age."

"Are they?" Voice harsh, he shook his head. "What does that even mean, Sophia? They're not even allowed to run and play outside."

"Of course, they are. Under strict supervision, of course, but they play."

"When? Since I've been here, I haven't seen a single kid. Not one. Not playing, not learning, not hanging out with their family, nothing. I'm not super into kids, but even I've noticed the complete and utter absence of childish laughter, the shouts of joy they make when running around outside, even their cries when they fall off their bikes."

"They have structured playtimes in an enclosed outdoor area inside the school."

"That's recess, not real playtime," he said.

Since she wasn't sure how to respond to that, she stayed silent.

Which apparently suited him fine, since clearly he wasn't finished. "Just like pets," he continued. "You have community dogs and cats. But where are all the hamsters, guinea pigs, birds…hell, even fish? What do you people have against pets?"

"I took you to the barn," she pointed out. "There were animals there."

"Livestock. There's a huge difference."

Again his words confused her. "Why? What are they good for? Ezekiel always says if an animal serves no practical purpose, it's unnecessary. We can ride the horses, milk and eat the cows and goats. The chickens provide fresh eggs."

"Are you serious? Haven't you wondered about having a pet? You love that mama cat, don't you?"

"No." She lifted her chin, finding his vehemence intriguing. "Maybe a little. But I don't understand what you mean about pets. Why don't you tell me?"

"Challenge accepted." His grin made her knees go weak. "I'll do my best but it would be so much easier if I could just show you."

Her breath caught when he leaned in close. "Show me?" she managed to whisper. This sparring… The jittery yet amazing way he made her feel. Was this flirting? For a second she closed her eyes. How could she not even know?

Again, the fleeting thought of how much her life was about to change brought her back to earth. She knew once she was married to Ezekiel, she'd never get to experience whatever this was right now with Jack. She took so much pleasure in this simple give-and-take. Honestly, Jack made her feel things she'd never imagined possible for her. The swooping tug of attraction racing through her veins when their eyes met. The way her insides tumbled when she got too close to him.

And more. So much more. This, finally, must be what it felt like to be falling in love.

Ever since she'd become an adult, she'd listened while her friends had discussed exactly this. She'd watched as, one by one, they were claimed then married. Slightly envious, she'd waited, just knowing that someday her time would come.

And now it had. Unfortunately, far too late.

"Yes, show you." Jack's breath tickled her skin. "Because, quite honestly, there's no way to simply describe the silky feel of your own kitten's fur or the unbelievable sweet smell of a puppy wiggling in your arms."

Enthralled, she swayed toward him, aching with a fierce, savage longing that he'd take her in his arms.

His gaze felt like a caress.

Behind them, someone coughed. Sophia jumped, a little cry escaping her.

"Hey, you two." A tall, beefy young man she recognized as Jack's roommate Phillip sauntered up. "What are you doing roaming around? Shouldn't you be home, getting ready?"

"I could ask you the same question," Jack countered. "And getting ready for what?"

Phillip's easy grin faded as he turned his gaze on Sophia. "Aren't you going to the cookout tonight? Your fiancé will be there."

Her heart fell. Once a month Ezekiel and his family hosted a huge barbecue in the center of the compound. They grilled steaks and chicken and all kinds of vegetables. In the past, she'd always looked forward to attending. This time, she'd managed to completely forget about it.

"Cookout?" Jack asked. "I love a good grilled steak. When and where?"

"I'll show you," Phillip said before turning his attention back on Sophia. "Girl, you'd better go get cleaned up. You know Ezekiel's going to do some kind of declaration in front of everyone tonight."

She struggled not to let her shoulders sag. "No, I didn't know. But you're right, I need to rush home and get ready. Thanks for the reminder."

"Sure thing."

Unable to resist glancing once more at Jack, she thought of something else. "Jack, about your earlier question. Tonight, everyone will be in the town square. Young and old. You were wondering when the children go outside to play. Tonight you'll get to see that in person."

He nodded. "Great."

Sickened by the sense of loss weighing her down, she nodded and spun around to head home. Even if the event tonight turned into a fiasco, she had to try to do her best, including making herself appear as pretty as possible.

When Sophia arrived at her little house, Rachel greeted her with a shriek. "You're running late," she admonished. "I laid out your prettiest dress. Jump in the shower and I'll help you with your hair after."

Too numb to do anything but as she was told, Sophia stepped into the bathroom, undressed and got into the shower.

She couldn't stop thinking about the comment Jack had made earlier. Asking her why no one found their lack of freedom odd. Maybe because this life, with all the rules and routine, was all any of them had ever known. They'd been born here, grown up here and raised their own families inside the compound. She supposed the one thing that might be most instrumental in pushing away any kind of doubt was the unshakable knowledge that they were Chosen. Children of Eternity, guaranteed a spot when the Others were not.

Since they weren't required to attend any kind of religious services unless they wanted to—aware being Chosen lived inside them and didn't need reinforcing—Sophia hadn't thought about the Others since learning this doctrine in school as a child.

Technically, Jack was Other. He'd come from outside. She wasn't sure exactly what he'd had to do to become Chosen.

This made her wonder how many Others had come into COE's fold. Was Jack the first or were there more? If there were, she hadn't ever heard of any.

Jack might very well be the first. She didn't understand why Thomas had brought him here, actually. Jack didn't seem to be actively searching for any sort of redemption and, as far as she knew, had never mentioned a desire to become Chosen.

As true to her status as Chosen, she should be worried for him. But she couldn't seem to summon up anything other than curiosity rather than concern. From what she knew of him, Jack was good and had a kind heart, not to mention ruggedly handsome.

And sexy, a little voice whispered inside her head. Ignoring it, she hurried through her shower so she could rush through the rest of her preparations for the evening ahead.

Ninety minutes later, wearing a flattering, long cotton dress that hugged her curves, Sophia surveyed herself as best she could in Rachel's hand mirror and nodded. "I guess it'll have to do," she said.

Rachel, wearing a similar dress in a darker color, sighed. "Soph, if you could only see yourself right now. I'd give anything to look as good as you do."

Both pleased and appalled, Sophia thanked her, unable to keep from thinking that maybe if she were less attractive, Ezekiel would never have noticed her.

Arm in arm, Sophia and Rachel walked to the town center. All around them, others were doing the same. Though darkness had not yet fallen, twinkly white lights illuminated the path, decorating the trees like the entrance to some sort of enchanted fairyland.

Huge, black, charcoal smokers were arranged in a semicircle, manned by several of Ezekiel's older sons. Long trestle tables had been set up nearby, practically groaning under the weight of multiple covered pans of food.

And children sat in circles with their age groups on

the ground, watching the activity around them with wide-eyed anticipation.

Rachel waved to her class, beaming with pride. "See how well behaved my kids are? They're doing so great."

Unbidden, Jack's words about how children should act came back to Sophia. She kept them to herself, aware Rachel would find them wrong and crazy.

Meanwhile, tonight Sophia would be meeting her fiancé for the first time. She inhaled, her mouth dry with nerves as she unobtrusively scanned the crowd for Ezekiel. When she didn't see him or his retinue of wives and children, she felt a little bit better. "Which one is the boy with the problem?" she asked, glad to have something else to focus on.

"There." Rachel pointed to a stocky, dark-haired kid near one of the attendants named Ralph, who appeared to be keeping a close eye on him. "That's Benjamin."

"He's cute," Sophia said, smiling in the child's direction. Instead of smiling back, the boy frowned before dropping his gaze.

"There's your friend." Rachel pointed at Jack. "He's waving. Oh, look, his roommate is with him."

Blushing, Sophia waved back. "Do you know Phillip?" she asked. "He sure is eyeing you."

Mouth curving in a pleased smile, Rachel nodded. "We've spoken a couple of times. I think he's cute."

A commotion had heads swiveling toward the north entrance. Sure enough, a procession headed toward them. With Deirdre and Ezekiel in the lead, Sophia couldn't keep from trying to count the numerous women walking behind them.

"Soon, you'll be there with them." Rachel sounded both proud and sad.

Bile rising in her throat, Sophia nodded. "Are all of those women his wives?" she asked, trying to count them.

"Surely not." Rachel noticed what she was doing and snorted. "You know some of them have to be his grown daughters. And the ones walking with the other guys must be his sons' wives." She giggled. "I wonder if they ever question why only their father gets to marry more than once."

"I doubt it. They all understand he's the leader." Sophia made the reply automatically. She noticed the instant Ezekiel's gaze began sweeping the crowd as if searching for something. Or someone. Most likely her. The thought made her nauseous so she maneuvered herself around enough that she had her back to him.

"What are you doing?" Rachel asked, her eyes wide. "You know he's looking for you. You need to go and greet him."

"Do I?" Sophia lifted her chin. "No. I won't. He can come to me."

Rachel gasped. Grabbing Sophia's arm, she steered her back the way they'd come. Only when they'd gotten past most of the crowd and numerous people separating them from the square did she let go. "What is wrong with you?" Rachel demanded. "Now is not the time for you to go insane."

"It isn't?" Sophia stood tall and straight. Now that rebellion had gone from festering inside her to erupting, she knew she couldn't go through with this farce of a marriage. Or could she?

"You have to," Rachel replied once Sophia told her. "Even if it's just to buy you time until you can find an alternative. Ezekiel is not only powerful and blessed, but he is proud. He won't allow you to humiliate him in front of everyone. You'll be punished, maybe even locked up. Then where will you be?"

She was right. Defeated and deflated, Sophia found herself blinking away tears. "I don't know how I'm going to deal with this. If he touches me…" She shuddered.

Rachel made a face. "He's not going to touch you too much, not now, not before the wedding. Maybe a quick, celebratory kiss or a hug. Surely you can deal with that."

Sophia made a face. "I'm not sure."

"Yes, you are. Put on a brave face." Rachel turned her around. "They're coming for you. You've got a fiancé to meet. Do me proud, my friend."

Jack watched all the color drain from Sophia's face before her companion turned her around and half pushed, half helped her face her fears. He glanced north to see what had so terrified her and froze. The huge procession heading their way had to be Ezekiel. The pudgy, bald, overdressed elderly man with an ornate cane who lead the group had to be COE's exalted leader. The equally stout woman marching at his side must be one of his wives, probably the first one. She at least seemed sort of close to his age.

He turned to ask his roommate who they were, but Phillip still continued to stare at Sophia and her friend.

"Ahem." Jack cleared his throat.

Finally noticing Jack watching him, Phillip gave a sheepish smile. "You know," he said, sounding dazed, "I've never seen a woman look that good in a dress."

"What?" Hiding his annoyance, Jack eyed his roommate. "Are you talking about Sophia?"

"No. The woman with her. That is Rachel, one of the teachers. She's really cute, don't you think?"

Jack nodded, aware he couldn't tell Phillip the truth. He hadn't noticed the other woman. He'd only had eyes for Sophia.

Damn, he was in trouble. Big trouble.

Needing something to distract him, he glanced back at the approaching procession. As soon as they'd reached the edges of the square, everyone shuffled for position. People had lined up to welcome them, in the same manner a crowd would stand to watch a parade.

Then he saw the children. His first thought was to wonder if they'd been drugged. Motionless, like little adults, they sat in an orderly circle watching the goings-on with quiet curiosity. They all wore matching uniforms—a crisp white shirt and plaid pants or skirts—reminding him of a private religious school.

For the first time he realized everyone else had dressed up, too; way too overdressed for a simple cookout, or at least in his world. Instead of shorts and T-shirts, all the men wore slacks and button-down shirts. The women, without exception, wore the same long dresses they always did, except these seemed to be made of a finer material.

Weird. Even stranger, Phillip hadn't said anything when Jack had pulled on a pair of well-worn jeans. Of course, maybe he'd understood Jack didn't own anything nicer than what he'd been given by Thomas.

As Ezekiel and his family neared the center of the commons, the rest of the crowd closed ranks, forming a circle around a raised wooden dais that resembled a stage. Transfixed by all the pomp and ceremony— really, where were the drums?—Jack watched as two younger men helped the elderly Ezekiel climb up on the platform. Once he'd been situated, the rest of his entourage flowed into place around him.

Apparently there would be a speech. Since no one had even remotely attempted to convert him to another way of thinking, Jack couldn't wait to hear this. For the first time he'd get an insight into the way the COE thought, which so far seemed more like a rigorously controlled commune rather than a cult.

And then, as Ezekiel and his people settled into their positions, two of the leader's men—Thomas and one other—moved out into the crowd, clearly searching for something. Or someone.

The crowd murmured, necks craning to see. Equally curious, Jack kept his eyes on Thomas's tall figure, noting when he stopped and bent to converse with a shorter person.

A moment later, as Thomas and the other man made their way back, they had someone with them. The instant he realized it was Sophia, Jack started forward instinctively.

"No." Phillip grabbed his arm, yanking him back. "Stay here. What the heck is wrong with you? You can't interfere."

Jack blinked. Of course he couldn't. Even though every cell in his body urged him to help Sophia, who appeared both terrified and, oddly enough, rebellious.

"Here she is," Ezekiel boomed, his tone jovial. For a man of his advanced years, his voice still reverberated with strength. "My lovely bride-to-be."

At this words, Sophia swallowed. Then she straightened her shoulders, lifted her chin and climbed the wooden steps to stand in front of her fiancé. Her remote expression revealed nothing but strength.

Marveling, especially since he had a pretty good idea how she must feel inside, Jack tried to mimic her stoicism. He relaxed his hands, which he realized he'd clenched into fists, and rolled his stiff shoulders to release some of the tension coiling there.

"Everyone, I'd like you to meet my next wife," Ezekiel declared, reaching out his age-spotted hand and pulling Sophia into his side, so he could gaze down lovingly at her. "Sophia Hannah, who has done me the honor of agreeing to become my bride."

As if she'd had a choice. As happy cheers and congratulatory shouts erupted all around him, once again Jack found himself wondering what the hell was wrong with these people that they could cheerfully celebrate forcing a young woman to marry a man nearly four times her age.

Not only did this infuriate him, it made him want to stand up and say something. Which not only might be dangerous and foolish, but definitely would endanger the reason he'd come here—to find the Bartletts' missing son.

Instead of worrying about Sophia, who clearly could take care of herself, he needed to figure out a way to talk to the children.

Judging by the stern-faced adults guarding them, doing so would be easier said than done.

But Jack was new and could always claim he didn't know the rules. As soon as Ezekiel's speech ended, Jack would make his way over to see what he could find out.

Meanwhile, Ezekiel had begun complimenting Sophia's beauty. The older woman on his other side watched him, her eyes narrowing and her lips growing tighter with each glowing word.

As for Sophia, her eyes had glazed over. She stood in place, a cool half smile fixed on her face as she gazed out at the crowd. Since he knew her, Jack could tell she'd switched to endurance mode. He doubted anyone else made anything of it.

It sounded like Ezekiel might be winding down. "As my family of Chosen, I want to invite every single one of you to my wedding in less than a month's time. We will hold it in the Sanctuary, of course. And then we shall celebrate here afterward."

The Sanctuary. Was that some sort of church? This was the first time Jack had heard any mention of such a structure. Interesting. Resolving to check it out if he could, Jack returned his focus to what he had to do next. Talk to the children.

As the Supreme Leader of COE finished his talk, he once again tugged Sophia into him, leaning hard on his carved and polished mahogany cane. "And now," he murmured, still loud enough to be heard, "we shall share a celebratory kiss."

When Ezekiel bent his head to cover Sophia's mouth with his, every fiber of Jack's being rebelled. He managed— barely—to keep his feet motionless, imagining them locked into place. Because of the angle, he couldn't see Sophia's face, just the rigid way she held her body. He found himself hoping she could hold herself together and refrain from doing anything that might give her repulsion away.

Finally, Ezekiel released her. Instantly she looked down, no doubt in an attempt to regain her composure.

"And now we eat," Ezekiel declared, waving his hand in a kingly gesture before motioning to Thomas to accompany him. Cane thumping, he moved away from Sophia without a backward glance, leaving her standing alone and rigid on the platform.

Though his first instinct was to go to her, Jack did

not. He turned and eyed the children, still seated so very politely. They looked like little robots, he thought again.

Glancing at Phillip, who'd refocused his attention on Sophia's friend, Jack shrugged and made his way toward the group of kids he judged would be around the right age as the Bartlett boy. He hadn't gotten within two feet of them before one of the stern-faced attendants stood and placed himself between Jack and the class.

"Can I help you?" the man asked, planting his legs in an aggressive stance and crossing his arms.

"What?" Jack pretended bewilderment. "I just wanted to greet the youngsters. I love children."

"Why?"

The question dumbfounded him, so he decided to answer in kind. "Why what?"

"Why do you want to talk to the little ones?"

Jack shrugged. "Do I have to have a reason? Is such a thing not allowed? I'm new here, so if there's some rule I don't know about, please fill me in."

For the first time since confronting Jack, the other man appeared uncertain. Then, as he considered, the calm certainty reaffirmed itself in his face. "Their experiences are carefully controlled," he said slowly. "We take pride in ensuring our offspring are raised properly. I'm afraid I can't allow you to upset that."

"Wow." The word slipped out, but once it had, Jack was glad. "That's really rigid."

"Maybe it is." The man's shrug made it clear he didn't care what Jack thought. "But I'm going to have to ask you to move away."

Aware he had no choice, especially since he couldn't afford to make a scene, Jack nodded and carefully made his way back to Phillip. His roommate no longer mooned after Sophia's friend; instead he'd fixated all his attention on the smokers and grills.

"Man, smell that?" Phillip sniffed the air in appreciation. "I'm craving some ribs. How about you?"

"I could eat," Jack admitted. But he found himself scanning the crowd for Sophia. Since he didn't see her, he figured she must have been hustled off to do something with the people who would soon be her new family group.

Glancing once more at the children, he finally gave up and followed Phillip over to one of the long tables, where food had been set out and lines were already forming. He'd scarf down some food and then try to find her. He had a hunch she might need a pep talk after what had just occurred.

Chapter 8

After Ezekiel's kiss and subsequent dismissal, Sophia knew she couldn't get away quickly enough. She suspected she might lose her fragile grip on self-control and explode if she had to endure one more thing, so she hurried down from the stage and pushed her way through the crowd. She moved fast, having picked up her long skirt in one hand so she wouldn't trip and add injury to insult.

While she wasn't sure where she was going—anywhere but here—she knew she didn't want to talk to anyone. Including Jack. Not yet, at least.

At first, she thought she might head home and lock herself in her bedroom for a good cry. But instead she found herself near the edge of the compound, near the fence that separated their space from the untamed forest.

Glad Jack had reminded her of this place, she stopped

and leaned on the rough-hewn timber. It had been far too long since she'd come here. Maybe she could regain some of the peace and joy the woods had brought her when she'd been younger.

Hitching up her dress, she climbed up to sit on the top rail. When she and her friends had escaped, as they'd called it, they'd all spoken in whispers about the possibility that there were cameras. That would mean their every move had been noted and recorded. But nothing had ever been found.

Glancing back toward the compound, she could see the smoke plumes from the barbecue grills and smokers. Everyone still gathered, celebrating. No one would notice if she disappeared for a little while.

Not even, she thought with a crushing sense of disappointment, Jack.

After she managed to climb over the fence without tripping on the hem of her long dress, she stood on the other side, feeling slightly foolish. Nothing had changed. Had she really expected it to? Since she'd never truly known freedom, she had no idea what it might feel like.

Still lifting the edge of her skirt with one hand, she took a deep breath and walked into the forest. She had no destination in mind. She just wanted to walk until she stopped hurting. Of course, the way she felt right now, she'd have to walk for days and weeks and months.

Careful to take note of her route, she continued into the forest. Once, she thought there might have been a path here, but undergrowth had reclaimed it.

She couldn't stop thinking about the flat assessment in Ezekiel's lizard-like eyes when he'd looked at her. Right then, she'd known that, to him, she wasn't a person, or even a woman, but a possession. A *thing*. His to do with as he pleased.

And she'd realized she'd rather be dead.

Shaken to the core, she wanted no part of his world. Not in three weeks' time, not ever. She didn't know what she was going to do or where she would go, but she wouldn't be marrying Ezekiel.

She knew she'd need to make a plan.

"Hey." Jack's voice, from a short distance behind her. She spun around. He'd found her. But how? How had he known where she'd go?

Though her heartbeat thundered in her ears, she worked hard to keep her face expressionless.

"Did you get a chance to eat?" Jack asked when he reached her.

"No. I wasn't hungry."

"I didn't think so." Holding out a paper-wrapped plate, he steered her to a fallen tree trunk. "Sit. I brought you some brisket."

"Oh. That's usually one of my favorites, but I'm not sure I can—"

"You can, you'll see." Once he'd helped her maneuver into a spot on the tree, he handed her the plate and pulled off the paper napkin cover. Immediately the irresistible, smoked scent of homemade barbecue assaulted her nose.

Her mouth watered. "Maybe I'll just have one bite," she said.

"I thought you might," he said as he handed her the plastic knife and fork. "The baked beans are really good, too."

Amazingly, she managed to finish the entire plate. Jack silently watched her eat, smiling.

The meal tasted wonderful and did not, as she'd feared, sour in her stomach.

Once she'd finished and used the paper napkin to wipe her mouth, he took the plate from her. Using his boot, he dug a slight hole and buried the plate in the dirt, along with the plastic utensils.

"Feeling better?" he asked, his eyes sparkling, making her body tingle all over.

She considered his question. "Maybe. A little." Taking a deep breath, she decided to tell him the truth. "I don't know what I'm going to do."

"It's tough," he agreed. "I'd hate to be in your position."

"Yeah." Her laugh came out sounding more like a cry. "But today made me realize something. I'm not going to marry him."

Her words, sent out into the universe, seemed to hover between them, taking on an existence of their own. She rushed on, aware she had to say it all now, before she lost her courage. "I'm going to have to leave COE. Go outside and figure out how to start a new life. And for that, I'm going to need your help."

Instead of responding, he continued to watch her, his expression giving nothing away. As the seconds ticked away, fear stabbed her. Had she completely misjudged him? Was he more into COE than she'd thought? And would he report her to Thomas or Ezekiel?

"Oh, Sophia." The intensity in his lowered voice confused her. "You have no idea what you're asking for."

"I do," she insisted. "At least part of it. By all that is just and right, you cannot tell me you expect me to marry Ezekiel." She shuddered. "If you'd seen what was in his eyes when he looked at me..."

He swallowed hard. "I can imagine. And, believe

me, I understand. But the life you have here, the sense of community, everything you love and value about COE—are you truly willing to give all that up?"

"Yes." She didn't hesitate.

"Forever?" he persisted.

"Once I marry Ezekiel, that life will be gone. I'll go live in his harem with his other wives. I'll no longer have any value other than as one of his possessions. Dr. Drew has told me this, and so has Deirdre, Ezekiel's first wife. I can't live like that. I won't."

Their gazes locked. Sophia could hear her heart beating, feel the thrum of her blood as it flowed through her veins.

"I'll help you," he finally said. "Things like this take some planning, though."

"I don't have a lot of time. He said less than a month, which is what I was told before." Her bitter laugh echoed the way she felt inside. "True." He glanced at his watch. "We'd better be getting back."

She balked. "Why? I'm not ready yet."

"Because." Offering her his hand, he helped her from the log. "Rule number one of planning to escape. Don't give them any hints something is up."

Since his words made sense, she allowed him to lead her back the way she'd come. She liked the way his hand swallowed up hers, and how the height and breadth of him made her feel protected. She liked *him*.

"Will you go back to the picnic with me?" Though his expression remained serious, the spark in his eyes pulled a small smile.

Even though she found the idea repulsive, she considered. "If we do, we should probably go separately. We don't want our being together to be noticed."

"Do you think it would?" he asked.

About to remind him of his earlier words, she stopped when she realized he was teasing.

Suddenly exhausted, she shook her head. "You go ahead and return to the cookout," she told him. "I'm going to go home and go to bed. I want this day to be over."

Gaze still locked on hers, he nodded. "I understand," he said.

They continued to hold hands until they reached the fringes of the forest. When he released her, she felt an aching sense of loss, which she pushed away. If she was going to do this, if she truly planned to leave her community and friends, she needed to learn how to stand on her own.

At the fence, she waved away his offer to help and climbed over by herself. Not gracefully, but she did it. Once she stood on the other side, she smiled at him. "Here's where we should part ways," she said. "I'll see you at work tomorrow."

As she walked away, he didn't follow. But she felt his gaze burning into her back until she was out of sight.

Because he liked to be early, Jack arrived at the medical clinic at 6:45 a.m., leaving his house well before Phillip had even started stirring. He was not surprised to find Sophia already there. She was the first one in and the last to leave and, as far as he could tell, she ran the entire clinic single-handedly. He wasn't sure what the other woman, Ana, actually did, but it seemed to mostly consist of sitting at the reception desk when she wasn't following Sophia around.

As far as the doctor, when he wasn't with patients, he spent his time sequestered in his private office with the door closed.

She hadn't been kidding about it being slow, except for that one busy afternoon. There wasn't much for Jack to do now that he'd organized the storeroom. As far as he could tell, the clinic would get along just fine without him. But so far, no one had appeared concerned about his conspicuous lack of duties. Of course, it had only been a few days.

Those few days made him feel like he'd been sitting still. Intellectually, he knew he needed time, but he didn't like the way he'd begun to feel comfortable inside the cult. Not only that, but pretty Sophia Hannah and her impossible situation tugged at his heartstrings. And there was also how badly he wanted to make love to her. If it had been another time and situation, he would have thought they were meant for each other. Truth be told, even the thought of another man—especially an elderly megalomaniac—putting his hands on her soft skin made Jack want to punch something.

None of that was good. His jaw ached from clenching it. He needed to find out if the Bartletts' son was here—and get out. Somehow, some way, he had to talk to the children. The fact that the cult apparently kept them locked away didn't bode well for him gaining access.

Sighing, he crossed the waiting room and headed back to the storeroom. Since he'd had to conjure up busywork, today he would be retaking inventory and letting Sophia know what items needed to be reordered. She'd told him she'd give the list to Dr. Drew, who would order from a medical supply clinic in Laramie. Jack wondered silently if the good doctor had a secret computer in addition to a cell phone. No doubt he did.

But he'd no sooner arrived in the storeroom when Sophia asked him to help her move a desk in the reception area. Apparently, Dr. Drew wanted the waiting room rearranged. Glad to actually have something to do, Jack pushed the desk to the opposite wall while she looked on. Something about the admiration in her gaze made him feel like he could do anything.

The next several minutes, he helped rehang pictures, move filing cabinets and a magazine rack. At seven thirty, Ana walked in. After jerking her head in greeting to them, she barely glanced at the new setup, instead heading straight toward the back bathroom. Her eyes were red, as if she'd been crying.

Right after she closed the door, two men entered. They both wore dark blue T-shirts and khaki slacks, and they carried themselves with authority.

"Jack Moreno?" one of them asked. When Jack nodded, the man stepped aside. "We'll need you to come with us."

Confused, Jack started forward.

"Wait." Sophia moved between him and the door. "What's this about?"

Both men turned identical disapproving looks at her. "You know better than to ask questions," the first one said. "And this is none of your concern."

Judging by Sophia's reaction, Jack guessed he might be in some sort of trouble. Since he hadn't done anything except walk with Sophia, he had to assume that was why. He moved past her and out the clinic door.

With one man on each side of him, they headed down the path. Neither of his escorts spoke.

As they continued on, the houses began to lose their boring similarity. One or two appeared larger, maybe a bit more ornate. Then he realized where they were taking him. Either to see Thomas or to meet Ezekiel.

Things had just gotten interesting. He sincerely

hoped it was the latter. He truly wanted to get a good look at the man who could inspire such blind devotion.

And maybe he could figure out a way to ask about the children. He'd heard offhand comments about family groups, but as yet he hadn't actually witnessed such a thing. Of course, he lived with another young, single man, which appeared to be what COE did once people aged out of the family group. He'd asked Phillip and learned that once a young man claimed a wife, which it sounded as if he did without consulting or asking her, they were wed and moved into a home with other married couples, which became their new family group. The family group helped raise any children.

From the way COE kept such a tight lid on all of this, Jack surmised they viewed children as a precious commodity. With so many strict rules, he couldn't help but wonder if any of them ever rebelled. Or perhaps they were all so brainwashed at an early age that bucking the system never even occurred to them.

One thing was for sure, he'd never be able to determine if the Bartlett boy was here unless he figure out a way to interact with the children, especially the troubled ones.

Finally his two escorts stopped. Jack knew this place. He'd been here before. "Here we are," the taller of the two said. "Thomas is expecting you."

Disappointed, Jack nodded and pressed the buzzer. A moment later the door opened and he went on inside.

This time, Thomas held out his hand for Jack to shake. "Welcome," he said, smiling. He led Jack into a small sitting room, gesturing toward a dark leather sofa. "Take a seat. I want to discuss a proposition with you."

Interesting. Careful to keep his face expressionless, Jack sat. The leather on the sofa felt soft and expensive.

"The other day you mentioned to Dr. Drew that you'd done some therapy work."

Jack nodded. He prayed they didn't have a source inside the military that would enable them to check his service records. If they did, he was screwed. They'd find out he'd completely made it all up.

"It so happens," Thomas continued, "that we have need of someone who can do some counseling. Have you ever worked with children?"

Though his pulse jumped, Jack knew he'd have to be extremely careful. "No, sir, I haven't," he answered. He figured he'd stick to as much honesty as he could. More difficult to get tripped up that way.

"I think you can give it a try. Dr. Drew has agreed to loan you to the school for as long as it takes. You'll be working with the primary teacher there. Her name is Rachel." Thomas's smile widened. "I think you'll find her very attractive. She's unclaimed, too, so if you think she's something you want, you'll need to jump in fairly quickly."

It took a moment for Thomas's words to register. "You want me to…claim her?" Jack asked, not sure what exactly the other man had in mind.

"Only if you want to." Thomas gave a jovial laugh. "You'll find we have plenty of unattached, pretty women here. So there's no need to go sniffing after any that are already promised. Do you follow?"

He meant Sophia. Jack carefully forced what he hoped was a casual smile. "I follow." He kept his voice light, despite the anger coiling inside him.

"I thought you would." Apparently satisfied, Thomas nodded. "Rachel will meet you outside her home at seven in the morning. She'll take you to school. Make sure you're there."

And with that, Jack was dismissed.

* * *

Thirty minutes after the two men escorted Jack away, a messenger rushed into the clinic and informed Sophia that Deirdre wanted to see her.

At the news the first wife was summoning her again, Sophia recognized the hard knot of panic that settled low in her belly. Dread.

She followed the messenger again. This time, Deirdre received her in the garden, which even Sophia had to admit was lovely. Spring flowers boomed in riotous color, and the ornate, metal patio furniture had been made to appear to blend perfectly with the landscape. In the back, she spied some sort of structure. A small house, half hidden by trees and shrubs and flowers.

Deirdre offered her lemonade. Sophia declined.

The meeting was brief. Deirdre just wanted to inform Sophia that all the arrangements had been handled, including the flowers and her dress. Sophia would need to be fitted, just to make sure the dress fit. But Deirdre felt confident it would because she was a very good judge of size.

Through it all, Sophia tried to smile and nod, but she ended up having to try to keep from crying. Finally, Deirdre finished and gestured toward the gate. "You can go now," she said, returning her attention to her drink.

Sophia spun around to do just that. "Thank you," she murmured, which seemed the final irony. As she made her way on the cobblestone path toward the exit, Deirdre called her back.

Careful not to show her reluctance, Sophia went.

"One more thing," Deirdre said, narrowing her eyes as she studied Sophia. "We've moved the wedding up a little. I know yesterday Ezekiel said less than a month, but that's incorrect. You're going to be married in two weeks. So get your affairs in order. I'm not sure if Dr. Drew will need a two-week notice or not."

Two weeks! Confused and horrified, Sophia froze. "What do you mean about Dr. Drew?"

This time there was no imagining the malice in Deirdre's smile. "You won't be employed there after you're married, sweetie. Ezekiel doesn't allow any of his wives to work."

"I see." Blinking back tears, Sophia managed a nod. Two weeks. As she stumbled away, she knew she needed to begin thinking about what she might have to do to escape. The outside world might be alien and frightening, but not even a tenth as much as the idea of her approaching marriage.

She needed to give her notice to Dr. Drew, but couldn't face anyone right now. So she took a detour and found herself in the barn. This time, instead of simply petting her favorite horse across the stall door, she let herself in. Smokey looked up, nickering in welcome. The clean hay felt soft underneath her shoes. She went to him and wrapped her arms around his neck, at long last giving in to her tears.

"I thought I might find you here." Jack's voice.

Startled, Sophia raised her head, wiping at her no-doubt red eyes.

His happy smile changed to a frown. "Are you okay?" he asked softly.

About to speak, she simply shrugged. The workers had entered the south end of the barn with a small tractor and wagon, continuing their daily routine of mucking out the stalls. Apparently they'd already finished the north side, since Smokey's stall was clean.

"Walk with me?" she asked, aware her desperation showed in both her voice and expression.

He nodded. "Sure," he answered without hesitation. "Though I should let you know I've been warned about hanging around with an engaged woman."

"Warned?" She hadn't thought her day could get any worse, but it just had. "By who?"

"Thomas." Waiting until she'd opened the stall door and slipped outside into the aisle, he held out his arm. "Don't worry. He wants me to check out your roommate Rachel."

The instant flash of jealously that knifed through her should have surprised her, but it didn't. "Why?" she asked. "Why Rachel?"

He waited until they'd left the barn before responding. "Because I'm going to be working with her, providing therapy for some of her students. He gave me a veiled warning about hanging out with women who were taken and mentioned Rachel was available."

"A veiled warning." The idea horrified her. "Maybe you'd better go."

"Not a chance." Again, the immediacy of his response gratified her. Because the truth was, if he left, she'd be all alone. And the misery festering inside her needed an outlet.

Still, she felt she needed to be up-front. "Jack, I honestly don't know what they might do if you're seen with me. Everything is spiraling out of control so quickly."

He turned to face her. For one heart-stopping moment she thought he might take her in his arms. Luckily for both of them, he didn't. "Is that why you were crying?"

"Let's go to the gardens," she said instead of answering. "At least there we'll have a small bit of privacy."

Since it was spring, the corn hadn't grown tall enough to hide in. The tomato plants had just been started, so she settled for taking him into one of the greenhouses, knowing they'd be empty.

Once the door had closed behind them, she let the entire story spill out. She told him everything.

Jack listened, the attentive look on his handsome face neither condemning nor shocked. When she finally wound down, ending with the earlier meeting with Deirdre, he shook his head. "They've moved the wedding up. Did she tell you why?"

Miserable, she shook her head. "I don't want to marry him," she whispered. "But I don't have a choice."

He gazed down at her, his blue eyes dark and hooded. "You always have a choice," he murmured. Then he covered her mouth with his and kissed her.

Stunned, she froze. The slow and thoughtful movement of his lips on hers filled her with a hunger like she'd never experienced. A delicious sensation, this kiss, forbidden and daring, making her burn. Alternatively both heady and tender, he seemed to be holding himself in check, as if he thought he needed to be careful with her.

Suddenly, achingly, she realized she didn't want *tender*. She wanted passion and fierceness, craving and wild desire. Everything she would be missing the rest of her life if she were to marry Ezekiel.

She wanted Jack. And she wanted him now. Her blood heated, her head pounded and her knees weakened.

Curling into the curve of his body, she gave herself over to him. Where he led, she would follow. And if he didn't lead, then she'd figure out a way to do so.

Her breasts ached for his touch, but since he didn't reach for them, she pressed them into the rock-hard muscle of his chest. Her heart pounded and her breath caught. Trembling, she tried to figure out how to ask him for more.

Continuing to kiss her, he moved his hands down to the small of her back, holding her in place. Still gentle, still restrained. As if he held a part of himself distant from her. But then she felt the swell of his arousal and realized he held himself in control with an iron strength of will. While she wasn't at all experienced, she knew enough to understand that a simple move, a wiggle and a squirm, could escalate his desire.

So she did. He made a low sound, something guttural, and raised his mouth from hers. She was gratified to see how hard he was breathing. "Sophia?" he asked, a thousand questions in the simple act of saying her name.

Chapter 9

"Yes," Sophia breathed, daring to use her hands to caress him. "Yes, yes, a thousand times yes."

"Someone might see us," he protested, though heat blazed from his gaze. "I don't know what the punishment is for something like this, but I have a feeling we don't want to find out."

"I don't care," she declared, her chest heaving. "I want this. I want you."

The heart-rending tenderness in his expression made her throat catch. "And I want you, Sophia. But not like this. Not standing in the dirt, with the smell of manure fresh in the air. We deserve more than this—hell, you deserve more than this."

Did she? Her body aching, she nodded. She buried her face in his broad chest, hoping she could hide her dejection. "You're right," she admitted. Though she hated the fact, it was the truth. If she actually did give in to temptation, the situation would need to be extra special. Not blind and crazed passion in a public greenhouse. "I don't know what came over me. I'm sorry."

"No." He cupped her chin in his large hand, raising her face to his so he could kiss the tip of her nose. "Don't apologize. Not for this. In fact, not ever. You're warm and beautiful and a damn desirable woman, Sophia Hannah. Don't ever forget that. And no matter what, don't you ever change."

She wanted to agree but couldn't. How could she not change, now that everyone she loved seemed to find it perfectly acceptable that she was to become the newest wife of a man old enough to be her grandfather? Did they not care or understand how her spirit would wither and die after she'd been relegated to a place in his harem?

Ever finding happiness didn't seem possible. Unless it was with Jack. The inexplicable connection that blazed between them gave her a glimpse at what might be possible, if she were to take a different path. And that somehow was worse, much, much worse, than never knowing.

"Baby, don't cry," he rasped. The endearment—or maybe the tone, or both—undid her, making it impossible to hold the tears in.

He held her while she wept, letting her soak the front of his shirt. And then he continued to keep her close while she attempted to get herself together, gathering her shredded composure around her like a cloak.

"I'm…" She shook her head. "Not going to apologize."

"Good." The approval in his warm smile lifted her spirits. "That's my girl."

If only she was, she thought. Right now, she'd give anything to be his girl.

And maybe such a thing might still be possible. Refusing to allow herself to even hope, she took a deep breath. Even if it was not, she needed his help. "Would you do me a favor?"

Without asking what, he nodded. "Anything."

"Tell me what it's like outside. I've never left COE and I'm curious. I need to know what to expect."

"Let's walk," he said, taking her arm and steering her toward the doorway. "I should warn you. I have no idea what it would be like from the perspective of someone innocent, like you."

Still wiping at her eyes, she grimaced. "Please, go ahead and tell me what's different out there from in here."

"I don't know where to begin."

"Please try."

And so he did, listing things succinctly, in a way she appreciated. While inside the compound they had vehicles and computers, their use was limited to people higher up in the organization. He told her about something called television and movies, and made comments on the different way women dressed out there. She listened, partly intrigued, partly appalled. Though she hadn't thought much further than escaping her impending marriage, the more Jack talked, the more she realized a completely different world would be opening up to her.

As long as she had Jack by her side, she thought navigating it would be amazing.

Later, after leaving Sophia and returning to his house, Jack gave himself a stern tongue-lashing. What the heck was he thinking? He'd actually been given the chance to talk to the children. He was so close to learning if any of them had been brought there from elsewhere, and specifically, if one of them might be the Bartlett boy. While Sophia Hannah made him feel things he'd never felt, he couldn't allow her to distract him from his mission inside COE.

But if she truly wanted to leave… The thought, like a seed sowed in fertile earth, took root. He couldn't discard it, couldn't let it go. Because not only was she sweet and beautiful, but her situation right now was terrible. As far as he could tell, she hadn't done a thing to deserve such a fate, other than being extraordinarily beautiful. Unfortunately that, itself, was often enough—whether in the outside world or here in COE.

But he knew one thing. If he could help her in any way possible without jeopardizing the reason he was there, he would. Until he found what he was looking for, he'd figure out a way to keep her safe.

The next morning he woke with a sense of anticipation. Today he'd be meeting Sophia's roommate Rachel and finally seeing the elusive children that were kept so isolated. But why?

Phillip strolled into the kitchen as Jack made himself a second cup of coffee. "Hadn't you better get going?" he asked, yawning. "You're usually gone when I get up. You're going to be late."

"I'm fine." Jack smiled. "I have a new, temporary gig. Today I'm meeting Rachel and going to the school to help with some of the kids."

Phillip did a double-take. "Really? That's kind of odd. Who decided this?"

"Thomas." As he'd suspected he would, mentioning Ezekiel's right-hand man's name immediately soothed

Phillip's fears. "I did some therapy work when I was in the military. He thought I might be able to help Rachel with a special situation."

"I see." Phillip nodded. "I really like Rachel," he said, a note of warning in his tone. "I've been thinking about courting her. Just so you know."

"So you're saying you've got dibs?"

Phillip's frown wasn't quite the reaction Jack had been expecting. "What do you mean?"

"Dibs. As in, you've got the first claim to her."

"Oh." Phillip's expression cleared. "Sure. But I promise if I change my mind, you'll be the first to know."

"What about Rachel?" Jack couldn't stop himself from asking. "Does she have any say in this at all?"

From his roommate's incredulous expression, apparently he found Jack's remark bizarre.

"Why would she?" Phillip asked. "I know you're new here, but I have to imagine it's the same everywhere. Women are just grateful to be claimed. That's all they live for. They can't wait to be a wife and hopefully a mother. That's fulfillment of their purpose in this world, the reason they were born."

Maybe a century or more ago, Jack thought, though he wisely kept the observation to himself. He finished his coffee and stood. "She's meeting me here," he said. "Just in case you want to come outside and speak to her."

For a second he thought Phillip might take him up on his offer. But then the other man shook his head. "No time. I need to shower and get ready for work."

Exiting the kitchen, he gave Jack's upper bicep a quick cuff. "Have a good day," he said. "And good luck with the kiddos. Being around that many children would give me a headache, that's for sure."

Once Phillip had disappeared down the hall, Jack took a deep breath and headed for the front door. Time to meet Rachel. He hoped he could convince her that he knew what he was doing. In reality, he didn't have the slightest idea.

Though he supposed he'd seen her from a distance, up close Sophia's roommate was not at all what he'd expected. Short and curvy, she strode toward him with a quiet self-assurance that seemed all business.

"Jack Moreno?" She spoke with a pleasing lilt to her voice. "I'm Rachel."

They shook hands. Her firm grip and cool skin made him smile. Already he liked her. He could see why Phillip had been considering dating her.

"I understand you're to be our new therapist?" she asked as they walked toward the center of the compound.

He nodded. "I confess, I've never worked with children. In fact, I've never been around many kids at all. Can you tell me a little bit about what this boy's issues are?"

Her smile lit up her entire face. "Oh, I can do better than that. I've got an entire file on him for you to read. After you've done that, I'll let you observe him in class. We'll take it slow, if that's all right with you. That is, as slow as possible. If he has another outburst, you may need to intervene."

"Sounds good."

Rachel stopped at a large square building. Though constructed from the same concrete material as the others, this one had only smallish windows, up near the top where they were way too high to be opened. They'd let the light in, but little else. He guessed the powers that be didn't want the little students to be distracted by being able to see outside.

"He's attempted to run away several times now," Rachel informed him. "He bolts and runs. Of course, with the way our school building is designed, he doesn't get far. But it's disruptive to the rest of the children. And worrisome. I've taught for seven years and nothing like this has ever happened before."

Thinking it better not to comment, he watched as she dug a key from her pocket and unlocked the door. Gesturing at him to precede her, once they were inside, she secured the lock after them.

"You lock them inside?" he asked. "Or are you locking them out until it's time to open the school?"

The cool, measuring look she gave him made him think she found his question out of line, so he decided to let it go.

When they entered the classroom, the noise level hit him. And the kids—there were so many of them. Some were seated, others were running and jostling each other, and yelling. Laughter, shouts and so many little voices all speaking at once assaulted his ears.

Or at least they did, until they caught sight of their teacher. Without Rachel saying a word, immediately every single student rushed to their desk, going as quiet as if a switch had been flipped.

"Thank you," Rachel said, her satisfied smile letting him know this behavior was expected. "Everyone, this is Jack."

"Hello, Jack," thirty young voices chorused.

"He'll be observing us today," she continued. "If everyone would get out their books and turn to page twenty-one, please."

The rest of the day passed uneventfully, though Jack

learned one new thing about himself. Being around this many kids *did* give him a headache. He and Phillip had that in common, at least.

Apparently, Rachel taught certain subjects to different groups of children, clustered together by age. She exhibited amazing patience, which he couldn't help but admire. She never pointed out the boy who needed counseling, so he had no idea which one it was or in which group. Though he studied each child carefully, he couldn't exactly pull out the sketch artist's rendition of what the Bartlett boy would look like now, so he couldn't tell if any of the boys might be him. He himself could barely remember it, even though he'd glanced at it before going to that fateful meeting where he'd met Thomas.

Despite doing nothing but observing, by the time the school day ended, Jack was exhausted. He watched as the children filed out of the room, wondering where they went. Finally he asked.

"To the dorms, of course." The matter-of-fact way Rachel answered let him know this was ordinary to her.

"Dorms? I thought the children stayed with family groups."

Continuing to straighten up her desk, she didn't even look at him. "They do, until they're old enough to start walking. They are sent to the nursery then and they live in the dorms. When they turn five, they start school."

"I bet the youngest ones have a hard time." He'd spoken without thinking. "Being without family."

She shrugged. "Sometimes they do. But the older children comfort the younger ones. And if things get really bad, one of us teachers make sure to comfort them and dry their tears." She flashed a rueful smile. "You don't know how many times I end up spending the night with the younger children at the beginning of the school year."

"That's dedication," he said, meaning it.

Cocking her head, she slowly nodded. "Yes," she answered. "Yes, it is." She considered him for another moment. "Do you mind if I ask you something personal?"

"Sure."

She glanced back toward the doorway as if she needed to make sure no one else was listening. "What are your intentions toward Sophia?"

At first he'd thought he'd heard wrong. Or, alternatively, that she might be joking. But her serious expression told him she really wanted to know.

"We're friends," he said. "I like Sophia. A lot."

Fixing him with a stern gaze, she swallowed. "I do, too. And she and I have known each other all our lives. And while you seem like a perfectly nice man, understand I mean this with every fiber of my being. If you hurt her, I will make you pay."

Fierce and fiery, just like Sophia. He liked that about her. "Rachel, the last thing I would ever do is hurt Sophia. I can promise you that."

After a moment her expression cleared as she appeared to accept his words. He wanted to ask her what she thought about Sophia's arranged marriage, but didn't dare. What he and Sophia discussed in private would stay between them only, and he felt certain Rachel felt the same.

"Now, about your class," he began, changing the subject. "When can I meet privately with the boy who needs counseling?"

"There are several, but we'll start with the most severe. That would be Benjamin." Apparently she'd decided to trust him.

"Which one was he?"

"The stout little boy with the curly dark hair. He insists on sitting alone at the back table."

Now he remembered. He'd thought it odd that the kid didn't interact with any of his classmates. He'd sat stone-faced, arms crossed, while he'd listened to Rachel's lesson. He'd listened, but that had been about as far as he'd gone. Even better, both the Bartletts had dark brown, curly hair. There might be a very real chance that this Benjamin was their missing son.

He struggled to contain his excitement.

"You're going to be here tomorrow, right?"

"Yes. I'll be helping here for however long it takes."

"Good." She smiled. "Then why don't we let you meet with him for a little bit tomorrow morning?"

"Perfect." It took an effort to appear calm, cool and collected, but he did it.

"All right, then." She seemed to be waiting for something, but he had no idea what. Since he didn't want to blow his one opportunity, he stayed silent.

Eventually, Rachel sighed. "You can go ahead and leave now. I've got a few things I want to do around here before I call it a day. Plus, I always check in with the children before I go."

"Could I go with you?" He'd love to see where the kids lived and what type of security features the cult employed.

"I'm sorry, but no." The watchful look had come back into her eyes. "You need to leave now. I'll see you again in the morning, all right?"

"Of course." Without waiting for a second prompting, he turned and made his way to the door.

He felt like grinning, but couldn't shake the feeling that someone could be watching. He wished he could share his good news with someone. More specifically, with Sophia. But he couldn't. Not yet. Not now. Maybe not ever.

The next day, with Jack once again back at the school with Rachel, the atmosphere at the clinic seemed dull, less interesting. Sophia missed having him at work far more than she knew she should. She actually ached for him, like a lovesick puppy or something. After the kiss they'd shared, she found herself wandering around in a daze.

The things he'd told her about the outside world seemed fantastical, almost like the kinds of dreams she'd once had as a small girl.

While she knew he hadn't made the details up, with her limited experience, she couldn't imagine them. Starting with this thing called television. Moving images on a screen? She didn't even know what a television was, until he'd explained it to her. There'd been more, so much more that she couldn't even remember. She'd seen Dr. Drew using his communication device, but she'd never asked to see it or how it worked. Jack had said these were numerous in the outside world, that everyone had communication devices you could use anywhere, something to do with blue teeth, and the idea that many people lived their lives in a mad rush.

He'd talked about places called zoos where animals were kept in cages and people came to see them. Restaurants where patrons paid money to eat food someone else cooked. Shops where one could buy anything and everything. The need to earn money to pay for rent and clothing and food.

Happiness and strife, war and love, different opinions, conflict and joy and more. Outside seemed like a confusing mishmash. Far different than her experience here in the quiet, well-organized compound. She could see why no one ever left. And, now that he'd gotten a taste of life inside COE, she found it difficult to believe that Jack ever could. Though she'd realized this was exactly what she was considering, she had a very good reason. If Ezekiel hadn't decided to force her to marry him, she'd probably have happily spent the rest of her life here inside COE.

Why would anyone ever want to go from *this*—paradise, where every need was taken care of—to that, to what seemed to be a hardscrabble type of existence? Jack had laughed when she'd asked that question. He'd kissed the top of her head, sending a shiver of delight all the way down her spine, saying, "That's just life, Sophia. Messy but beautiful. At times it can be challenging, but most times it's exhilarating."

All she'd been able to think about after that was how she'd do anything if she could have a chance to live that life with him by her side.

Since once again it was a slow day at the medical clinic, time crawled. Sophia felt jumpy and out of sorts. When Dr. Drew wandered into the reception area and suggested they go ahead and close early, Sophia busted her butt to finish up so she could get out of there. She couldn't wait to get home and hear what Rachel had to say about Jack.

Since the school finished up before the clinic, Rachel always beat Sophia home. Even though Dr. Drew had let her go early, Sophia knew Rachel would already be there. So she rushed. She started out walking briskly, but ended up jogging home.

"Rachel?" she called out as soon as she'd pushed open the front door. Nothing but silence greeted her.

Sophia stopped, jealousy and doubt clawing at her chest. "Rachel?" she called again, quieter this time.

"I'm in my room." Rachel's voice, shaky and so completely unlike her normal, confident tone that Sophia's heart sank.

"I'm on my way."

"No. Wait," Rachel ordered. This time she sounded a bit more normal.

Sophia froze. "But—"

"I'll be right out. Give me a minute. I'm…not alone. Just wait there."

Not alone. Jack? Sophia's heart sank. That had happened fast. No. She refused to believe it. Rachel knew how she felt about him. It had to be someone else. But who?

A minute later Rachel came into the kitchen. With her hair all mussed and her lips swollen, it seemed perfectly obvious what she'd been doing. And then Sophia saw that Rachel's eyes were red, as if she'd been crying.

"Are you all right?" Sophia asked. "Have you been crying?"

"I have. Happy tears." Rachel smiled, the brilliance of that grin making joy spark in her eyes.

Sophia swayed. She swallowed hard, forcing herself to smile back. "Are you going to tell me what's happened?"

"I can do that!" a masculine voice—one that did not belong to Jack—said. A man appeared. A large man, with broad-shoulders and sun-bronzed skin. His brown eyes crinkled when he smiled. And he only had eyes for Rachel.

"Sophia, this is Phillip," Rachel said, blushing. "We've talked a few times and—"

"Kissed," Phillip interjected, grinning. "I promise

you, I did not take advantage of your roommate. I respect her far too much for that."

Looking from one to the other, Sophia could have sworn Rachel appeared regretful at his words. She knew Phillip. He was Jack's roommate. She didn't think he and Rachel had ever met.

"I really like her," Phillip continued. "And I think she likes me."

His words made Rachel blush harder. "He's asked if I mind if he courts me," she blurted. "I told him I don't mind at all."

Courting was one step before claiming. This meant Phillip was serious. A quick glance at her friend showed Rachel practically glowing from happiness.

Stunned, ashamed of her earlier thoughts, and honestly thrilled for her friend, Sophia squealed. "Oh, my stars!" Rushing over, she hugged Rachel tight. "That's wonderful."

After a moment, she released her friend and stepped back. Rachel looked past her and held out her hand.

With his gaze locked on his new girlfriend, Phillip grabbed her fingers and pulled her to him. He kissed her, hard and quick, before letting her go. "I'll see you later," he said, dipping his chin at Sophia on the way out.

After the front door had closed behind him, Rachel dropped down onto the couch. "What a pleasant surprise. After the day I've had, too. Even though he'd just finished work and hadn't time to shower, Phillip was waiting outside the school for me when I got off work. At first I thought he'd come to see Jack, but he said no. This is like a dream come true!"

"I'm so happy for you," Sophia said, meaning it. "This seems really…sudden."

"We've talked a few times." Rachel shrugged. "There's always been a spark between us, kind of like you and Jack."

"Speaking of Jack, how'd that go today?"

Rachel shrugged. "Since yesterday was his first day, I just let him observe. Truthfully, I don't think he knows anything about children. At all. But maybe he's a good therapist. Today I let him have an hour alone to talk with Benjamin. Jack reported the boy wouldn't talk and let me know earning Ben's trust was going to take some time. I sure hope he can do it. Goodness knows, I need some help with this."

"True," Sophia agreed, even though she had no idea. "I wonder if he'll ever come back to work at the clinic."

"I don't know." Rachel met her gaze. "I think he's needed more at the school. Why?"

Sophia took a deep breath, deciding to share her own truth. "Because I like Jack. I like him a lot."

"Really?" Then Rachel's eyes narrowed. "When you say 'a lot,' what exactly do you mean?"

Sophia sighed. "It's complicated."

"No. It. Is. Not. You are about to be married to our leader. He is the Anointed One of the Children of Eternity. Please tell me you're not seriously considering stepping away from your path."

Emotion clogging her throat, Sophia looked down. "You're right," she admitted, her voice rusty. "But sometimes I feel like I'm suffocating."

Rachel froze. "That word."

Looking up, Sophia cocked her head. "What?"

"Suffocating. The little boy in my class—Ben—he says that. And the other night…" Expression troubled, Rachel hesitated. "I had a dream. Between you and me…I've been struggling with my beliefs lately."

That made two of them. "Oh, Rachel. I had no idea. I have, too."

"You have a reason, though." Though Rachel only spoke truth, still her words stung. Something of Sophia's feelings must have showed on her face.

"I'm sorry, Soph." Rachel squeezed her shoulder. "You know I love you. And I love knowing I'm one of the Chosen." She took a deep breath. "But I'll be honest. Seeing what's happening to you has made me really think about life here in COE."

Sophia swallowed. Was Rachel testing her? Though it went against the grain to mistrust her lifelong best friend, why would Rachel say this? Especially since now more than ever, Rachel had a very real chance of having a bright and happy future with Phillip, something she seemed thrilled about.

When Sophia didn't respond, Rachel sighed. "Come on, now. Can you honestly tell me you believe what they're doing to you is 100 percent right?"

"No." Heart pounding, Sophia could barely push out the word. She couldn't make herself say more. It was one thing to think about leaving inside her head, but totally another to actually say the thought out loud. Except to Jack, she amended silently. Jack was different. Unlike her or Rachel, he'd actually lived most of his life outside COE.

"Come on." Rachel shook her head. "I want to show you something I confiscated from one of my students. Before I do, you have to promise me you won't speak a word of this to anyone else. Not even Jack."

Chapter 10

Intrigued, Sophia agreed. She followed Rachel back to her bedroom, studiously ignoring the rumpled sheets on the bed. Rachel glanced at her once or twice, her nervousness apparent, before getting down on the floor and reaching underneath her dresser. She fumbled around for a moment before straightening, a long rolled-up piece of black velvet in her hand.

"What's that?" Sophia moved closer.

"Just a sec." Rachel looked from Sophia to the door, swallowing hard. "I just need to make sure you understand that no one can know I have this. I'm supposed to turn this kind of stuff in immediately. I usually do, but something about this…" Silently, after unwrapping the velvet roll, she handed a glossy brochure over.

Sophia stared. Pictures of water and sand, sun and palm trees. Happy, tanned people wearing miniscule swimsuits, holding colorful drinks with umbrellas.

Slowly, she unfolded the paper, gaping at the rest of it. "Where is this place?" she breathed. "I want to go there."

"Me, too." Hand shaking, Rachel took the paper back. "It says Miami, Florida. I have no idea where that is. Of course, I have no idea where anywhere else is beside COE." She bit her lip. "I've always found it odd that all our textbooks are produced by us and don't say anything at all about the outside world."

"When I was small, I wondered about that, too. I even dared to ask the teacher. For punishment I had to clean the girls' dorm bathroom for a month."

"Yeah." A thread of bitterness crept into Rachel's voice. "We're taught early on not to question anything. Now that I'm a teacher, I do it, too. And I hate every second of it."

"I had no idea." Sophia hugged her friend. "I thought you loved your job."

"Oh, I do. At least, most of it. I adore the children, and the way I'm helping to mold them into good citizens. It's just... There's more."

Stunned, this last comment rocked Sophia back onto her heels. "I never thought about that," she admitted. "Basically, I've been pretty content, until right now." Something Rachel had said earlier bothered her. "Do you have any idea where your student got this?"

Rachel shook her head. "No. I'm not supposed to discuss it with them, just report it."

"How often does that happen?"

It took a moment for Rachel to answer. "Not much, but often enough. A couple times a year, maybe."

An interesting—and terrifying—thought occurred to Sophia. "Are these mostly new students?"

"New?" Rachel's frown showed she didn't understand what Sophia was asking.

"As in, they came from somewhere else?"

Rachel's expression cleared. "Oh, you mean like transferred from another class. As a matter of fact, yes. Every single one of them."

"And you're sure they came from another class?" Sophia persisted.

"Of course. Where else would they have come from?" Then, horror filled Rachel's eyes as understanding dawned. "Are you suggesting what I think you are?"

This time Sophia was the one who glanced at the door, as if she expected Thomas or one of his assistants to rush through and grab them. "You know Thomas brought Jack in from outside, right?"

Slowly, Rachel nodded. "Yes."

"Do you think it might be possible that Thomas brings in kids?"

"If you'd asked me that question a few years ago, my answer would have been an emphatic no. But now…" Rachel bit her lip. "I have to say the thought has occurred to me. But I have no proof. What I wouldn't understand is why. Surely we have enough young couples getting married and having children, don't we?"

"I have no idea." For the first time, Sophia realized how restrictive their focus seemed to be. "Do you?"

"No." Rachel's troubled expression revealed she'd come to the same realization. "If you think about it, we're programmed to focus only on our own lives and our family group. No one worries about what anyone else is doing. Or not doing, as the case may be."

"We always just assume that Ezekiel—and by default Thomas and the other top tier—are looking out for us. And we all keep on doing what we're supposed to, confident that it's right for COE." Sophia thought of her impending marriage to their leader and grimaced. "No one seems to care if it's right for us individually."

Despite his resolve not to, Jack couldn't stop thinking about Sophia. Seeing her, being with her, breathing in her scent, touching the ivory softness of her skin. And kissing her. The way she'd wrapped herself around him had started a fever in his veins. He wanted her, wanted her with a fierceness stronger than anything he'd ever felt for anyone before.

She was unique and lovely and special. She needed to experience what it felt like to be loved by a man who recognized and celebrated all of that within her. She deserved the chance to find her own happiness, to raise a family if that's what she wanted, and be given a chance to weather the often stormy sea of true love with all its joy and sometimes pain.

Instead, these bastards planned to marry her off to an eighty-year-old man in less than two weeks. The thought made him want to grab her and run, far and fast, to a place where the COE could never find them.

Then he'd make hard, passionate love to her. Like he'd wanted to with every single breath he took, every second he was around her.

He told himself to focus. The sooner he found out if COE had abducted children from outside, the quicker he could help Sophia get out of there.

But his first therapy session with young Benjamin hadn't gone well. For most of the sixty minutes, the boy had refused to speak. He wouldn't answer a single question, so Jack had resorted to talking about his own life.

It hadn't been until the hour was nearly up when Jack had managed to get any kind of response. And that had only been due to a casual remark he'd made about his life outside COE.

Even then, he wasn't sure if he'd imagined the flare of interest he'd seen in Ben's eyes. Because the kid still hadn't said a single damn word.

After the session, Jack had gone back to sit in the classroom and observe, as Rachel wished. He'd tried, but had to stand and pace a little to keep from dozing off.

When the school day ended, he'd told Rachel goodbye and left. Surprised to see Phillip waiting outside, he'd actually been relieved to learn his roommate had come for Rachel. Jack's frustration level had been way too high to try to make small talk with Phillip.

He knew his impatience wasn't realistic, so he planned to schedule talks with Benjamin every single day if he had to until the boy spoke.

Checking his watch, he saw he had at least another hour until the medical clinic shut down. So instead of going home, he headed out there to see if they needed his help with anything. At least that way he could pretend not to be seeking out Sophia.

When he arrived, the place appeared deserted. He walked through the reception area toward the back, but saw no one. One of the examination room doors was closed, which meant Dr. Drew was attending to a patient. Sophia might be assisting, so Jack found busy-work tidying up the general supply area right outside the exam rooms.

The door opened and Dr. Drew came out, nearly walking into Jack. As Jack started to apologize, the other man frowned. "What are you doing here?"

"I finished up early at the school, so I thought I'd

come by here and see if there was anything you wanted me to help with."

"Whew." The doctor relaxed. "I thought maybe things hadn't worked out for you at the school. That'd be on my head, because I'm the one who recommended you."

Surprised, Jack shook his head. "No, I'm only on my second day there, and my first counseling session. These things take time."

"True, true." Turning, the older man dismissed him with a wave of his hand. "You can go home now. And until your work at the school is finished, there's really no need to come back here."

Disappointed, Jack nodded. "Okay," he said easily. "I'll leave. But first, do you happen to know where I might find Sophia?"

"Why?" Dr. Drew narrowed his gaze. Though Jack suspected the doctor knew the answer, he knew there was no way he could tell the truth.

"I just wanted to thank her," he said. "Her help was invaluable to me as a new person here in COE."

"I gave her the afternoon off."

"Thanks." Without a backward glance, Jack strolled to the door. He hoped Dr. Drew didn't suspect how close he and Sophia had become.

Since Phillip had been waiting for Rachel, Jack figured she wouldn't be home yet. Which meant if Sophia had gone home, she'd be there all by herself.

Heaven help him, his heart rate sped up at the thought.

Quickly, he covered the short distance to the bungalow where Sophia and Rachel lived.

Unsure of protocol, he rapped on the front door.

A moment later it swung open. "Jack? What are you doing here?"

"May I come in?"

"Of course." Sophia stepped back, motioning him inside. "What's going on? Is everything all right?"

"Yep. Everything's just fine." As soon as the door closed, he reached for her, yanking her up close without even pausing to think. She gasped and jerked away, glancing around wildly.

"Are we alone?" he asked.

"Yes." She smiled. "Rachel and Phillip just left." Unable to help himself, he grinned back at her. Again, something electric sparked between them, undeniable and strong. As she moved away, he had to wonder if she felt it, too.

He glanced around the small living area, looking for a distraction, anything, to keep from reaching for her again.

"Jack, you should see your face." Then she laughed, the pure sensuality in the sound catching him low in the gut. "I'm so glad to see you. I've missed you."

Her words had his heart stuttering. "I've missed you, too," he admitted, feeling as if he were treading on dangerous ground. "Your friend Rachel is nice but..."

Again she chuckled. "I know what you mean."

Something in her manner suggested she had something on her mind. She flitted around the room like a butterfly, not landing in any one spot. All he wanted was for her to come close to him.

Sad state of affairs when merely being in the same space with her—alone—had him full-on aroused. He couldn't think, couldn't move. He wanted her so badly he ached with it.

"What's wrong, Sophia?" he asked gently. "Is there something on your mind?"

She flashed him a look of surprise, her lush lips

curving into a smile. "There is. I'm just not sure how to go about saying it."

Charmed and intrigued, he waited.

"Listen, I have a favor to ask you," she murmured, stopping her pacing a few feet from him. Gazing up at him, hope warred with worry in her big eyes.

His heart full, he looked down at her, riveted as she licked her top lip.

"I'm sorry, I'm nervous," she added. "This is not easy for me to say."

Damn. He went still. Had he completely misjudged? Was she about to cut him loose?

"What is it?" he prodded gently. "Go ahead, you can do it. You know you can tell me anything."

"I can, can't I?" She exhaled, color suffusing her face. "I'm just going to blurt it out. Okay?"

He nodded.

"Would you make love to me, just once? Right now?"

Flabbergasted, he couldn't reply. Actually, his body responded for him. Every cell, every fiber of his being, came amazingly, gloriously alive. Every thought in his mind disappeared into a blaze of arousal.

While he battled for self-control and the right answer, unfortunately Sophia took his silence for refusal.

"Never mind," she mumbled, head down. "Clearly, I misjudged. Forget I said anything."

He realized there were no words adequate to relay everything he felt. So he went to her, slipped his hands up her arms and gently pulled her closer, letting her feel how much he wanted her. "Look at me," he said.

With a troubled expression, she raised her face to his. "I'm sorry..." she began.

"Don't be." His voice came out harsher than he intended. And then, because he was helpless to speak, helpless to do anything but cover her mouth with his, he kissed her.

Burning, the press of his mouth on hers demanding, his heart pounded as fiercely as his arousal. When she kissed him back, her reckless abandon nearly undid him. Openmouthed, her lips warm and moist, her tongue demanding as she hungrily drank him in. The wanton way she pressed her lush body into his made his head spin.

"Slowly," he rasped as he slid his hand down the curve of her hip, then inside the buttons of her dress, parting them so he could caress her silken belly. She shuddered under his touch.

One move and they fell back onto the couch, bodies still entwined and, to his regret, still fully clothed. Wait. What the hell was he doing? Through a red haze of desire, he forced himself to stop. "Sophia, we need to discuss this…" he began.

"I don't want to talk," she protested. "I don't want to think. I want to feel. Something—anything—other than numb." Then, as she gazed at him, her eyes filled with tears. She covered her face with her hands, her shoulders shaking.

He held her while she wept, unsure what, if anything, he could do or say to make her feel better.

When her sobs finally diminished, she scrubbed angrily at her eyes with the backs of her hands and twisted out of his embrace. Jumping to her feet, she stalked to the window, peering outside. "I'm a terrible person." When she turned to face him, he saw regret and anger in her expressive face. "I'm not like that, I swear."

Not sure what she meant, he waited.

"I was brought up to remain pure until I married,"

she said. "I swear, I'm not a fallen woman. I've never done anything like this before."

He froze, unable to believe his ears. "'Anything like this'?" Taking a deep, shaky breath, he went to her and gently pushed her hair away from her face. "Sophia, do you mean you've never made love to a man?"

Though her face flamed with color, she didn't look away. "Yes. I mean, no. I'm a virgin."

A kind of primitive joy exploded inside him, shocking him. While he'd never considered himself a caveman, the idea of being her first humbled and aroused him. "I see. I consider you wanting to make love with me a high honor, Sophia."

Her eyes widened, letting him see the depth of her hurt. "Then why don't you want me?"

While he knew he needed to be careful, the way she looked at him, so sadly resigned with her heart in her eyes, he had no choice but to give her the truth.

"Oh, I want you all right," he said grimly. "With every fiber of my being, I want to show you what lovemaking feels like."

Still, he saw she didn't understand.

"But if that's the case, why won't you?"

How to answer? She deserved nothing less than the truth. "Because you mean too much to me—"

The words had barely left his lips when the front door crashed open. Two burly men rushed in, stopping in front of Jack and Sophia.

"Jack Moreno," the first one barked, "by order of the Anointed One, you're coming with us."

Ezekiel. How had he known? Or had he? One look at Sophia's terrified face and Jack knew he wouldn't resist. Not now anyway.

"Lead the way, gentlemen," he said, refusing to be

alarmed when they fell into place on either side of him. Flashing Sophia what he hoped looked like a reassuring smile, he left her house, waiting patiently when one of the men carefully put the door back into place.

Sophia thought she might go mad with no one to talk to. She just knew Ezekiel coming for Jack had something to do with her. Thankful they hadn't been caught in a compromising position, she checked the front door for damage and tried to calm her frazzled nerves.

Was Jack all right? What would Ezekiel do to him? How had he known? Technically, she figured no one outside would know or care if Jack simply disappeared. And here inside COE, no one ever remarked on a member's sudden disappearance. They never knew if the missing person had simply decided to leave or if something more sinister had happened.

Sinister. What an odd word to apply to the Anointed One. Yet once she'd thought it, she found she couldn't call it back. Ever since her sudden engagement—and Jack's appearance, if she were to be totally honest—she felt like her blinders had been ripped off.

The instant Rachel came through the front door, Sophia filled her in, trying—and failing—to rein in her rising hysteria. Talking in short, furious bursts, she couldn't stop pacing.

"Whoa." Rachel held up her hand. "Slow down. First off, why exactly do you immediately assume Jack's in trouble? He's doing vital work at school. Maybe Ezekiel just wanted an update?"

"So he sent two huge guys crashing through our door?" Sophia pointed to where the wood had splintered in the frame. "They didn't knock or anything. Just busted their way in."

Now Rachel frowned. "In here? You and Jack were alone inside our house?"

"Yes. We were alone a lot at work, too. How is this any different?" Except even she knew it was.

"Come on." Rachel knew her too well. "Tell me. What could Jack have possibly done that could get him in trouble?"

Sophia's face colored. "I had just asked him to make love to me."

Her words made Rachel gasp. "You didn't."

"I did." Sophia swallowed hard. "But nothing actually happened."

"Because they knocked in the door?"

"No." Ashamed, Sophia grimaced. "I got cold feet. I started crying. Jack was comforting me when those men showed up."

"Do you think...?" Glancing around wildly, Rachel moved closer and lowered her voice to a whisper. "Is there a chance someone is listening in on us?"

Sophia's heart skipped a beat. "It's conceivable," she allowed. "I'm beginning to think anything is possible. Ever since Ezekiel claimed me..." She couldn't finish.

"He's keeping an eye on you," Rachel finished for her. She moved closer, so she could whisper directly into Sophia's ear. "That means they might know about my brochure. And about everything we've discussed here."

And everything she and Jack had talked about, like leaving. Sophia winced. "Let's go for a walk," she said, using a normal tone of voice.

Once outside, the two women looked at each other. "Do you think we're being paranoid?" Rachel ventured.

"I don't know. How else would they have known Jack was there with me?"

"Good point." Rachel kept looking over her shoulder as if she expected to be followed.

"Stop," Sophia hissed. "You're being way too obvious. Act normal, act casual. For all we know, they could be watching us."

At her words, Rachel winced. "I hadn't thought of that." She started to swivel her head to look around again, but caught herself. "You're right. This is crazy."

"I hate that everything has changed." Sophia didn't bother to keep the sadness from her voice. "Before this, I was happy. I still had a future. I believed in our lifestyle and our leader. I never felt fear—not for me or for anyone I knew."

Rachel stared straight ahead as they walked. "And now?"

"None of that applies."

Alert and on edge, Jack took care to keep his posture relaxed and his expression friendly. As he and his escorts walked toward where the higher-ups lived, they passed Thomas's home. The next one, which was by far the largest, had to be Ezekiel's.

So the Supreme Leader of the COE really did want to see him. Part of him had suspected Thomas was behind this, but apparently not. If Ezekiel had taken issue with him, there could really only be one reason. Sophia.

At the gate, one of his escorts punched in a code. The ornate black metal slid open soundlessly.

"After you," the taller man said, gesturing for Jack to precede him.

Once inside the courtyard, the gate closed behind them. Jack took care to check out his surroundings, looking not only for a way to escape should it come to that, but places he could take shelter if need be. Sometimes his old military training came in handy.

Inside the house, he was escorted down a long, tiled hall. At the end there were two massive, mahogany doors with pewter handles. "This is where we leave you," the tall man said, then rapped sharply on the wood.

"Show him in," a querulous voice ordered. "And then go."

The door swung open to reveal a room that reminded Jack of photos he'd seen of the president's Oval Office. Certainly the massive desk and the curtained windows suggested their design had been borrowed from the White House. Intentionally, he supposed. Of course, Ezekiel would view being the holy leader of a cult on a par with the President of the United States.

The two men, having done their duty, quickly backed out of the room, closing the door behind them.

Jack faced the desk. The elderly man seated behind it didn't greet him or rise. Fine. Jack decided to take the initiative.

"Good evening, sir," he said, moving forward with his hand outstretched. "I'm Jack Moreno."

Ezekiel's eyes narrowed. He made no move to take Jack's hand. "I know who you are. Tell me, why do you think you can move in on my woman?"

So this *was* about Sophia.

Not bothering to pretend he had no idea what the older man meant, Jack shook his head. "We're friends. Nothing more."

"You must consider me to be an idiot, Mr. Moreno. Let me reassure you. I may be old, but I'm not stupid."

Since he wasn't sure how to respond to that, Jack didn't.

After a moment Ezekiel continued. "I see you sniffing around her, and you have to know she's been claimed. Not by anyone, either, but by me. She is aware what a great honor that is. I'm thinking you do not."

"Actually, I—"

"Be quiet," Ezekiel cut him off. "From now on, you are to have nothing to do with my fiancée. You will no longer work at the medical clinic at all. You work full-time with the school. Do you understand?"

A warning? He was getting off with a simple warning? Aware the wisest answer would be to agree, Jack slowly nodded.

"I don't believe that you do." The smile on the old man's wizened face sent a chill down Jack's spine. "I want to make sure you understand the consequences if you disobey my direct order. You will be punished and put to death. Slowly and agonizingly. Are we clear?"

Damn. Jack knew he needed to remember the reason he was there. He had one chance to locate the Bartletts' son. "Clear as day," he said cheerfully. "Rest assured, you will have my full cooperation."

The double doors opened and his two escorts stepped inside. Damned if Jack had seen Ezekiel give any sort of signal, but he must have.

Once they reached the outer gate, his two escorts waved him through. Once he'd gone, the gate closed, leaving him alone.

Jack didn't go directly home. Not yet. He needed to get himself under control. Anger had begun simmering inside him as he considered what had just occurred. If Ezekiel really believed Jack could now so easily abandon Sophia to marriage with him, he had another thought coming.

Pulse pounding, he realized he now had two objectives for inside the cult. Not only did he need to locate and prove that one of the children in Rachel's class had not only come from outside but was the Bartletts' missing son, he now needed to convince Sophia to flee with him. He'd get her away from this place or die trying.

Chapter 11

Though Jack had come to enjoy his walks, he couldn't take the chance of running into Sophia, so he went straight to the compound's border. A quick climb over the fence and he disappeared into the trees. The same spot where Sophia had gone after the cookout.

Thinking of her made his chest ache. He had no doubt she was pretty freaked out right now. That's how people like Ezekiel regained control, through fear and bullying. More than anything he wished he had a way to contact her without anyone knowing, but the only way he could do that here would be through Rachel.

The next morning when he walked to the school, a pale and jumpy Rachel let him in.

"Is Sophia all right?" he asked, trying to keep from sounding too alarmed.

She jumped. "Yes," she said, then leaned in close

so she could whisper in his ear. "She and I think we're being spied upon. So be careful what you say or do."

He wasn't surprised, just annoyed that he hadn't thought of that possibility sooner. Slowly he nodded.

"Today I've received permission to have you meet with three of the more troubled children," she told him out loud, her voice clear and professional. "You'll have one hour with each and you're free to split them up however you prefer. Just make sure that you allow time for lunch and for recess."

Recess. At least, contrary to his previous belief, the kids got to play outside. Sure, it was in a large, inner courtyard, but they were under the sun and in the fresh air.

Since he'd already met with Benjamin, he decided he'd talk to him last. Maybe if the kid saw him talking to some of his classmates, he'd open up a little. Ha, Jack amended. Maybe he'd actually speak.

Once the class was assembled and every child at his or her desk, he asked Rachel who the other two were. She quietly pointed out a little blond boy and a sullen, red-haired girl. "Theodore and Samantha."

He decided he'd take Theodore first. In light of what Rachel had said about possible listening devices, he asked her if it would be all right to talk with the boy outside.

Understanding flashed across her face as she pretended to consider his request. "I don't see why not," she finally said. "There's no way to leave the courtyard without one of the guardians letting you back in."

Again, he realized how much this school resembled a prison for children.

When he called Theodore's name, the boy jumped up so quickly he knocked over his chair. After hurriedly picking it up, he ran over to Jack, barely skidding to a stop before barreling into him.

"Walk, Theodore," Rachel admonished. "You know we don't run."

"Yes, ma'am."

"Let's go outside and get some fresh air," Jack said in a friendly voice. The boy nodded his head so violently Jack nearly winced.

Once outside, Theodore took off as soon as Jack told him it was okay to get some exercise. Running, running, running, as if trying to escape the inescapable. Jack let him go, even though it was cutting into his allotted time. Eventually the boy would run out of steam. Maybe once he'd burned some energy, he'd be more willing to talk.

Sure enough, after about five minutes, the youngster jogged over to where Jack had taken a seat on a stone bench.

"Sit." Jack patted the spot next to him. Instead, Theodore shook his head and dropped to the grass at his feet.

"Why do you want to talk to me?" the boy asked, meeting Jack's gaze with open curiosity.

At least he was talking. Jack gave a casual shrug, deciding to wing it. The bench was far enough from any structure wall that he doubted he could be heard. "I just thought since I came from outside of this place, you might have some questions to ask me."

At that, Theodore jumped up, moving closer before tentatively taking a seat next to Jack on the bench. "You came from outside?" he asked in a low voice, his eyes wide.

"Yep." Jack smiled. "Did you?"

To his shock, the boy's eyes filled with tears before he angrily wiped them away with his small fist. "No.

Maybe. I don't know. I have lots of dreams of another place. They're like nightmares, but not really scary. Just different." He swallowed hard and looked away for a moment before raising his gaze back to Jack's. "The other kids make fun of me."

"That's tough." Jack nodded in sympathy. "Kids can be mean if they don't understand."

"Yeah. Ben and Samantha are the only ones who leave me alone. I think that's because they have dreams, too."

Jack struggled to contain his excitement. Finally, he might be getting somewhere. "Can you tell me about one of the dreams?" he asked.

For a second Theodore appeared uncertain, but then he slowly nodded. "You won't make fun of me?"

"Of course not," Jack scoffed. "Why would I do that? I'm from outside, remember?"

His disclaimer appeared to soothe the boy. Theodore took a deep breath. When he started to speak, words poured out of him so quickly that Jack had to struggle to make sense of them.

In true dream fashion, the kid relayed a mishmash of events, some realistic, some fantastical. But some of what he said brought up some possible red flags. Theodore remembered a room with a crib and a rocking chair, bright and colorful, describing what sounded like a typical nursery in great detail.

Jack interrupted then. "Is that like where babies are kept here?"

Theodore shook his head violently. "No. The nursery is a big room with a bunch of clear plastic bin things. All the babies are kept in one place—I've seen it. This other place, the one in my dream, makes me miss my mom. Sometimes I think I can hear her voice, but then I know I'm crazy. No one has just one mom. No one."

"They do where I come from. Outside, that is," Jack said, keeping his tone casual. "Are you sure you've never been there?" He knew he had to be extremely careful here. It wouldn't be good to get the boy all riled up and have him go around spouting that he'd come from outside because that nice man Jack said so.

No, that wouldn't be good at all.

Regretful, Jack asked Theodore a few more questions, and then talked about how sometimes dreams were our inner self's way of showing us what we secretly longed for. He said maybe Theodore had been feeling lonely lately, so he'd begun to wish he could be different, more than just one of many kids. As he wound down, he wondered if the boy would pick up the one anomaly of his words—that there was no way Theodore would know what it was truly like outside unless he'd actually been there.

Checking his watch, Jack saw that the hour was nearly up. "You can run around for a few more minutes before we go back inside," he said.

Immediately, Theodore jumped up and did exactly that.

Jack watched him, surprisingly drained. For the first time, he saw far-reaching implications that might arise from his investigation. What if the Bartlett boy wasn't the only child who'd been abducted and brought to the cult?

How many might there have been? How long had it been going on? And was it possible some of them might even be adults now?

Walking back into the classroom with Theodore, he gave Rachel an impersonal smile before taking his usual seat at the back of the classroom. He decided to wait a little bit before taking Samantha outside to talk. He needed to process the information Theodore had given, to sift through it and decide what was valuable and what could be discarded.

Again he found himself wishing he could discuss this with Sophia. No doubt she'd have some insights to share that would help him.

But with Ezekiel and his people apparently watching her like a hawk, he simply couldn't take the chance. He would have to stay away from her for both their own safety.

Right before lunch he took Samantha outside. Unlike Theodore, she was quiet and timid. She shook her head when he asked her if she wanted to run around and play, and she immediately sat when he patted the bench next to him, crossing her feet primly at the ankles.

"Is there anything you'd like to talk to me about?" he asked, keeping his voice soft and friendly.

She shook her head no, refusing to even look at him.

"I understand you've been having some bad dreams?"

Again she shook her head no.

The rest of the hour went exactly the same way, with Jack trying everything he could think of to draw the little girl out and failing every single time. Like Benjamin, she'd apparently withdrawn into herself.

He returned her to the classroom, struggling not to show his frustration. When they all went to lunch, Rachel asked if she minded if she joined him at his table.

"Why not?" With a shrug, he gestured at the empty chair across the table.

"I have recess duty an hour after lunch," she told him, smiling. "I know you've been outside a lot today, but you're certainly welcome to join me."

That way they could talk without anyone listening.

"I'd like that." He kept his answer casual. "I can never get enough fresh air."

They ate their lunches in relative silence, making the occasional small talk about the beautiful spring weather or how good the meal tasted.

A bell rang and Rachel's class lined up next to another group of kids. "Follow me," Rachel said, leading them all back to the classroom.

He managed to keep from watching the clock as he waited for recess. Exactly one hour after they'd returned to the classroom, a bell rang again. Finally. Rachel waited until all the children had lined up again before leading them outside. Jack followed.

Standing away from the walls and any possible listening devices, Jack and Rachel watched the children play.

"Any luck?" Rachel asked, pitching her voice low.

He outlined what Theodore had told him and let her know Samantha had refused to speak. "Just like Benjamin," he said. "It's very discouraging."

"Well, I'm sure you must have run up against roadblocks before," she told him, smiling. "Keep after it, I'm sure you'll eventually make progress."

Of course, he couldn't let on that he didn't have that much time. His certainty continued to grow that one or more of the kids might actually be from outside. If not the Bartletts' child, someone else's. And while he still didn't understand why Ezekiel and his people felt the need to kidnap outsiders' children, he suspected it had something to do with introducing new blood into the gene pool.

"When are you going to speak with Benjamin?" Rachel asked.

"This afternoon." He kept to himself his belief that meeting would be as unproductive as the previous one. If he'd been an actual therapist, maybe he would have received training techniques to help draw the boy out. Since he hadn't, he could only continue and hope for the best.

The children seemed quieter than normal after recess. Rachel assigned them reading and Jack watched as Benjamin heaved a sigh before getting his book out from inside his desk.

When Jack walked up to him to ask the boy if he would come with him, he could have sworn a look of relief flashed across Benjamin's face. But his words didn't sync up.

"I guess," the kid said, his tone surly and his posture defensive.

Once again Jack led the way outside. Since they'd just had recess, he figured Benjamin wouldn't want to run around, so he pointed to the bench. "Sit with me?"

Benjamin sat. Jack didn't speak, simply waited, hoping the boy might feel the need to fill the silence with words.

"Why'd you leave me for last?" Benjamin eventually asked. "Is it because I'm the least interesting?"

Elation filled him. Finally the boy was talking. Though his first instinct was to reassure the child, instead Jack pretended to consider the question. "Well, you won't hardly talk to me," he eventually answered.

"Did Theodore and Samantha talk?"

Jack smiled. "You know I can't discuss them with you. Just like I wouldn't talk about you with them."

"Oh." Benjamin again fell silent.

Once more Jack waited him out. Even though he

hadn't wanted to get his hopes up, he felt pretty good. Already the boy had said more than ever before.

"Did Theodore tell you about his dreams?" Benjamin swallowed hard as he spoke again.

Since Jack had already said he wouldn't discuss anything the other two might have said, he turned the question around. "Do you have dreams about another place?"

Benjamin looked down. He twisted his hands over and over while he considered Jack's question. "I don't know." He shot to his feet. "And if I did, why would I want to tell you about them?"

That said, the boy moved away. He didn't run, just walked a few feet from Jack and stood with his back to him, hands shoved into his pockets. His posture resembled that of a weary old man more than a young child.

Pushing slowly to his feet, Jack crossed the space between them. He half expected the boy to run off when he reached him, but Benjamin didn't move.

"If you ever want to learn about what life is like outside, I can tell you," Jack said quietly. "And if you have some memories or dreams that make you think you might have been there, I'd be happy to sort through those with you."

"Why would I think that?" Frowning, Benjamin stalked toward the school entrance. "I want to go back to class. I have some reading to do."

Jack nodded. Without another word, the two of them returned inside.

Deirdre swept into the medical clinic shortly after Sophia unlocked the doors at the start of the day. Both Sophia and Ana looked up from the reception desk, where they'd been going over the patient list of appointments.

"You," Deidre declared, pointing imperiously at Sophia, "are coming with me." She swung her gaze to Ana. "Tell Dr. Drew that she won't be in at all today."

Then, before either Sophia or Ana could utter a single word, she spun on her heel and marched back out the door, clearly expecting Sophia to follow.

Which, since she had no choice, Sophia did.

Outside, Deirdre barely contained her impatience. "Hurry. We don't want to be late. We have a lot to attend to today."

Though Sophia knew Deirdre expected her to simply do as she was told without question, she decided to ask anyway. "What are we going to do?"

The older woman stopped short—so suddenly that Sophia nearly ran into her. Looking down her rather prominent nose, her annoyed expression softened. "Normally, I'd reprimand you for daring to ask questions, but with all the fuss going on, I forget it's your wedding, too. Today we are going to get you fitted for a dress and discuss what colors we want. I'll also need a few names of your best friends—the ones you want in your wedding. We'll need to get them fitted for dresses, too."

Though Sophia had spent nearly the last decade fantasizing and planning her wedding, her stomach turned. With all the craziness of thinking she'd actually be marrying Ezekiel, she hadn't thought about ordinary things like choosing a dress and colors. Now, though she knew it would be a waste of time since she had no intention of going through with it, she couldn't say anything to Deidre.

She licked her lips, aware she might be pushing it, but feeling she had to try to stall anyway. "Is there enough time to have a dress made? I would think the dressmaker would need more than two weeks."

"Honey, you aren't any ordinary bride," Deidre answered, her mouth quirking with amusement. "We'll have four or five dressmakers at once working on your gown. Once we have the fitting and choose the material, it should be done in less than forty-eight hours. Then we can have it adjusted so you have a perfect fit."

All of which, from what she remembered hearing from her already married friends, usually took weeks or months.

Deidre resumed moving forward, this time at a more leisurely pace, the rich material of her long gown sweeping the path. "Are you excited?" she asked, her tone casual.

Aware she couldn't tell the truth, Sophia nodded.

"Good, good." Another sideways glance. "Did you give any thought to the advice I gave you last time we talked?"

As if Sophia would be foolish enough to tell her if she did. "I heard your wise words," she said slowly, "and considered them, but in the end I must always act with the honor expected of someone in my position."

Unexpectedly, Deidre laughed. "Whatever. Honey, if you only knew what kind of fresh hell awaits you, you'd reconsider. But because I know you expect it, I'll say what I'm supposed to say. You did the right thing. You're a good girl."

Confused, Sophia didn't know how to react. She'd supposed that Deirdre's advice had only been a test.

Then again, if Ezekiel had people watching Sophia as she suspected, Deirdre might already be aware that Sophia had asked Jack to make love to her. Luckily for both of them, nothing had happened. Who knew? All this intrigue had her head spinning.

They were now in an area of the compound where Sophia had never been.

"This," Deirdre said, sweeping her arm in a grand gesture, "is where the seamstresses live. And the bakers, so we'll stop in and order your cake, as well."

Though Sophia nodded, she wanted to close her eyes and wish all this away, as if it were a bad dream. In a way, it was.

Feeling as if she were somewhere outside her body, she sat through watching as the white-haired designer sketched some samples of what kind of wedding gown she felt Sophia would look best in. After that, Sophia had to hold herself motionless for what seemed like hours while the seamstress directed multiple assistants to take her measurements.

When they finally declared themselves finished, Sophia hoped she'd be allowed to sit for a moment to rest, but Deirdre marched her down the street to consult with the baker.

Having no preferences about what kind or size of cake, Sophia told Deirdre she trusted her judgment and found a chair. She watched while Deirdre and the head baker discussed what sounded like a huge and pretentious confectionary masterpiece.

Sophia simply leaned back and closed her eyes. Misery filled her, misery and a kind of desperation that made her wish she could simply jump up and declare this all needed to stop. Right this instant.

Again she thought of Jack and the way he made her feel. She tried to picture outside, her thoughts going back to that brochure Rachel had hidden away. While she knew it wasn't all so beautiful, Miami would be one place she'd want to see.

"Wake up, dear." Deirdre's voice, sounding both

amused and exasperated. "We've still got places to go and people to see. But first we'll go have a nice lunch to refuel us for the afternoon."

Dutifully, Sophia nodded. Clearly when Deirdre said they were spending the day together, she meant all day.

Deirdre led the two of them down an alley to a small courtyard. "My household chef teaches here," she said. "His students need to practice their cooking techniques. They'll be preparing lunch for us today."

Inside the courtyard were several round tables made out of iron. Deidre took a seat at one and motioned for Sophia to do the same. "In the world outside, they call places like this restaurants," Deirdre confided. "Except I hear one must pay to sample the food."

"Pay what?" Sophia asked, genuinely curious. "Do they barter services or goods in exchange for the meal?"

Deirdre shrugged. "I'm not sure. I've heard Ezekiel talk about something called cash. I don't know what that is exactly, and I certainly couldn't ask."

Which meant even once she'd obtained as powerful a position as the Anointed One's first wife, she still wasn't permitted to ask questions.

Again Sophia found herself battling despair.

Several young men, all wearing white jackets, came out to greet them. Both Deidre and Sophia were given tall glasses of ice water. A bowl of some kind of breaded vegetable was placed in the center of the table. Sophia eyed it dubiously.

Noting her expression, Deidre laughed. "I promise you, it's good." To prove her point, she took a piece, dipping it into a small bowl of white sauce. "Delicious."

"But what is it?" Sophia asked, hoping the older woman wouldn't mind yet another question.

"Fried zucchini. With ranch dressing for dipping. Try it for yourself."

Gingerly, Sophia picked up some and, following Deirdre's example, dipped it in the white sauce and took a tiny bite. To her surprise, it was delicious. She finished it off quickly, wondering if it would be rude for her to reach for more.

"Help yourself." Deirdre smiled, proceeding to do exactly that. "This is called an appetizer. You don't get food like this in the regular dining hall."

She was right about that. In short time, the two of them demolished the appetizer.

"Now for the main course!" Deirdre rubbed her chubby hands together in glee, making her numerous rings flash in the sunlight, including the large one proclaiming her Ezekiel's wife.

Deirdre must have noticed Sophia eyeing her rings. "Don't worry," she said. "Ezekiel will give you some baubles, too, if you please him."

It took a major effort, but somehow Sophia managed to keep from shuddering. She'd lived her entire life without any jewelry and figured she could continue to do so. In fact, very few women in COE wore any kind of adornment other than the choker proclaiming them to be married. The only one who did was Deidre.

Before she could frame a suitable comment, the main course arrived. Some kind of painstakingly arranged pasta dish, with cut-up mushrooms and tomatoes and green peppers. Sophia didn't recognize the protein that had been arranged in a neat circle on top. She stared, anxious to ask but even more afraid to eat.

Again, Deidre must have correctly interpreted Sophia's expression. "It's shrimp, honey. Seafood from the ocean. We have it flown in every so often. Try it, it's delicious. Seafood is another one of the perks you'll enjoy living in the Chosen household."

"Perks," Sophia repeated, picking up her fork and trying to summon the nerve to dig in. She watched as Deirdre ate, practically shoveling the food into her mouth as if she hadn't eaten for days.

Telling herself she needed to start slow, Sophia ate some of the pasta first. It was delicious, with just the right amount of garlic and oregano and some other seasoning she couldn't quite identify.

Encouraged, she stabbed one of the shrimp.

"Don't eat the tail," Deirdre cautioned, pointing to a little pile she'd made on her bread plate.

Though the sight nearly made Sophia gag, she opened her mouth and popped in the shrimp, holding the tail with her fingers and separating it with her teeth, the way she'd seen Deidre do.

The taste wasn't bad. Garlic and butter, maybe olive oil. The texture? Now that was another story. She wasn't certain she liked it.

Somehow she managed to eat most of her entrée, saving time by cutting off the tails with her fork and then chopping the shrimp up into tiny little pieces to mix with her pasta.

Full, she pushed the plate away. "That was delicious," she told Deirdre, smiling. "I'm stuffed. I can't eat another bite."

Eyeing Sophia's half-eaten plate, Deirdre pushed it back toward her. "You can and you will. You're way too thin by far. Ezekiel prefers his women a bit plumper."

Staring, Sophia waited for the other woman to laugh and tell her she was only joking. Instead, Deirdre continued to eye her, expression unreadable. "Eat," she ordered. "Hurry up, because I want dessert."

Disbelief warred with—surprisingly—fury, which Sophia managed to contain. She choked the rest of the food down, eating with methodical precision fueled by humiliation. This, she thought, was a hint of how her life would be if she went to live in Ezekiel's household. She'd be the lowest woman on the totem pole and, as such, subject to all the various whims of every wife who'd come before her.

Once she'd cleared her plate, she felt like she might vomit from too much food. Taking small sips of her water, she concentrated on keeping everything down.

At that moment, the assistant brought out two huge pieces of chocolate cake. Deirdre clapped her hands together in delight. "That looks amazing." Her voice trilled. "My compliments to the chef."

Eyeing the triple-layered monstrosity before her, Sophia wanted to cry. While she loved cake, especially chocolate, she didn't think her stomach could hold another bite.

Gamely, she picked up her fork and dug in. The cake tasted wonderful, the texture so light it melted in her mouth. But two bites were all she could manage, though this time she wasn't foolish enough to push the plate away.

Deirdre didn't have the same problem, naturally. Watching her devour her dessert, Sophia had the oddest thought of asking if the other woman wanted hers. Because if she tried to eat the rest of it, Sophia knew she would lose her entire meal.

"Is there a problem with your dessert?" Deirdre asked, brows raised.

"Of course not," Sophia answered, attempting to sound cheerful. "My stomach is so full, I think I'm going to take this home with me and eat it later."

"Eat it. Now."

What the…? "No." Sophia crossed her arms. "I'm full. If I try to force this down, I'll get sick. It won't be pretty. And that's not the way to honor an amazing meal like this."

At first, judging from the speculation in Deirdre's gaze, Sophia thought the first wife might slap her. Instead the older woman stared at her, considering.

"You've got spunk," Deirdre finally said, surprising her. "That could be good or bad, depending on how you use it. You'll need to be careful, though. Ezekiel will enjoy beating that right out of you."

The matter-of-fact way she spoke made Sophia briefly doubt her own ears. "Did you say…?"

"Yes." Deirdre nodded. "I did. And that's the least of it, I promise you."

Horrified, Sophia could only stare. Beatings? Could it even get any worse? Or was the older woman trying to scare her. Suddenly she knew she didn't want to find out.

Before, while she'd been serious when she'd talked with Jack about wanting to escape, she hadn't gone so far as to make actual plans. Now she realized that was exactly what she'd have to do. She thought of Jack and the way he'd been dragged off to see Ezekiel. Hopefully he'd only been given a verbal reprimand, but in view of Deirdre's mention of beatings, she couldn't be sure. If he'd been hurt because of her, she didn't know how she'd live with herself.

Rachel would know. She couldn't wait to see Rachel after school let out for the day to find out how Jack had weathered the meeting.

Though she kept her face expressionless while Deirdre eyed her, her insides were a mess. In view of the definite possibility that she was being watched and listened to, she'd have to use Rachel as a go-between, asking her to deliver messages to Jack. They'd all have to be very careful. Life in COE had suddenly become dangerous.

Chapter 12

After school let out, Jack went for a walk. Despite himself, he couldn't help watching for Sophia. It was early yet and no doubt she was still at the clinic; a place he'd avoid like the plague from now on. He wasn't sure what he'd do if he saw her out, as well, but for right now, it seemed best to avoid her entirely. Hopefully she'd understand.

He saw quite clearly that he'd been a fool. Ezekiel had no intention of ever letting Sophia leave COE. In less than two weeks' time, he'd make sure she'd be marrying him and taking her place among the numerous women in his harem.

Acknowledging that fact made Jack want to punch something. As long as he lived, he'd never forget that moment when she'd gazed into his eyes and softly asked him to make love to her.

And for the rest of his life, he'd regret not taking her up on it.

He loved her. Damn, he loved her. Once again proving he'd become a consummate idiot, he'd fallen in love with another man's woman. And it hurt like hell.

Though the best course of action would be to focus on the real reason he was there—trying to find the Bartlett boy—he knew he'd do whatever he could to help Sophia escape.

Resolved, he pushed away the constant ache inside him and rehashed his meetings with the three children. He couldn't stop thinking about what Theodore had told him about his dreams. Before he'd left, the Bartlett family had given him a copy of a sketch for reference. They'd hired an artist to do a rendition of what their son Ryan would probably look like now at the age of seven. Their desperate hope had moved him. Five years had gone by and they'd never given up.

But he'd studied Rachel's entire class and not a single boy resembled the sketch that he'd left behind with his wallet in his hotel room. For the first time since coming inside the cult, he wondered if the Bartlett family might have gotten it wrong. Maybe their son wasn't inside COE. Perhaps someone else had abducted him.

Either way, the possibility remained that some of these children had been brought there from outside. Whether this had been done illegally or not, remained to be seen.

At the rate this therapy thing was going, it could take months to learn anything truly useful. He didn't have that long. While he'd let the Bartletts know it would take a month or so if he managed to infiltrate the cult, now that he was there, he realized it could take much longer.

There had to be another way. Mentally, he ran through his options. Thomas knew all the answers. Therefore, he needed to cozy up to him. But how?

And then it dawned on him. COE. Ostensibly he'd been brought inside the compound to join the cult. Since his arrival, not one single person had spoken to him about their beliefs, invited him to any kind of religious service or given him COE reading material.

He would seek Thomas out as his spiritual guide. Ask to be allowed to spend time with him, maybe flatter the other man's ego some.

Resolve quickening his steps, he made a sharp left turn and headed toward Thomas's house.

Arriving at the door, he pressed the buzzer. At first, there was no response, which indicated to him that Thomas wasn't used to receiving visitors in the middle of the workday. He buzzed again and a moment later an irritated voice responded. "Who is it and what do you want?"

Hmm. No cameras, then. He filed that information away for future knowledge. Giving his name and expressing his need to speak with Thomas, he waited.

After a moment the voice said he could enter and the gate clicked open.

Mentally rehearsing his words, Jack was just about to open the door when Thomas stepped outside, arms crossed, sunglasses hiding his eyes, he waited for Jack to approach him.

"What do you need?" Thomas asked, his tone simultaneously annoyed and bored. "I'm in the middle of working on financials."

Financials? Another interesting tidbit.

Arranging his expression into something he hoped look humbled, Jack bowed his head. "I've been here a couple of weeks now," he began. "And I'm thinking you were waiting as a sort of test of my resolve."

As he'd hoped, Thomas took the bait. "Waiting for what?"

"To see if I was ready to learn," Jack said enthusiastically. "I've observed and I've listened, and I feel like I'm making a difference. I'm ready to go all in."

Slowly, Thomas nodded. "I see."

Did he? Just in case he didn't, Jack continued, "Where do I go to get your book, your bible or whatever it's called? And I'd like to attend worship services, if you have them."

Thomas reared back, his expression shocked. "If we have them? Don't tell me your roommate never invited you to attend service at the Sanctuary? Or offered to loan you his *Volumes of Choice*?"

Crud. The last thing he wanted was to get Phillip into some kind of trouble. "He might have mentioned it, sir," he lied. "But I didn't feel ready. I do now. And I'd really like you to teach me."

"Me?" Now the older man regarded Jack as if he thought he might have lost his mind. "I'm not a spiritual teacher."

"You're Chosen, right?" Jack had heard that word bandied about often enough to use it with a fair amount of confidence. "And one of Children of Eternity's leaders. What better way to lead than by example?"

He could see the wheels turning inside Thomas's mind.

"I really admire you, sir," Jack continued. "After all, you came to me and saw my need. You chose me to become one of you. I'm truly Chosen. Because of you, I'll be among those ready for eternity. Please, don't turn me away now."

Thomas simply eyed him silently. Jack stared right back, imploring.

Finally, Thomas sighed. "Fine. We'll schedule a few learning sessions. It'll have to be during the day, so you'll have to work your therapy with the children around our meeting. I'm thinking three times a week at first, for one hour each time."

Since that was so much more than Jack had even hoped for, he nodded eagerly. "When can we start?"

"How about tomorrow?"

"Perfect." Jack wanted to high-five the other man, but didn't, of course.

"Wait here one second." Thomas turned and went inside. When he returned a moment later he held a small, paperback book. The pages were rimmed in gold leaf. "Take this home tonight and study it," he said. "It's yours. A gift from me."

Accepting the gift with the appropriate amount of reverence, Jack saw the words *Volumes of Choice* emblazoned on the cover. The Children of Eternity's bible. Which, as far as he'd been able to ascertain, had nothing to do with that of any other religion. Supposedly, Ezekiel, as the Anointed One, had been given the words from some divine source. The book was a source of speculation, as no one outside of COE had ever seen a copy.

"Thank you," he said. "I'll begin reading it immediately."

Thomas smiled. "Good."

Once he left Thomas's, he went home. Not only did he want to make himself familiar with their sacred book, but he needed to come up with some well-framed questions that might give him more insight into what COE might be doing as far as bringing people in from the outside. Here, he had an unusual advantage, since he was—as far as he knew—the only adult member brought into the fold from there.

But he really needed to skillfully turn the focus on the children. As a "therapist," that should be relatively easy to do.

Phillip breezed in, showered and stopped by Jack's room to inform him he wouldn't be home tonight. "Rachel and I are going out."

"Great." Jack smiled. "I'm curious. What do you do around here when you go out on a date?"

"We walk, maybe go hear some music. Someone is always playing an instrument or singing down at the center park—you know, where we had the cookout—when the weather is nice. There are benches or we spread a blanket on the grass and have a picnic. Some girls like to visit the flower gardens while others enjoy the barn. The possibilities are endless."

Jack nodded, thinking of Sophia and how much she loved the farm animals. As soon as he did, he pushed the thought away.

"What kind of things did you do?" Phillip asked, expression curious. "Before, when you lived outside?"

"Mostly we'd go out to eat at a restaurant and maybe go see a movie." Realizing Phillip would have no frame of reference for either of those things, Jack continued, "Sometimes we also go to listen to music or attend a sporting event, like a baseball game."

"You need to read that book, brother." Phillip pointed to the *Volumes of Choice* in Jack's hands. "Though I'm really not sure what movies or baseball games are, those two are specifically mentioned by name as forbidden."

"Oh." Hoping he appeared properly chastised, Jack hung his head. "I didn't know. I just got this from Thomas today and have been paging through it."

"It's okay." Phillip stepped inside and cuffed Jack lightly on the shoulder. "You're here now. Away from all that. You'll be among the true Chosen before you know it."

Jack wondered if Phillip realized how ominous that phrase sounded.

"Thanks," he said. "Is there anywhere you recommend I start?"

Phillip chucked. "In the beginning," he answered. With that, he left.

Interesting. Jack took a deep breath and continued to page through the book, scanning. The first part appeared to be a history of how Ezekiel had become the First Chosen, the Anointed One. He read a few pages and then skipped ahead. Read a few more and did the same. After a while, he started skimming. The more he read, the worse he felt for all of the people he'd come to consider his friends.

He needed fresh air. Aware he couldn't walk around the compound now because he might run into Sophia, he headed for the fence and the forest. There, even though he was only yards outside the boundaries, he felt free.

Leaving his small house, he took the *Volumes of Choice* with him. From this day forward, he planned to take the book with him wherever he went so he could at least give the appearance of trying to begin his journey toward becoming a devout and truly Chosen.

All the way to the boundary, he felt like his skin had been stretched too tight. Nervous. He guessed finding out that someone seemed to be watching his every move could make him that way, and he sure didn't like it.

Actually he didn't like any of this. If his entire future

wasn't dependent of solving this case, he'd grab Sophia and cut his losses now and get out.

But he hadn't gotten this far by being a quitter. And something was off with those kids. Even if none of them turned out to be the Bartletts' son, he had to find out what had happened to them. Somewhere, maybe they all had parents who were still desperately searching for them.

The sound of dried leaves crunching underfoot alerted him to the fact that he was no longer alone.

"I thought I'd find you here." Sophia's voice.

Though his heart skipped a beat, he steeled his resolve. "You can't be here," he said. "Seriously."

"But then, I am." She sounded supremely unconcerned as she moved closer to him. "Rachel told me you were okay."

"I'm fine." Keeping his distance proved more difficult than he'd thought, especially when every fiber of his being ached to touch her. "However I've been warned by no less than the Anointed One himself to stay away from you."

Just like that, her exuberance vanished. Part of him hated to be the one to snuff out the joy in her eyes.

"Did he hurt you?" she asked, her voice grave.

"No. Of course not."

"There is always that possibility," she said. "Deirdre informed me that I should expect to be beaten."

Rage flashed through him, which he stifled. "What did you say when she told you that?"

"Nothing." Instead of hanging her head, she lifted her chin and locked her gaze with his. "Because there was nothing to say. Jack, you know I want out. We've got to start making plans immediately. They're fitting me for a wedding dress." She took a deep, shaky breath, crossing the last few feet between them. "I need to know if you will really help me escape within the next few days."

Heaven help him, he could only blink. "You're serious?"

"I am." She seemed poised on the balls of her feet, as if she wanted to either leap into his arms or run away. "And as you know, I really don't have much time."

"Come here," he said, his voice gruff as he held out his arms. When she flung herself toward him, he caught her and held her close, breathing in her scent. "Sweetheart, you need to be very, very certain. Life isn't always easy outside, but I'll do whatever I can to help you."

She looked up at him, her eyes shining. "Thank you."

"Are you sure this is what you want?"

She didn't hesitate. "Yes. I'm positive. I can't be what they want me to be. I don't want to live like that."

Though he wanted to kiss her more than he wanted to breathe, he didn't. They both needed to keep their heads clear to deal with what lay ahead, especially him. He realized he could trust her the same way she did him. That would have to be enough for right now.

"Take a seat," he told her, gesturing at the fallen log. "And let me fill you in on the real reason I'm here."

She listened silently while he told her about Mr. and Mrs. Bartlett and their missing son. When he got to the part about his talks with the three children in Rachel's class, she nodded. "She's been talking to me about them. She's worried, too."

When he finished talking, he noted she didn't appear surprised. "Do you think there's a possibility I'm right and they're bringing infants in from outside?"

"Stealing babies? It's something that's occurred to

me a few times." She hesitated. "Actually, I've wondered if I was one myself. I've always had memories
that don't fit in with the way of life here."

He stared. "Really?"

"Yep." Lifting one shoulder in a quasi shrug, she
grimaced. "I convinced myself I was just being weird.
Now, I'm not so sure. It's a very real possibility."

"Do you have proof?"

"No," she admitted.

He remembered her saying something once about
seeing his file. Reminding her of this, he asked her if
she knew where COE kept the main files on everyone
in the cult.

"I hate that word," she said, wincing. "We've been
taught from childhood that we aren't a cult. As for the
files, I'm not sure. Wherever they're kept, you can bet
they're under lock and key. That's information Thomas
and Ezekiel wouldn't want getting into the hands of the
general public."

"That's for sure." He thought for a moment. "Do you
have a library?"

"A what?" Clearly the word wasn't in her vocabulary.

"A place where books are kept."

"What kind of books?" She tilted her head. "Do you
mean textbooks for the children or extra copies of the
Volumes of Choice?"

Was that the only book they were allowed to read?
That would explain how Ezekiel kept such a firm hold
on them. No TV or radio, and now no books. "Fiction?"
He tried anyway. "Or reference materials? Books of poetry or photography?"

Her blank look told him she had no idea what he
meant. "Never mind," he said. "Let's try another direc-

tion. If someone comes into your clinic and you need to look at their personal file, what do you do?"

"Look it up on the computer in Dr. Drew's office," she answered quickly. "We each have a special code to put in and that lets us into the database."

He felt a little thrum of excitement. "Do you have a computer at home? Like a laptop?"

Her laugh told him she thought he was joking. "Of course not. The only computers are where they need to be—at places like the clinic that need them. What would we do with something like that at home?"

"It'd be easier not to tell you." He thought for a moment. "Can you look up those three kids tomorrow at work?"

"Sure." She didn't appear worried.

"Does anyone monitor what you do on the computer? I want to make sure you're safe."

"I don't know. The subject has never come up. But Rachel has access to a computer, too. Since she's their teacher, wouldn't it make more sense to ask her to do it?"

"Rachel doesn't know. And I'm not sure I trust her enough to fill her in."

"I trust her," Sophia said. "I've known her all my life. She's my best friend."

"I understand." He had to ball his hands into fists to keep from touching her. "But for now, please don't say anything to her about what we've discussed, okay? We can't risk it."

Slowly she nodded. "I understand, so I won't say a word. But I should let you know, I do plan to tell her goodbye before I leave. Even if it's at the last second."

"That's understandable." He wanted to kiss her almost as much as he wanted to breathe. "Maybe I can get her to let me take a peek at her computer."

"Do you even know how to use a computer?" she asked. "I can show you if you'd like."

He hid a smile. "We have those outside," he told her. "I'm actually pretty handy with them."

"Oh. Well, if you want, I can try to pull their records tomorrow."

Considering, he shook his head. "Hold off. I don't want to take the chance of someone noticing and getting you in trouble. Let me see what I can work out with Rachel before you go risking your job."

"I want you to be careful, too." She pushed to her feet and crossed to him. He stood absolutely still, afraid to move, while his heart hammered in his chest.

Leaning in, she kissed his cheek, the warmth from her breath tickling his ear. "Promise me you won't take any unnecessary chances."

Too close, he shuddered. Unable to keep from touching her, he settled for squeezing her shoulder, letting his hand linger. "I'll do my best. But I've got to find out about the children. Even if the Bartlett boy isn't here, if those others were stolen from their parents, they need to be reunited and the practice stopped."

"It's illegal, isn't it?"

"Yes. If COE has really been abducting children, there will be charges against them. Ezekiel and Thomas and whoever else might be involved would be facing serious jail time."

Her grimace had him searching her face. "It's wrong, Sophia. What if you were abducted as a baby? You might have parents, people who care about you and have been searching for you all these years."

The look of anguish in her eyes did him in. Despite

his promise to himself, he pulled her close, smoothing her hair away from her beautiful face and wishing she was his.

Dangerous. Before he did something foolish, he let her go. "You'd better head back," he said, shoving his hands into his pockets. "Before you're missed. I'll go later, just to make sure no one figures out we were together. That kind of trouble we don't need."

She nodded. "When do you want to meet again?"

"I want to make sure it's safe. How about tomorrow evening? Here, around the same time?"

"As long as no one sees us."

"I feel confident they don't watch beyond the perimeter. As long as we arrive separately and from different locations, I think we'll be fine. Just to be sure, I'll leave the compound farther south, then loop around once I'm in the forest. You just come directly here."

Again she nodded. As she turned to go, she opened her mouth and then closed it. "Be careful," she finally said. And then she was gone.

The next morning when Sophia went into work, Dr. Drew waited in the reception area. Since this had never happened the entire time she'd worked there, Sophia stopped short. "Good morning," she said, registering the solemnity of his expression.

Instead of replying in kind, he nodded. "Sophia, please take a seat." He gestured at one of the chairs.

Puzzled and a bit worried, she sat. "Is Ana all right?"

"She's fine." His frown deepened. "Sophia, I'm afraid I'm going to have to let you go."

Whatever she'd been expecting, it hadn't been this. "What? Why?"

"Ezekiel doesn't want you working here any longer.

And Deirdre has informed me that you'll need to begin your training."

"My what?" Tension coiled in her belly, making her feel ill. "I just spent the day with her and she didn't mention anything about training. Training for what?" But before she'd even finished speaking, she knew.

"Training to be Ezekiel's wife." Dr. Drew's answer confirmed her thoughts. He scratched the back of his head and shifted his weight from foot to foot. "He requires this of all his wives."

Numb, she manufactured a smile as she nodded. "I didn't know. Did Deirdre say where I'm to go instead of here?"

"No. I'd suggest you return home and wait. I'm sure she'll be sending someone for you soon." He gave her a kindly smile that she could have sworn contained a trace of pity. "Now go ahead and collect your things. I'll have to ask you to turn in your key before you leave."

It only took her a few moments to gather up her belongings. A coffee mug, a potted plant and a framed photo of the sunset Dr. Drew had given her for her fifth work anniversary. Tears stung her eyes as she walked through the clinic one last time. The leaving was bittersweet, because even if she hadn't been forced out of her job by Ezekiel, she would have been leaving anyway. Just not so soon.

As she walked toward the front door, she remembered her key and detoured by Dr. Drew's office.

He cleared his throat awkwardly when she entered. Removing her key from the small ring, she placed it in front of him on his desk. She decided not to mention she was keeping a second key she'd taken when she'd worried she might lose the first. "I've enjoyed working for you," she said.

"As I'm sure you'll enjoy your new position of honor as wife of the Anointed One."

"Of course." Her answer came smoothly, surprising her. "I hope Ana arrives soon, so I can tell her goodbye."

He shrugged. "She should be here at any moment. If she's not, I'll tell her for you." He seemed nervous for some reason. "Let me walk you out. I really think you should go."

Then he stood and led the way toward the front door, and she wondered why he appeared so worried. Had Ezekiel threatened him, too? If so, why?

As they reached the entrance, he held the door open for her. Once she'd stepped outside, he followed her, glancing both left and right before leaning close. "You've been a great employee, Sophia. Just be careful, okay? Don't do anything foolish."

Was that a warning? Before she could respond, he turned around and went back inside, closing and locking the door behind him.

Since there was no sign of Ana yet, Sophia debated waiting for her and decided to go home instead. Juggling her mug, plant and picture, she headed that way.

When she got there, Rachel was in the kitchen, packing her lunch for the day before she left for work. She shook her head when Sophia told her the news, but was careful not to say anything even remotely negative. The night before, Rachel and Sophia had searched the entire house, looking for anything that might indicate they weren't paranoid and were actually being spied upon or listened to, but they hadn't found a single thing. Of course, they had no idea what they were looking for, either.

"Would you like to walk with me toward school?"

Rachel asked, meaning so they could talk without fear of being heard.

Sophia almost said yes, but then she remembered that Deirdre would be sending someone for her. "I don't want to be gone when whoever is coming to get me arrives," she said, letting her regret show. "We'll catch up at the end of the day."

Hopefully. But first, she had to meet up with Jack. If she could. She wouldn't be surprised to learn she was supposed to move into the big house prior to the wedding. If that happened, escaping would be much more difficult.

Chapter 13

Deirdre herself knocked on Sophia's front door thirty minutes after Rachel left for work. The older woman, accompanied by two large men wearing all black who appeared to be her bodyguards, swept inside. She looked around dismissively before settling her pale gaze on Sophia.

"Are you happy you don't have to work anymore?" Deirdre asked, clearly expecting Sophia to jump for joy.

"Of course." Sophia knew better than to answer with the truth. She also knew better than to ask what was on that day's agenda.

"Pack all your things," Deidre ordered. "And do it quickly. I'll wait here until you're finished."

Sophia's heart sank. Now what? Though she found doing so nearly impossible, she managed to keep her mouth shut as she pivoted on her heel and went to her room.

As she threw her clothing into a duffel bag, she told herself this was a good thing. Being packed would make for a much more efficient leaving. Except the only reason Deirdre would ask her to pack would be if she were being sent to live in Ezekiel's house, which would complicate things.

Finally she thought she had everything. Hoping her expression didn't reveal her worry, she hefted her full bag and went back to the main living area.

"That's everything?" Deidre tilted her head toward the bag.

Slowly, Sophia nodded.

"Good. Larry, take that from her."

One of the big men stepped forward, holding his hands out. Once she'd handed everything she owned over, he lifted it to his shoulder as if it weighed nothing.

"Take that to the residence," Deirdre directed. "Sophia and I will be there later."

"'The residence'?" Sophia repeated, realizing too late that she'd managed to ask a question.

"Of course." Deirdre didn't seem offended. "Tonight we women are having a little ceremony. We do this for every new wife-to-be, at my instigation. Since you're going to be starting a new life, we have a symbolic 'letting go' ceremony." Deirdre winked. "Some women find it quite shocking but others have said it's liberating."

Confused and worried, Sophia swallowed, hoping the other woman would tell her what she meant.

But no, Deirdre apparently decided she'd said enough. "Come along," she directed. "We've got things to do and people to see."

Try as she might, Sophia couldn't seem to get her feet moving properly. There was one thing she had to know, so she decided to risk punishment and ask. "Will I be coming back here?"

Instead of answering, the first wife held up her hand. "No more questions. Let's go. I don't want you to be late for your appointment."

Over the course of the next several hours, Sophia found herself shuffled between various women who were intent on making her into something she was not. *Preparing her*, as one of the women said. She was shuffled from one room to another inside a wing of Ezekiel's house. She had what they called an exfoliating body scrub, a massage, a facial, a manicure, pedicure and a sauna that made her feel ill from the heat. Then she was made to shower and sit still while someone else cut and styled her hair.

Finally, nails buffed and polished, skin glowing, she clutched the white robe she'd tied at her waist and eyed herself in a large mirror, barely recognizing the woman gazing back at her.

And they weren't finished.

"Pay attention," Deirdre barked. "Simone here is going to show you how to apply makeup. You'll be taking the products with you and be required to use them, so you'd better pay attention."

For the next thirty minutes, Simone slathered stuff on Sophia's face. Something called foundation and powder, then blush and eye shadow. Her brows were darkened and her eyelashes curled and coated with mascara. "It's important to do the mascara more than once," Simone said. "Now look! How beautiful are you?"

A stranger peered back at her in the mirror. Oh, she knew it was her from the heart-shaped face and dimple in her chin, but still. Her brown eyes appeared huge, framed by long and sooty lashes. Her lips were colored in some reddish pink that highlighted their bow shape.

All the other women oohed and aahed, telling her how pretty she looked. Personally, Sophia felt she appeared garish. Like one of the clowns in the children's stories they'd read to her as a child.

Deirdre entered the room and everyone fell silent.

"Let me see," she ordered, pushing her way through the others. When she caught sight of Sophia, her lips thinned and her eyes narrowed. The makeup artist audibly caught her breath, clearly terrified that the first wife wasn't pleased with the results.

"Perfect!" Deirdre declared. "You made her look exactly the way Ezekiel prefers. Sophia, did you pay attention? You'll need to be able to recreate this look whenever you're required to."

"Yes," she said firmly. "I listened. I'm sure I can do this again." Though if she had her way, she never would. The sooner she could get away from this madhouse, the better.

"Perfect. Now we need to outfit you for tonight." Deirdre snapped her fingers. Two women rushed off, returning with a rolling clothes rack full of dresses of every color. Most of them looked a lot shorter than those Sophia was used to wearing.

Deirdre began flipping through the dresses, dismissing them with a critical eye. "No," she said. "I don't think so. No, no, no. Aha. Here we go." She pulled out a mustard-yellow frock that appeared to have been cut from a flour sack. Not to mention that yellow really wasn't Sophia's favorite color.

"This one, I think," Deirdre said. "Though, of course, I'll need to see it on you."

Forcing a smile, Sophia nodded. She'd seen several

lovely blue dresses and even a nice green one. But she didn't dare question Deirdre's judgment. Heck, for all she knew, the first wife might have deliberately chosen something unflattering. No matter. Sophia didn't want to appear pretty around Ezekiel. The uglier, the better.

Everyone stared, clearly waiting. Sophia looked around for a place to change, but there was none.

"Try it on," Deirdre ordered, clearly expecting Sophia to simply drop the robe and do so. Even with an audience. Despite the massage and other pampering Sophia had received, the attendants had made sure to keep her tastefully covered.

Accepting the dress from an attendant, Sophia turned her back to them and untied her robe. If she maneuvered herself just right, she should be able to slip the thing over her head, let the robe fall to her waist, and end up dressed without showing any excess flesh. Or at least she hoped.

Mostly, that's what happened. It wasn't the slightest bit graceful, and she might have flailed about a bit like a catfish on the end of a fishing line, but when she turned around to face Deirdre, she was dressed. Sort of. Her lower legs were bare. Used to dresses that came to the floor, she felt exposed. Vulnerable. To cover, she bent over and picked up the white robe pooled around her feet, forcing a smile.

"That's very nice," Deirdre declared.

Of course, Sophia nodded. Contrary to her expectations, the material felt soft and comfortable and the way it hung seemed as if it might be semi-flattering. It was almost the right length, hitting her right below her knees at the calf. Just a little short. She wasn't sure if she should say she liked it, having a feeling that to do so would ensure Deirdre changing her mind and picking out an even more hideous dress from the rack.

"We need shoes." The first wife snapped her fingers. Immediately the two women who'd wheeled in the rack of dresses rushed from the room. They returned a moment later carrying several boxes.

"All of these are your size," Deirdre told Sophia. "Have you ever worn a pair of high heels?"

Slowly, Sophia shook her head, aware Deirdre already knew the answer. Here, every woman was issued the same basic flat-soled shoes, one pair of black, one brown, as well as boots. Sophia had only seen high heels on one of Ezekiel's female family members. They looked uncomfortable.

"There's a trick to walking in them." Was that malice making the older woman's eyes gleam? Or simple amusement? "But since I'm sure you'll be required to wear a pair in your wedding, it's time you learned how."

Again, Sophia simply nodded.

Deirdre chose a box and held it out to one of the attendants. "Let's see how she does in these."

The woman nodded, carrying the shoes over to Sophia. "Please sit, ma'am." She indicated a small, ornate chair.

Would this never end? Sophia took a seat, careful to move the dress to avoid smashing it. The shoes were brought out—they were black and shiny, with red soles and a dangerous-looking, long-spiked heel. Once they'd been fitted onto Sophia's feet—a perfect fit—the attendant pushed herself up and held out her hand. "Please stand."

Eyeing the other woman, Sophia swallowed hard and did exactly that. She wobbled a little bit, but managed to keep her balance, as long as her knees were bent.

Her smile widening, Deirdre crooked her finger. "Walk toward me."

Sophia wanted to take the shoes off and fling them at the first wife. Reminding herself that soon she'd be escaping from all of this and all of them, she lifted her chin, held her head high and took a step.

Her ankle nearly gave out from under her. *Strength of will*, she told herself. She could do this.

And so she did. Not neatly, not even with the tiniest degree of skill. She wobbled and weaved, but she crossed the room to stand in front of Deirdre, pleased to note how the shoes made her at least three inches taller.

"Well done." Again, the older woman's brittle expression was at odds with her patently false smile. "Let's see how you do on the walk back to the big house."

Sophia nearly groaned out loud. She honestly didn't think she could do it. Already both her ankles and the balls of her feet ached.

"Don't worry," Deirdre said, apparently correctly judging Sophia's apprehension. "You'll get the hang of it. And it's a perfect intro for the rest of what's going to happen tonight."

Clenching her jaw, Sophia nodded. She knew the other woman's words were meant to bait her. Despite that, her stomach roiled and she had to clamp her mouth shut to avoid asking a forbidden question.

"Let's go." Deirdre strode off without a backward glance.

Tempted to simply stay put, Sophia followed, though much slower.

Outside, she saw Deirdre had already traveled fifty yards. Of course she had, since she had on flat, comfortable shoes.

The heck with it. Sophia kicked off the high heels

and picked them up, hurrying after the first wife in her bare feet.

When she caught up with Deidre, at first the first wife's jaw clenched when she saw what Sophia had done. Her narrow-eyed gaze traveled from Sophia's dirty feet to the shoes she clutched in one hand.

And then, surprising Sophia, Deirdre laughed. "You're a resourceful little twit," she said. "I should be furious, but I actually find you entertaining."

They continued on. Deirdre did not ask Sophia to put the shoes back on, so she didn't.

When they reached the big house, they went through the front gate and into the garden. "I keep a little place back here," Deirdre informed her. "It's mine and mine alone. Ezekiel built it for me when we were first married. No one else is allowed entrance except by my invitation. We hold the new wife initiation ceremonies here."

New wife initiation? Not sure she liked the sound of that, Sophia hurried after Deirdre. They traveled through vine-covered trellises, well-tended flower beds full of riotous color and trees. Finally, at the back of the garden near the boundary wall, a small cottage sat. Unlike all the residences inside the compound, this structure had been built from wood and painted a beautiful pale blue.

Inside, Sophia could hear a chorus of voices, all of them feminine. She hesitated, earning a sideways look from Deirdre.

"Come on," Deirdre said, not bothering to hide her impatience. "We all have to go through this, so don't worry. Well, everyone went through this except me. I was first, so I'm the one who came up with this idea."

Noting the other woman hadn't said it was fun, Sophia exhaled and took a step forward. "It's still afternoon," she said, trying to stall. "Don't you want to wait until dark?"

"No. We do nothing after dark, because that's when Ezekiel looks for us. We need daylight, no shadows to hide in, so we stay safe."

Safe. Another interesting word. "I see," Sophia said, even though she didn't.

"First, put your shoes back on," Deirdre ordered. "Then keep your head high and your shoulders back. It's not wise to let them sense your fear."

Fear. Great.

Deirdre opened the door, beckoning Sophia to precede her. Sophia stepped into a brightly lit room full of women, all of them staring at her.

"Do you think I could have a look at the kids' files?" Jack asked, helping Rachel organize some folders.

"Files?" she asked, frowning.

"Yes. I'm assuming you have files on each student, right?"

Eyes wide and cautious, she gave a slow nod. "Well, yes, we do. But I'm not sure if you're allowed to view them."

"Why wouldn't I be?" He kept his tone reasonable. "I'm a therapist trying to help them. There might be information in there that can help me break through."

She considered. "I might need to check with my boss."

"The principal?"

"The what?" She peered at him, her brow wrinkled in confusion.

"Maybe you call it something else here. The person in charge of all the teachers and the entire school."

"My boss."

Okay, so they didn't have a name. "Who is your boss?" he asked, figuring it would be someone higher up in the ranks like Thomas.

"Her name is Yvonne. She's very busy, but she takes orders directly from Thomas and Ezekiel."

"Good. Then ask her, please. Since Thomas is the one who brought me here and hired me to do therapy, I'm sure he won't have any problem with me viewing the files."

Considering him, Rachel nodded. "We'll see," she said.

Right before lunch, while the children were busy writing a descriptive story, Rachel motioned him to her desk. "I couldn't reach Yvonne, but I thought about what you said and it makes sense. You're the official thera- pist, so of course you should be able to access the chil- dren's records. We'll stop by the shared computer room after we have our noon meal. My time is always the last ten minutes before classes resume in the afternoon."

"Ten minutes? That's all you get?"

"Yes." She eyed him. "We don't do much on the com- puter, except for entering grades into a spreadsheet. Is ten minutes not long enough for you?"

"It will have to be." He kept his voice casual. "I'll just have to read fast."

"Oh, that shouldn't be a problem. The files are not very large."

He wondered if he was about to be completely dis- appointed.

He'd brought his lunch—a sandwich and some of Phillip's homemade macaroni salad. He scarfed it down, nearly unable to contain his eagerness.

Rachel noticed him trying not to fidget in his chair and grinned. "Are you ready?" she asked.

"Is it time already?"

His feigned surprise made her laugh. "It is. I sure hope you're able to find something helpful."

"So am I, Rachel. So am I."

They left the lunchroom and walked down a long hallway, their footsteps echoing on the linoleum floors. "Here we are," she chirped, unlocking the door to a small room. Inside was a folding metal table and an ancient computer with a huge, old monitor.

"I hope it's on," she remarked. "If not, sometimes it takes forever to come up."

He hoped so, too. He didn't want to waste the entire ten minutes waiting.

Luckily, the last user had left it on. Rachel logged in and waited. "Here we are," she said. "I've accessed the record."

At his direction, she opened Benjamin's file first. Once she'd pulled it up, she vacated the chair and motioned for him to take a seat. "Here you go."

"Thank you." Gingerly he began to scroll through the document. He didn't even mind that Rachel stood directly behind him, watching his every move.

There was a plethora of information on the boy. His nightmares and communication problems had begun in early childhood, when he was two years old. Try as he might, Jack couldn't find any information prior to that.

He turned in his chair to ask Rachel.

"That's weird," she said, reading over his shoulder. "That would make this an incomplete record."

Meeting her gaze, he nodded. She knew what he was thinking, but didn't dare say it out loud, just in case anyone might be listening.

Theodore's and Samantha's files were similar, only Theodore's started at age four and Samantha's at three.

"Can you pull up one more child—a random one who's not having any problems?" Jack asked. "I just want to make sure they're not all like this."

"Sure." She keyed in another name. When the records came up, the observation started at the age of two months, stating the child had been a happy, active baby. There were several more notations such as the age when the child had first crawled and also walked. Every lost tooth was noted, along with sicknesses and recoveries.

"They're radically different." Eyes wide, Rachel appeared shocked. Then, just for the benefit of anyone who might be eavesdropping, she cleared her throat. "I'll mention this to my supervisor. Clearly there's some glitch in the system."

"Clearly," he drawled. As far as he was concerned, this was a pretty strong indicator that the three children had been brought in from outside. Not yet proof—he had to believe that would come later, with DNA testing, after the child had told his or her story.

Now he just needed to get one of them to talk. If he could just find the right words so they'd open up. Luckily, he'd scheduled two of their meetings in the afternoon. The boys—Benjamin and Theodore. He'd met with Samantha in the morning and hadn't learned anything new. He had high hopes of doing better now that he knew what age to focus on with each of them.

True to the previous attempts, Benjamin sat sullen, refusing to answer any questions or to acknowledge Jack's presence. Until Jack brought up what he'd learned from reviewing Ben's records.

"Tell me one thing you remember happening when you were one or two," Jack asked. Since Ben's records started at two, he hoped going back a year might jog the kid's memory.

Though Ben darted a quick glance at Jack, he still didn't respond.

"Now most people don't remember anything much before they were three or four," Jack continued. "And you might be like that, too, I don't know. But sometimes we have one or two flashes of something. A memory that meant a lot to us but nobody else." Careful not to reveal his anticipation, he waited.

Still, Ben didn't speak.

Jack sighed. "I guess you didn't have any flashes of memory. That's okay, we'll work on—"

"I did," Ben interrupted. "More than one. But I'm not sure I want to tell them to you."

"Why not?"

"Because you'll punish me. I'm not stupid. I've made that mistake before." The boy spoke with force, pushing the words out with a vehemence that reminded Jack once again of where they were.

"You can't take them away from me," Ben continued. "No matter what you do. She was my mommy and I loved her." His eyes widened and he clamped his lips together as if he meant to keep anything else from spilling out.

"I had a mommy, too," Jack said softly, his heart aching. "And I loved her very much. She was always there for me. I miss her to this day."

Now a flash of interest gleamed in the child's eyes. "Did they take you away from her, too?"

Aha. Something concrete. Aware he needed to be extremely careful as to how he reacted, Jack looked down. This gave him time to gather his thoughts. He hesitated to speak the truth—his mother had died from cancer—because doing so might make Ben shut down even more.

Instead he deflected the question back to the boy. "Did someone take you from your mom?"

Ben looked away, no doubt fearful of the repercussions that usually followed him declaring something like this.

"I won't tell anyone, I promise," Jack said. "And I won't let anything happen to you for telling me the truth." He prayed he could keep his vow.

But clearly Benjamin didn't trust him that much. "I'd like to go back to class now," he said. "Don't you need to talk to Theodore?"

Jack stood, both disappointed and amused at the way the kid managed to deflect. "Sure, you can go back. Just remember, though, I'm from outside, too." The *too* was deliberate. "I understand better than anyone else what you're going through."

Again Ben cut his eyes to Jack, then toward the bench. Jack suddenly realized that maybe the boy was trying to tell him something. Like the possibility that if he'd look underneath the bench, he might find some sort of listening device.

Heart pounding, Jack led the way inside. When he got out there with Theodore, he'd have to figure out a way to check.

Five minutes later, as he marched outside to start his final session of the day, Jack pretended to trip just before he reached the bench. He landed a few feet from it and crawled forward slightly so he could get a good look.

He saw nothing. Aware that there could be cameras watching him, he slowly climbed back to his feet and made a show out of clutching his knee. "That hurt," he said cheerfully to Theodore. "That's what I get for being so clumsy."

Theodore smiled. Jack hobbled over to the bench and took a seat, patting the spot next to him. He'd need to be careful. Just because he hadn't found anything that looked like a listening device didn't mean there wasn't one.

Still, he said the exact same thing he'd said to Benjamin, except modifying the age to three. Theodore, always a talker, began ruminating about some bright yellow toy truck he'd gotten at Christmas, how Santa had left it under the tree, and how much he'd loved it.

It took Jack a few seconds to realize what the boy had said. As far as he knew, COE didn't celebrate Christmas—or any holiday for that matter. And he'd yet to see a single toy truck—or any toys, actually.

"You remember Christmas?" Jack asked, keeping his tone casual.

Theodore nodded. "Oh, yes. And the Christmas tree, with all the lights and sparkly decorations. Mom let me help hang them up, too. My favorite was—" Eyes widening, he broke off with a quick gasp. "You can't tell anyone I said that. Talking about stuff like *before* only gets me in trouble."

"'Before'?" Repeating the word, Jack smiled. "I promise you, Theodore. What we discuss between us stays with me. I won't repeat it to anyone else in here. You have my word."

The child's expression remained fearful. "Not even Miss Rachel?"

"Not even her."

Theodore held his gaze, clearly not certain if he could believe what Jack said.

"I'm your therapist," Jack reassured him. "We're not

allowed to tell anyone what you say in private." Unable to help himself, he glanced down at the bench. Of course, this made Theodore do the same.

"There's nothing there," Theodore whispered. "Me and a couple of the kids found the listening thing when we were playing a few weeks ago and broke it. Stomped it to pieces. So far, they haven't replaced it."

Jack let his relief show in his smile. "Thank you for letting me know. I think Benjamin believes it's still there."

"Oh." Theodore nodded sagely, too wise for an eight- or nine-year-old. "He still won't talk, huh?"

"I can't discuss him with you," Jack said promptly, secretly amused at how quickly the boy put him to the test. "You know that."

Theodore's sly smile told Jack he did. "I remember more than Christmas," he said. "My parents gave me a birthday party once."

This time Jack pretended not to understand. "In your family group here? I didn't know we celebrated birthdays."

"Not here." Theodore swallowed, clearly fighting to hold on to his bravado. "Before they brought me here. At home. My parents invited other kids from somewhere—day care? And we had cake and balloons and lots of presents."

"Day care?" Jack frowned, pretending not to understand the word.

Theodore shrugged. "I'm not sure what that is. I just remember it. I think it's where I went when my mom and dad went to work."

Thinking fast, Jack figured most kids were taught to memorize their address and phone number by the age of four. "Do you know your address and phone number?" he asked, glad he had his trusty therapist pad and pencil.

"Sure." Theodore rattled off an address. "It's 164 Oak Street, Fort Collins, Colorado." He followed this with a phone number.

Careful to hide his growing elation, Jack jotted both of them down.

Finally proof. He'd need to be careful, but this could be investigated. If only he still had access to his cell phone.

Since there were still thirty minutes left in the "session," Jack chatted with the boy about other things like snow and summer. As they wound down, Theodore grew wistful. "I miss them, you know," he said. "I still don't know why they sent me away."

"Sent you away?" Chest aching, Jack swallowed. "Why do you think that?"

"That's what Mr. Thomas told me. It's the reason I live here now. My parents didn't want me anymore."

Chapter 14

"Welcome." The voices were soft and loud, happy and monotone. Gazing around the semicircle of feminine faces, all of them Ezekiel's wives, Sophia assessed which would be allies and which enemies. If she were staying, that is. Since she wasn't, she didn't intend to spend too much time worrying about who to befriend.

Sophia counted at least twenty women. Some were older, others appeared to be closer to Sophia's age. One or two wouldn't even look at her—they kept their heads down and their faces averted. All had painted their faces and wore brightly colored dresses. Some, the normal long length, others short. And yes, she saw lots of heels as high as the ones Sophia had crammed on her aching feet.

As she stood facing them, the women moved once more, almost in unison, as if by some hidden cue. Behind them, a set of open French doors revealed a large wooden deck outside, surrounded entirely by tall bushes. A fire blazed in a beautiful stone fire pit. Next to that, Sophia saw her duffel bag.

Unsure what was expected of her, she hesitated, wobbling slightly in the high-heeled shoes.

Again acting on some unseen signal, the women began to flow through the doors and out onto the deck. As they neared Sophia's bag, each reached down and pulled out an article of clothing. Mystified, Sophia knew better than to protest.

"Come," Deidre ordered, sailing toward the others, clearly expecting Sophia to follow. Of course, Sophia did.

As soon as she'd made her way to Deirdre's side, the first woman lifted her arm high, waving one of Sophia's dresses. Then, with great ceremony, she tossed the blouse into the fire.

All the other women quietly cheered.

Not sure what to think, other than that maybe they'd all lost their minds, Sophia glanced at Deirdre. Wearing the fixed, grim smile she always wore, Deirdre nodded. "Continue," she ordered.

And then, one by one, each woman burned an article of Sophia's clothing. Heart sinking, Sophia realized they'd systematically destroyed every garment she owned.

When all had taken their turn, Deirdre marched over to the duffel bag and inspected it, probably to make sure it had been emptied. She pulled from inside Sophia's favorite sleep shirt, a well-worn and faded garment that Sophia loved.

Since she had a pretty good idea what Deirdre meant to do to it, Sophia worked hard to keep her expression impassive. Even when Deirdre tossed it into the fire.

"Your old life is now behind you," Deirdre intoned. "Start forward into the new."

"Start forward into the new," all the other women chanted. Some of them appeared bored, while one or two had a rapt countenance that Sophia found really disturbing. The rest—a vast majority—watched Sophia, as if hoping for some kind of exciting reaction.

Of course, Sophia knew better. She kept a pleasantly vacant expression on her face.

As her clothing burned and they all watched silently, Sophia wondered what would happen next. Deirdre had forced her to spend the day primping and being made to look like someone she wasn't. Surely all of that hadn't been just for this little ceremony.

Her feet were aching and, while she longed to remove the torturous shoes, her instinct told her Deirdre wouldn't be nearly as forgiving in front of this group of women.

Since they'd harped about her new life, Sophia wondered if they were about to bring her some new clothing to replace the stuff they'd destroyed. Not that she cared, but if they didn't, that meant she'd be stuck wearing this dress for a while. At least until she could get Rachel to loan her something.

Assuming she even got to go home.

Someone nudged her elbow. Deidre, holding out her hand. Bracing herself, Sophia took it. As she did, she realized all of the women had formed a large circle, clasping each other's hands. Another wife stood on Sophia's other side, clearly waiting for Sophia to complete the link.

Apprehension building, Sophia slid her fingers into hers.

And then, just when she thought things could not get

any stranger, they all began to sing. Since she had no idea of the words, Sophia didn't even attempt to follow along. She listened.

Though the melody was reminiscent of a hymn, the words were anything but.

"Sisters we are, united in hope. True to each other, until our last breath. Vowing to fight, stay strong and stay true. Keeping hold of our hearts, united together until our death."

While Sophia puzzled over this, she realized what they sang was a quiet battle cry. Stunned, she tried to process this.

She must have let some of the shock she felt slip through to her face, because Deirdre hugged her. "Tonight, we will swear an oath to each other," she said in Sophia's ear. "We promise to always help one another, no matter the circumstances, no matter the cost."

The others finished singing and now watched her, listening.

"If you have a question, ask it," Deirdre said, her smile genuine.

Sophia nodded. "Why?" she asked. "Why is such a thing necessary? What can happen in that house?" She shivered. "Is it really that bad?"

Several of the women grimaced, more than a few nodded, and one or two looked down.

"You remember I mentioned beatings?" Deirdre asked. "Well, there are actually worse things than that. Enalia, come forward."

Enalia, a petite, dark-haired girl who'd been one of the downcast women, moved toward them. She didn't raise her face until the very last moment. When she did, Sophia took an involuntary step back and gasped.

A network of scars crisscrossed one of Enalia's cheeks. Angry mutilations that hadn't healed well.

Immediately ashamed of her reaction, Sophia's eyes filled with tears. "I'm so, so sorry." She hugged the other woman. "What happened to you?"

"Ezekiel." Though Enalia spoke in a flat voice, the hatred in her eyes revealed her true emotion. "He finds pleasure in hurting others."

Immediately, Sophia's gaze flew to Deirdre. "Is that…is that true?"

Swallowing hard, Deirdre nodded. "All of us have been marked in some way. I was lucky—he stopped when I had his son. That is why I advised you to get with child if you could. While I was pregnant was when he took his second wife, Cassandra."

A tall, slender woman with a single, long gray braid strode up. "He branded me," she said, both her eyes and her voice dull. As if she'd checked out mentally long ago, leaving only the shell of her body to finish out her life. She turned slowly and lifted her skirt, exposing a horrid scar on her right buttock in the shape of an E. When she turned back around to face Sophia, a tear rolled down one perfect cheek.

Again, Sophia hugged her. She struggled to find the right words, but in the end realized there were none.

"He's branded more than one woman," Deirdre said. "As well as various forms of mutilation and torture. He even cut out poor Hallie's tongue."

A curvy redheaded woman who must have been Hallie nodded vigorously. She moved her fingers in some kind of sign language. When she stopped, Deirdre nodded. "She says it was all very painful and degrading."

Degrading. Now that word perfectly summed all this up.

"Don't any of you ever fight back?" Sophia asked. "Surely there has to be something you can do. What about the others—Thomas or some of Ezekiel's sons? Surely they can't be aware? Why would they allow this to happen?"

"Wife number four tried," Deirdre said, the corners of her mouth turning down in remembrance. "Ezekiel killed her, then burned her body and scattered her ashes to the wind. That was the first time he publicly punished one of his women. Of course, he lied about the reason, so no one would know the truth about what he'd done." Deirdre took a deep breath. "Oh, and Thomas is aware. He simply chooses to look the other way."

"We have no allies but each other." Enalia's eyes flashed. "Now that there are so many of us, we try to look out for the newer ones."

"Are you able to stop him?" Sophia swallowed. "You don't let him hurt them anymore, right?"

Deirdre and some of the other women shared a long glance. "We do what we can," the first wife said. "But there are definitely limits."

Sophia shivered. "That's horrible." Though she knew they'd think her revulsion and fear was for herself, in reality she didn't plan to be there to experience any of Ezekiel's twisted tortures. No, she worried for them. Why hadn't any of them ever tried to leave? She thought of wife number four and realized some of them might have, and ended up paying the ultimate price.

Though this bonding ceremony or whatever it was might be interesting, she still didn't trust them enough to reveal her own truth.

"It's time to take the oath," Deirdre declared. "You

can never speak of this again, unless Ezekiel takes another new wife after you."

Surprised, Sophia nodded. "Is that likely?"

Most of the women let out a collective groan.

"Yes," Deirdre said, the disgust in her face answer enough. "Now kneel, Sophia."

"Okay." Sophia did as the older woman asked. One by one, each woman came to kneel with her, pledging to always have her back. To each, she pledged the same. When Hallie's turn came, she used her fingers to sign the oath and Deirdre repeated it out loud for her.

Finally the last of the wives had taken their turn. Knees aching, Sophia was allowed to stand.

"You may return to your dwelling now," Deirdre said.

Sophia thought of her clothing, now ashes. What would she wear? As she opened her mouth to ask, Deirdre handed her a duffel bag, similar to Sophia's but brand new and red.

"There's new clothing in here," Deirdre told her. "Everything you will need to start your new life. I'll see you the day after tomorrow for the bridal dress fitting."

Her wedding date kept creeping closer. Time continued to march on, way too fast. Accepting the bag and finding it heavier than she'd expected, Sophia managed to nod. "Thank you," she said. She turned to face the others, finding them watching her with varying degrees of both sadness and pity. She looked for malice, like what she'd once thought she'd seen in Deirdre's eyes, but saw none.

"Thank you all," she repeated, her eyes filling with tears. Deirdre took her arm and led her out.

At the front gate, Deirdre eyed her up and down. "If you want any food, I'll be picking some up later at the place we had lunch. Probably around dark. You can meet me there if you'd like. I'll get extra."

Surprised, Sophia nodded. "Thank you."

"I'll watch for you." Looking around quickly, Deirdre reached out and squeezed Sophia's shoulder. "I'm sorry to spring so much on you at once, but I wanted to get to know you before I gave you your new reality. You seem like you have a strong spine, girl. You'll need it, that's for sure."

And then the gate buzzed open. Sophia stepped through and it clanged closed after her. On the other side, Deirdre had already turned away. Sophia watched for a moment until she'd vanished from sight and then took a deep breath and began the walk home.

The sun had barely begun to set. Since she was meeting Jack soon, she thought she might take Deirdre up on that offer of food later. After all, it had certainly been delicious. For now, she'd go home and think about everything she'd learned. Maybe some of the women she'd met might want to leave COE with her. But could she risk asking them?

Jack couldn't wait to see Sophia. As soon as school let out, he took off, deciding he'd jog around the perimeter of the compound before heading to their meeting place in the woods outside the fence. He didn't want to take a chance of being discovered. Not now, not when he was so damn close to the truth.

Despite the run—and he made two laps around the entire compound—when he finally climbed over the fence and walked into the woods, he was still early. The sun had barely begun to make its way toward the horizon. With birdsong as background music coming from the treetops, he walked into the little clearing and took a seat on the fallen log. Sophia should be getting off work fairly soon. The thought of seeing her again had his heart skipping a beat. He whiled away the time making plans for their new life in the outside world.

Eventually, he heard the rustling in the underbrush, letting him know she'd arrived. Jumping to his feet, he caught his breath at the first sight of her. As she rushed forward, he caught her in his arms and twirled her around, feeling complete now that she was there.

They clung to each other, neither willing to move. As he held her close, he thought he could do this every day for the rest of his life.

Until reluctantly, they broke apart.

"What a day," they both began at exactly the same moment.

He laughed, she laughed. "You go first," she said. "I'm still trying to process my news."

"Me, too." He told her everything, starting with viewing the three children's records and the discrepancies in them. When he finished relaying the conversation he'd had with Theodore, her amazing eyes went wide.

"That's unreal."

"It's a genuine breakthrough," he said, not bothering to keep the excitement from his voice. "The question is, where do I go from here? This information makes it pretty clear this boy at least came from outside. He believes, because that's what Thomas told him, that his parents didn't want him anymore, but I doubt the truth of that. He even remembers Christmas and his birthday. And I know you don't celebrate either of those things in COE, do you?"

Sophia shook her head. "No." She frowned. "I don't even know what they are, though I can guess about the second one. Celebrating one's birthday sounds like fun. But that first word…" Her frown deepened. "It's vaguely familiar to me. I don't know where, but I've heard it before." She shook her head, as if clearing her mind. "Christmas. It has a happy sound."

"Do you think you might possibly have memories, too?" He watched her closely. "Let me give you some more related words. Christmas tree, decorations, lights, tinsel, presents, caroling. Joseph, Mary and baby Jesus. The three wise men and the little shepherd boy. Snow and shopping and 'Joy to the World.'"

She listened to each word, clearly concentrating. Waiting, he made sure to contain his rising hopeful excitement. If someone like her, an adult, could recall a life before COE, then that could mean the cult had been abducting children for a very long time.

"I can't remember," she said. "They sound familiar, but I can't be sure if it's only because I want them to be."

Struggling to contain his disappointment, he took her in his arms. "Maybe it'll come to you," he told her. "Now tell me about your day."

Snuggling into his side, she sighed. "I'm not sure where to start. It began with me getting fired from my job at the clinic. Dr. Drew said Ezekiel doesn't let his wives work. Deirdre had told me that, as well, but I thought I could stay until after the wedding."

"I'm not surprised," he said. "You had to know it was coming, sooner or later."

"Maybe. I just wasn't prepared. And then shortly after I got home and Rachel left for work, Deirdre showed up. She—"

"Don't move," a stern, masculine voice ordered. Rustling came from the thick brushy undergrowth to the left of them and two men came into view, both holding rifles. They were the same two who had escorted Jack to see Ezekiel.

Jack froze, sending Sophia a quick look and hoping she understood she needed to do the same.

"What are you doing outside the perimeter?"

Maybe this wasn't as bad as it appeared.

"We like to walk," Jack said, his tone easy. "We're friends. And neither of us wanted anyone to think I was moving in on Ezekiel's woman, so we decided to meet here so no one would gossip."

Facing him, Sophia winced, which let him know that maybe that hadn't been the right thing to say.

Well, they were stuck with it for now.

The taller man slid his gaze dismissively over Sophia before turning his attention—and his rifle—to Jack. "You were warned and you chose to disregard the warning. Now you must pay the price."

Jack wondered if the other man realized he sounded like a bad actor in a B movie. But then, since no one in COE even owned a television, he doubted it.

"Wait." Sophia stepped forward, lifting her chin as she faced the large man. "We haven't done anything wrong. Jack and I are simply friends."

Her words didn't appear to even register. "Sir, you'll need to come with us. Ezekiel will want you to be punished."

Sophia gasped. "No. He's done nothing wrong, I swear to you."

The second man sighed. "Ezekiel has given orders as to what must be done. Your friend will not be killed."

"No," she shot back. "But from what I've heard, he'll wish he was dead."

"Torture?" Jack asked, keeping his tone even though

his mind raced. "I thought Children of Eternity is all good."

"Cut the crap," the first man snarled. "Now get moving." He gestured with the rifle as if to punctuate his order.

Just as Jack turned to do as he was told, Sophia jumped forward, slamming her slender body into the giant and grabbing for his gun. "Jack, run," she screamed.

As if he would turn away from her like a coward. Instead he leaped for the second man, using his head like a battering ram. Caught by surprise, the guy fell backward, gasping for air since Jack's hit had knocked the breath out of him.

Jack grabbed the rifle. Once he had it, he swung the butt like a club, knocking the assailant out. Then he turned to help Sophia.

To his surprise, while Sophia continued to struggle with man number one, she appeared to have the upper hand. Maybe because the guy had been given strict instructions not to harm her. Either way, Jack saw it to their advantage. He swung. The rifle butt connected and the man went down.

"Thanks," Sophia said, trying to catch her breath. "Now what?"

He didn't see where they had a choice. "Do you know how to use that thing?" he asked, gesturing at the other rifle.

"Well, no," she admitted. "But I'm a fast learner."

"I'll show you later. Grab it and let's go. We're going to have to make a run for it."

"Now?" Expression horrified, she stared. "But I'm not ready. I want to say goodbye to Rachel."

He checked his weapon and then grabbed some

ammo from the unconscious man. "We don't have a choice. We've got to go now. If Ezekiel was furious that you and I were together, imagine what he's going to do once he learns we took out two of his armed goons. I'm sure he has a special sort of punishment reserved for situations like this."

Slowly she nodded. "You're right."

As they turned to go, a shot rang out. He felt the bullet tear into his thigh with a sense of shock. A moment later, the searing pain had him doubling over.

"Run, Sophia." Choking out the words, he managed to lift his arm and point. "Run. Now."

Despite the urgency in his voice, still she hesitated. "But…you've been shot."

"Yes." Teeth clenched, he shoved her. "You've got to go. Now. Or they'll get you, too."

Finally, to his relief, she took off, disappearing into the forest before the first man reached him. He knew he'd need to do his best to distract them so they didn't go after her. Despite the awful burning in his leg, he launched himself up at his assailant, head-butting him in the stomach. The man went down, rolling to the side in what clearly was a practiced move, before jumping to his feet. Then he swung the butt of his rifle. Jack barely saw it coming before it hit him and then he saw nothing at all.

Sophia ran, trying to go as quietly and quickly as possible. She could hardly breathe. They'd shot Jack. Though her insides felt paralyzed with shock, somehow her legs kept moving. As each bare foot made contact with the earth, she swore every beat sounded out his name.

COE, the only place she could ever remember living, was no longer safe. If they'd been willing to shoot Jack, what exactly would they do to her? Horrifyingly, she thought she knew. Whatever it was, it wouldn't be pleasant. And Ezekiel was sure to be involved.

Now what? She couldn't go home. Even if she'd had a disguise, which she didn't, asking Rachel to hide her would involve her friend and potentially ruin Rachel's life.

But she couldn't leave Jack at the hands of someone who thought nothing of scarring and branding women. She could only imagine what Ezekiel would do to a man he believed had wronged him.

Sophia knew she'd die before she'd let that happen. Escaping, starting a new life in the outside world, none of that meant anything without Jack.

She loved him. More than life itself. She had to get to him, to figure out a way to free him. But how? Who could she trust beside Rachel?

And then, she thought of the oath she'd sworn with the other wives, who'd all sworn the same to her. Would that promise apply to something like this? Surely the answer had to be yes. It was a huge risk, but what did she have to lose? And who knew, maybe some of them would actually want to escape with her. They'd have to, if they helped her free Jack. Right now, she couldn't see that she had any other choice.

Decision made, she knew she'd have to be careful sneaking back in. Once she made it, she couldn't actually go ring the buzzer at Ezekiel's gate and ask to talk to Deirdre. Then how would she contact any of them? She'd never noticed any of the other wives out and about unless it was for a formal event like the cook-out. Of course, she didn't hang around that part of the compound, either. For all she knew, the women could be meeting at the park every day for lunch.

But now the sun had almost finished setting and it would soon be dark. Most of Ezekiel's women would likely be at home, doing whatever it is they did for the night. Her heart sank. She didn't know what condition Jack was in. She couldn't afford to wait until morning. If she could get to him, she knew where to find everything in the medical clinic to get him patched up. She could only pray his injury wasn't too bad.

Her stomach growled, reminding her she hadn't eaten. Deirdre! Of course! Deirdre had mentioned she planned to pick up food that evening. Maybe Sophia could still engineer a run into her there, if the timing was right. Yes, there were too many what-ifs, but she didn't have a choice. First, though, she needed to find Jack.

With every heartbeat, she could practically hear a clock ticking. How long before Ezekiel killed Jack? Since Jack had been shot, would Ezekiel's henchmen bother to take him to the medical clinic? If so, she still had her second key and could let herself in.

It was a start. For now, the only choice she had. If she didn't locate Jack there, she'd have to regroup.

The clinic then Deirdre. Decision made, she headed north in the woods, intending to make a circle around so she could reenter the compound near the medical clinic. If she could get inside there, sight unseen, she might have a prayer of pulling this off.

Chapter 15

When Jack opened his eyes, he realized he was in the exact same hospital bed where this all had begun. He tried to sit up, but the agonizing pain in his thigh had him falling back onto the bed, wincing. Real pain? Or imaginary? Then he remembered. He'd been shot.

"So you're awake." Ezekiel's voice, full of a strange sort of pleasure.

Jack turned his head, eyeing the older man. He didn't bother to speak since the answer was obvious.

"You really care about that stupid little twit, don't you?"

Was he talking about Sophia, his wife-to-be? Jack blinked. The disparaging words were confusing. So was Ezekiel's weird devilish delight.

"I'll take your silence for a yes." Now, Ezekiel's eyes glowed with a gleeful malice. He grinned, rubbing his hands together. "You have to be punished, you know."

"I figured." Struggling to move, Jack realized he'd been shackled to the bed. Of course. He eyed the bandage on his leg. Same damn one. "What I don't understand is why you bothered to fix me up."

"I had Dr. Drew take care of your wound. It's been cleaned and closed up." Leaning hard on his cane, the older man circled Jack slowly. "The bullet went through. He gave you a shot of antibiotics and says you're going to be just fine. Of course, you'll have one more scar. But I'm sure that won't matter to you."

The answer made absolutely no sense. But he figured Ezekiel would tell him. And he was right.

"I could have killed you. Or let you continue to suffer and slowly die as your leg got infected and rotted." Ezekiel's smile broadened. "Of course, Thomas tells me you were once addicted to painkillers. Would giving you just one bring that craving back in full force?"

Jack struggled not to show his horror. He'd been through hell and back kicking his addiction. He shuddered to think what could happen if Ezekiel forced a pill down his throat.

"And then, once I got you good and hooked, I could simply cut you off. I've heard it's a horrible, slow sort of death. Shakes and sweats and pain."

This time, Jack could not suppress his shudder. It had been all that and more. Much, much more. Ezekiel's smile widened when he saw Jack's reaction.

"Instead I have a better punishment," Ezekiel continued. "I'll find my little bride-to-be and marry her anyway. And then, I'll let you watch as we consummate the marriage. You might not know this about me—" he leaned in, lowering his voice "—but I enjoy pain. Agony excites me. I'm very fond of branding them. I'm thinking the letter *A* branded right onto her forehead might be especially appropriate to mark her shame. You know, like *The Scarlet Letter.*"

Stunned, Jack tried to fathom what Ezekiel had just said. "Branded?" He didn't bother to hide his horror and revulsion. "Surely you're not serious."

"Oh, but I am," Ezekiel said. "You should see some of my other wives. But this? I predict this will be the best wedding night yet."

Then, while Jack gaped at him in shock, Ezekiel turned away. For the first time Jack noticed one of the two men who'd brought him there. He stood next to the door, his pistol neatly holstered but easily accessible.

"Keep an eye on him," Ezekiel ordered. "I've sent six more men out to search for sweet little Sophia. Once she's found, I'll have us married in private first. We'll hold the public ceremony later." He chuckled. "I'll need to make sure she wears a veil for that. It wouldn't do for others to see what I plan to do to her face."

Sophia made it back into the compound without any trouble. She guessed that if Ezekiel had people looking for her, they'd be combing the woods outside the perimeter. Certainly no one would be expecting her to return.

Though she kept her head down, she walked with purpose, as if she had someplace to go, things to do.

"Sophia," someone called, the low-pitched voice barely catching her ear.

Cautious, she glanced in the direction of the voice, her heart stuttering in her chest when she realized who it was. Cassandra, one of Ezekiel's wives, the woman who'd been branded. With her was Enalia, the one whose face had been marked with a horrible web of crisscrossed scars.

Sophia allowed hope to flare inside her. They had,

after all, sworn loyalty to one another. "Please, come this way," she said, gesturing to an alley behind one of the buildings. Since full night had not yet fallen, the outdoor lights hadn't yet come on and the shadows would be better at keeping her from being seen by anyone else.

As she'd hoped they would, Cassandra and Enalia followed her without question. Quickly, Sophia explained what had happened. Enalia shook her head while Cassandra crossed her arms. "What are you going to do?" Cassandra asked.

"Escape," Sophia answered. "But first I've got to save Jack."

"Seriously?" Cassandra raised one arched brow.

"Yes, seriously."

"You've got courage, I'll give you that," Enalia interjected. "Remember, Ezekiel isn't kind even when you're obedient. I'd hate to see what he does when you're not. Your death will be slow and painful."

"Well, hopefully he won't catch me." Taking a deep breath, Sophia looked from one woman to the other. "Will you help me?"

Neither woman responded. Sophia's heart sank. "Okay. I understand, I guess." Steeling herself, she lifted her chin, meeting each of their gazes individually. "Even so, I have to ask. If Jack and I—*when* Jack and I—are successful, do you want to go with us? Strike out for freedom, too?"

Enalia gasped. Clearly the idea of running had never occurred to her.

"You know what?" Cassandra swung her long silver braid over her shoulder, almost angrily. "I'll help you. So will most everyone, once they think about it. We've all spoken our vows to each other. It's time to take them more seriously."

Enalia made a sound, as if she wanted to protest, but Cassandra silenced her with a hard look. "Don't tell me you didn't wish someone had stopped him before he did that to your face?"

Clearly stunned, Enalia took a step back. She stood silent, her hands clenched into fists while she considered. Finally she bowed her head. When she looked up again, tears streamed down her cheeks. "You're right," she managed to say. "It's time for this to stop. I'll help."

"What do you want us to do?" Cassandra asked.

"Right now, go home and talk to the others. Only those who you think might want in. We can't take a chance of one of them going to Ezekiel with this."

"No one would do that," Enalia said, bitterness coloring her voice. "We all hate him. Some of us more than others."

"You never know." Cassandra grimaced. "I'm pretty sure there are one or two of the newer ones who still have feelings for him."

Impatient to get moving, Sophia shifted her weight from one foot to the other. "I've got to try to locate Jack. Keep your eyes and ears open. I'll be in touch."

"Gotcha." Cassandra took Enalia's arm. "Come on, hon, let's go."

Sophia watched until she could no longer see them, then she stepped out from the alley and resumed her purposeful walk.

She made it to the medical clinic without being stopped. The clinic appeared shut down, the same as it always did when she walked by it after hours. She went around to the back, using her key to let herself in. Once inside, she locked the door behind her and stood still, giving herself a moment so her eyes could adjust to the darkness. Luckily, after all the years she'd worked there, she knew the place like the back of her hand.

She didn't want to turn on any lights in case someone noticed, so she made her way quietly down the hallway. As she turned the corner that would lead her to the examination rooms, she realized two things.

One, she could hear voices. More than one. And two, the lights were on in exam room number two.

Crud. She froze. Afraid to move, glad of the dim light, she listened. Her heart gave a skip as she realized one of the people speaking was Jack. He was alive!

Then another person spoke. Ezekiel. Her blood turned to ice as she heard him tell Jack exactly what he had planned for her. She shuddered, thinking of how narrowly she'd escaped a life worse than hell.

Of course, she hadn't escaped it yet. She had to save Jack and get out of the compound first.

Still, she listened as Ezekiel continued to gloat. When he finally wound down, she heard him bark orders to someone to keep an eye on Jack. Which meant, of course, that Jack was under armed guard.

Since she wasn't sure which exit Ezekiel would use, she slipped into a small storage closet to wait until he'd left. Good thing, too, because a few seconds later Ezekiel and one of his goons marched past her.

Heart hammering, she listened as he went outside and someone locked the door behind him. Another guard? Or the same one? Was Dr. Drew here, too? She hated that there were so many unknown factors.

Maybe she needed to rethink her plan. There was no way she alone could overpower an armed guard, and there might even be more than one.

But then again, she had the element of surprise on

her side. Maybe she could do this without having to attempt to seek out and involve Deirdre.

While she dithered, she heard footsteps walk down the hall. To her horror, they seemed to stop right outside the storage closet door. Had she been discovered? If so, how?

"I know you're in there." Dr. Drew's voice. "I was watching, and my cameras are everywhere in this clinic. Ezekiel's gone and I've injected his guard with something to knock him out for a few hours. If you want to help your Jack, don't waste any more time."

Your Jack. Swallowing hard, she stepped out of the closet and into the hall.

"You're quite resourceful," Dr. Drew commented with a faint smile. "Now, come on. Believe me, we don't have very long."

She followed him into the exam room. One of the men from the woods lay slumped over on the floor, his handgun kicked out of reach. And on the bed, Jack, shackled with some sort of metal handcuffs, his leg wrapped with a large, white bandage.

His eyes lit up when he saw her. "Sophia!" But then he frowned. "I told you to run. You should be far away by now."

"I couldn't leave you—" she began.

"Ezekiel has people searching," Dr. Drew interjected. "If she'd remained in the woods, she would have been caught by now."

Jack glanced sideways at the other man. "Whose side are you on? Ours or his?"

"Yours, of course." Dr. Drew smiled. "Otherwise I would have turned little Sophia over to Ezekiel when he was here. My security cameras caught her entering the building. Luckily, I'm the only one that saw."

"Why are you helping us?" Jack asked, clearly still suspicious.

"Because I've had enough. I've spent years patching up and trying my best to help the women he's hurt. His wives." The bitterness in his voice told her he meant it. "I can't let him do that to Sophia. I refuse to be a part of this any longer." He sighed. "Once, this group stood for good things. Ezekiel truly believed and he did his best to help others. After a while, I guess the power went to his head."

"From what I've seen," Sophia interjected, "he's been torturing his wives for years. How does such a thing go unnoticed? Though I confess—I've seen them at all kinds of public events and never had the slightest idea."

"Because Ezekiel has people like Thomas—and me—who make sure no one ever sees. But he doesn't have me any longer." Dr. Drew glanced at the door. "We've got to get moving. I don't want to take a chance that someone might come back. Plus, the drug I slipped this guard only lasts a few hours. Safer that way."

"What about these?" Jack rattled his wrists. "Do you happen to have the keys?"

"I do." Moving swiftly, Dr. Drew freed Jack. As soon as the last shackle fell with a clatter, Jack sat up, wincing slightly. "How bad is my leg?"

"Actually, not too bad. The bullet passed right through without hitting bone or any vital organs. This type of gunshot wound causes a lot less damage. You just need to continue to take the antibiotics and change the dressing every day and it should heal fine."

Jack nodded. "Thanks. Now, what's your plan for us to escape?"

"Here." Dr. Drew tossed him a pair of sweatpants. "Put those on. I'm thinking I can hide you in the back of my van. I'm supposed to go to town in the morning to pick up more medical supplies. No one would look for you there, because they don't suspect me."

Dismayed, Sophia shook her head. "I'm not sure it's such a good idea for us to spend the night locked in the back of your van. Is there any way you can leave now?"

Eyeing her, Dr. Drew considered. "I think they might find that a little suspicious," he said. "If you have a better plan, then tell me."

The idea that had been building in her all along had taken root. "I want to free them all," she said slowly. "All of his wives. At least those that want to go."

Before she'd even finished speaking, Dr. Drew started shaking his head. "That's crazy. There's no way you'd succeed."

Though she still wasn't 100 percent certain she trusted him, at this point she didn't see where she had a choice. Taking a deep breath, she told both Jack and Dr. Drew about her meeting with Ezekiel's previous wives. "I have to believe if they were given a choice, most of them would take freedom."

"Most of them?" Jack asked. "What about the others? Any chance they might see an opportunity to improve their standing with Ezekiel by revealing the plan?"

Considering the oath she'd taken with all the other women, she shook her head. "I vowed to try to help them. And they me. I gave my word, Jack. That's not something I take lightly." And then she told him about the woman who'd been branded and what Ezekiel had done to many of the others.

"I remember," Dr. Drew began. Before he could finish, they heard the sound of the front door opening. Dr. Drew swore under his breath. "Hide," he ordered, pointing to the tall lockers where patients' belongings were stored. "Now!"

Sophia yanked the door open and slid inside, closing it quietly behind her, though she left a tiny crack. She was afraid if it clicked shut, she wouldn't be able to open it from the inside, a thought that made her heart race. Though normally she wasn't claustrophobic, the tight space with only three tiny vent lines at the top made her want to hyperventilate.

"Dr. Drew?" Ana's voice, sounding surprised. "What are you doing here so late?"

"I might ask you the same question." Dr. Drew must have been standing to block entrance to the exam room.

"Who's in there?" Ana asked. "We didn't have any patients when I went home for the day."

"I have a special patient I'm looking after for Ezekiel." He'd put his customary arrogance back in his voice. "Who that patient might be is none of your concern. What do you need?"

Inside the closet, Sophia hoped Dr. Drew realized exactly how unusual it was that Ana had come back to the clinic. She had to be up to something.

Silence. Then Dr. Drew's surprised question. "What are you doing, Ana? Put that gun away."

Gun? Ana? Though she had to be careful not to be seen, Sophia widened the crack a tiny bit, hoping she could see what the heck was going on. But the only visible thing seemed to be Dr. Drew's back as he faced the hall, still using his body to block the door.

"Don't make me have to shoot you," Ana said. "Move into the examination room and stand against the wall."

Slowly, Dr. Drew complied. "I don't think you have it in you to shoot me," he said, using the calm tone he usually reserved for patients in pain.

"You'd be surprised at what I can do," Ana responded. Her voice was grim and determined.

"What is it you want?" This came from Jack, apparently still pretending to be shackled to the bed.

"You," Ana told him. "And Sophia, if we can find her."

"Why?" Jack again, his mild and disaffected tone completely at odds with what Sophia knew he must be feeling.

"Because I consider Sophia my friend," Ana said. "I want to help her."

Everything inside Sophia screamed at the men not to believe her. Whatever agenda Ana had, she wasn't telling them the truth.

"How do you even know she's missing?" Dr. Drew asked, cutting to the heart of the matter. "For that matter, how did you know Jack was here? Only Ezekiel and his close staff are privy to that information."

"None of your business," Ana snarled, but Sophia could tell that Ana knew she'd been found out. "What did you do to my Ivan?"

"Ivan?" Dr. Drew asked. "Oh, you mean him, Ezekiel's security guard. I injected him with a sedative. He'll sleep for a little while."

"You'd better not have hurt him," Ana declared.

"So that's how you knew," Jack said. "You and Ivan are...?"

"Lovers. And Ivan says Ezekiel will pay dearly for his missing fiancée. We're going to get that money and get out of here." Ana had moved around to stand right in front of the locker. From what little Sophia could see, Ana's gaze appeared to be fixed on her boyfriend, though she still held a pistol pointed at Dr. Drew. Clearly, she had no idea that Jack's hands were free.

Or that Sophia was right behind her.

Now or never. Not giving herself time to think, Sophia shoved open the locker door into Ana hard. As Ana staggered, Sophia jumped and tackled her, knocking the gun from her hand, praying it didn't go off. Luckily, Ana either still had the safety on or her finger wasn't on the trigger, because the pistol hit the floor without discharging. Dr. Drew snatched it up and helped Sophia subdue the woman.

"You're here?" Eyes wide, Ana stared. "Are you crazy?"

"Maybe," Sophia allowed. "But I couldn't let Ezekiel torture Jack. So I came back to get him."

"You'll never get out of here alive." Ana sounded certain. "Ezekiel and Thomas have mobilized all their men searching for you."

"Outside the compound." Sophia and Jack exchanged satisfied looks. "Like you, they'd never expect me to be inside."

Ana swallowed, her defeated expression making Sophia actually feel bad for her.

"One thing I don't understand," Sophia said. "You're married? What about your husband?"

"I don't love him. I love Ivan." Ana's mouth turned down at the corners.

"We've got to go," Jack interjected, his tone urgent. "What do you want to do with her?"

"Lock them here in the exam room," Sophia answered.

"But she knows." Dr. Drew stepped forward. "Ivan has no idea that I drugged him. But Ana here… She'll turn me in. I won't be able to continue to live and work here, helping others."

"Then you'll have to leave," Jack said. "You can come with us."

Still, Dr. Drew didn't move.

"You can't kill her, man." Jack sounded exasperated. "You're a doctor."

"Not only that." Sophia touched his arm. "But you're one of the good guys. With your medical education and training, you have an excellent chance of making a life in the outside world. Come on, let's go."

Seconds ticked by while Dr. Drew considered. Finally he nodded. "Fine."

The two men helped Ana climb up on the exam table. Then, using the same handcuffs that had restrained Jack earlier, they quickly secured her.

"You won't get away with this," she told them. "You know that, right?"

Sophia eyed her for a moment. "I hope you're wrong. But I've got to try. Even if I die trying, it's better than living the kind of life I would have had here."

And then she slipped out the door, using her key to lock it. "I never would have guessed. Who knew there were other unhappy people?" she mused.

Jack caressed the back of her neck. "Are you sure you want to do this?"

She glanced back at him, hoping her love for him showed in her eyes. "It's not a matter of me wanting to," she explained. "But this is something I feel I have to do."

"We don't have time to discuss anything," Dr. Drew said, his agitated body language matching the urgency in his voice. "We've got to go."

"I agree," she said, looking from one man to the other. "What's the immediate plan? Still the back of your truck?"

Dr. Drew winced. "Yes. If I pretend I need to make an emergency run for supplies, maybe with everything else that's going on, they won't notice."

And everyone knew without saying that it was entirely probable they would.

"And then what?" Sophia asked.

"We try to get you both away from the compound."

"No," she said. Now both men were staring at her as if they thought she'd lost her mind. "I told you, I want to free the other wives. We've got to make a stop at Ezekiel's house first."

From the sideways look Dr. Drew sent his way, Jack knew the other man thought they should simply pretend to humor Sophia and then do whatever they wanted. Because, quite frankly, her idea of going to Ezekiel's home with its locked gate and tight security, sounded crazy. He understood she wanted to free the other women, but she'd need a better plan and reinforcements.

Right now, they had to get somewhere where they stood a chance of being safe. Briefly he weighed his options. He didn't want to lie to her. But he also didn't want to fight. And, even worse, he needed to prevent her from doing something completely crazy.

They could talk about freeing the others once they were away from COE and safe. Then and only then, could they discuss rational options.

He took her arm. "Lead the way," he told the doctor. In all of this, the fact that Dr. Drew was helping them was what he found the most shocking. He would have bet the farm that the doctor was firmly in COE's camp of devout believers.

"This way." They headed for the back door.

"This is how I came in," Sophia said. "I didn't see a vehicle parked out here."

"It's around to the side," Dr. Drew responded. Just as he reached to unlock the door, they heard a commotion outside. "Damn it," he swore. "They're back. We'd better hope it isn't Ezekiel. You two—in the laundry room. Hide. I'll distract him. If worse comes to worst, run out the door and take my truck." He tossed Jack the keys.

Neatly catching them, Jack shook his head. "Stay safe," he said before grabbing Sophia's arm and pulling her into the laundry room.

Once inside the dark room, Jack pulled her up close, nestling her body against his. Unbelievably, even in these circumstances, his body reacted. He shifted slightly to keep her from noticing.

The back door opened and Ezekiel strode in. "We can't locate the bitch," he said. "I'm thinking maybe I should torture Jack Moreno and see if he knows more than he's letting on."

Not good. If Dr. Drew let Ezekiel get back to the exam room, he'd know everything. Jack hoped the doctor had a plan.

Ezekiel kept talking as they walked past the laundry room.

"He left the door partly open," Sophia whispered. "Do you think he wants us to…"

"Run. Yes. Come on." Without giving either of them time to think, Jack yanked on her arm. They tore out through the open doorway. Darkness had finally fallen, which meant any more searching would be called off until morning.

They made it through the open door, moving fast, but careful not to make a sound.

Outside, still holding on to her hand, he tugged her around the corner toward where Dr. Drew had said he'd left his vehicle. But there was nothing there.

Chapter 16

"What the hell?" With his heart thundering in his chest, Jack skidded to a stop. Next to him, Sophia did the same.

"It's got to be here somewhere," she said, her breath catching. "He must have forgotten where he parked it." But there weren't any other places, at least not nearby.

"Or someone else is using it." He cursed, pulling the key fob from his pocket. He hit the lock button twice, listening for the accompanying beep of the vehicle horn.

Nothing.

He swore again. "Come on. Looks like we're on foot. Let's go." Giving her hand another tug, they moved away from the clinic.

"Where are we going?" she asked.

He swallowed. He didn't want to tell her that he had no idea, but he kind of had to. "I don't know. The woods?"

"That won't work. That's where they're looking for me."

Damned if she wasn't right. Maybe they could steal a car. He figured if it wasn't a new one, he could hotwire it and they'd still have a prayer at making it out of there alive.

"Who else has a vehicle?" he asked her. "I'm thinking Ezekiel? Thomas? Anyone else?"

"I don't know," she answered. "I think most of those in the upper echelon have personal vehicles, but I have no idea where they're kept."

Despite the lack of destination, they kept going. His leg throbbed, making it more and more difficult to move without a limp. He didn't want to stop because that would be like admitting defeat. Which he sure as hell wasn't ready to do. Not yet. Not as long as they had a chance.

"Ezekiel is our best chance for a vehicle," she told him. "He has several. And, since I already told you I had to stop there, we'll have help. Come on. His house is the last place they'll look for us."

Though she might be right, he didn't like it, not one bit. "How are we going to get in?" he asked her. No longer holding hands, they both walked at a brisk pace, but kept their heads down to lessen the chance of anyone recognizing them. Though from what he'd seen of Ezekiel, the only ones who would have been told Sophia and Jack were wanted would be his own people. The Anointed One wouldn't want the general population knowing anything they didn't need to know.

"Have you forgotten the locked gate?" he asked. "How are we going to get in? We can't just buzz and expect them to admit us."

She flashed a mysterious smile. "I've got people on the inside."

Though he still hated the idea, he went along. For now.

When they reached the outside gate—closed and locked, of course—he squeezed her arm. "Promise me, if this goes bad, you'll run. Don't worry about what happens to me, or anyone else. Just go somewhere and hide. I'll do my best to find you and get us both out of here."

Slowly she nodded. "I might say the same thing to you."

He peered at her. She meant it. He had to give her points for that. After all, she'd made it back to the medical clinic for him. "Fine," he said, conceding.

"Thank you."

"What's your plan?" he asked, hoping to hell she had one.

"I'm going to ring the buzzer and ask for Cassandra. She's one of his wives and has promised to help me."

"But what about the guards?"

She shook her head. "Ezekiel won't have told anyone in the household what's going on. It would make him look too bad. It'll be fine."

"I hope you're right," he responded.

"I guess you'll have to wait and see." Chin up, she strode over to the gate. He braced himself, wondering what would happen once she'd pressed the buzzer.

Hoping she appeared to have a lot more bravado than she actually did, Sophia hesitated before pressing the buzzer. Though her heart hammered so hard it made her feel dizzy, she knew she needed to sound carefree and confident. Or at least moderately unaffected.

An instant after she pushed the buzzer, the guard, sounding bored, answered. When she identified herself and told him she had something for Cassandra, he pushed the unlock button and the gate swung open.

So far so good. Turning around, she motioned for Jack to follow her. From the expression on his handsome face, she knew he thought they were going straight into the lion's den. In a way, he was right. But he didn't know there were a lot of lionesses willing to fight with her.

Or at least two, she amended silently. Cassandra and Enalia. Hopefully they'd had time to speak to some of the others.

Cassandra appeared, moving like a graceful wraith out of the shadows. Silently she gestured that they were to follow her. She took off toward the garden, striding down the winding path as Sophia hurried along after her.

Jack caught up, limping slightly. "Damn leg hurts," he muttered. "Sorry. I can't move as fast as I'd like."

Immediately she felt terrible. But they'd reached Deirdre's little private house, so she gave his arm a quick squeeze instead.

At the door, Cassandra turned to face them. Her gaze slid over Jack dismissively before settling on Sophia. "Are you sure you want to do this?" she asked quietly. "Because a lot of people's lives are going to be irrevocably changed. I need you to be certain."

"Are you?" Sophia asked back. "Because I am. There's no way I want to live my life the way—" She stopped, horrified at what she'd almost said.

But Cassandra got it anyway. "You're right," she said. "We should have put an end to this a long time ago. This is no way to live."

And she turned the knob and opened the door and stepped inside. Swallowing hard, Sophia squared her shoulders and followed.

Inside she saw more than half of the women who'd been there before. Cassandra, of course. And Enalia.

Hallie, her red hair flowing down past her shoulders. And seven others, most of whose names Sophia didn't know.

She didn't see Deirdre, which shouldn't have surprised her, though she felt disappointment rise up in her like a lump in her throat. In fact, all of the women in attendance were among the younger wives. Other than Cassandra, none of the older ones had come.

Had Cassandra invited them? Or decided not to, out of an abundance of precaution. She turned to Cassandra to ask, but before she could, more women came through the door. Deirdre led them in.

Despite everything, Sophia's eyes filled with tears. "You came," she said. And then she saw how all the others stared at the first wife with shock and horror.

"I came," Deirdre answered. "Not to turn you in, like some of you seem to think." She let her gaze drift around the room. "But because I, too, have had enough. None of us, myself included, deserves to be treated this way."

Murmuring came from the assembled women. Some of the voices sounded welcoming. Others, not so much.

Cassandra moved toward her. "You're the first. And you gave him a son. Because of that, you've been treated differently than those of us who came after."

"Have I?" Deirdre shook her head. Giving them her back, she asked Cassandra to help with the buttons. Then, she parted the dress, revealing her back. Welts, some old, some newer, crisscrossed her skin. "He was just learning when I married him. He used whips then, instead of brands. Yes, he hasn't touched me in years, but I've never forgotten. I want out."

At that, Cassandra moved forward, holding out her

arms. As she enveloped the older woman in a hug, she recited the words Sophia remembered from earlier.

"Sisters we are, united in hope. True to each other, until our last breath. Vowing to fight, stay strong and stay true. Keeping hold of our hearts, united together until our death."

"Which is what this might come to," another woman put in, "if we don't get a move on. The longer we're here, the greater the likelihood of being discovered."

"She's right," Jack said. Every single woman eyed him with varying degrees of suspicion. "Sophia mentioned one of you might have access to a vehicle."

"I do," Deirdre said. "I'm one of the few he trusts enough to let go into town." She looked around, counting heads. "But nothing big enough to fit all of us at once."

"If you have access to more than one, I can drive," Jack said. "But we need to go. Now. Last time I saw him, Ezekiel was at the medical clinic intending to torture me. Once he finds out I've escaped, he's going to up the intensity of his search."

"Let me see what I can do." Deirdre headed toward the door. "Wait here. I'll be back in a minute."

The instant the door closed behind her, women started talking. Several of them were worried Deirdre had left to turn them all in.

Meanwhile, Sophia moved closer to Jack. "What about Dr. Drew?" she asked. "We can't just leave him there at Ezekiel's mercy."

He groaned. "You're right. But I think we need to get these women to freedom first. Then we can come back for him."

"No. He could be dead by then. We'll just swing by the clinic and pick him up."

"Sophia." He pulled her close and wrapped her in his arms. "We can't save everyone, at least not this instant. We've got to get outside and notify the authorities. When we come back, it'll be with reinforcements."

"But…" She started to protest and fell silent, breathing in the beloved scent of him. "You're right," she said. "Except Dr. Drew put himself at risk for us. Ezekiel could kill him before we get back."

Jack's silence was in its own way an acknowledgment.

"I don't want him to die for us," she protested, her face pressed against his chest.

"I don't, either. But we have all these people to think about now," Jack told her, the deep rumble of his voice against her ear making her shiver. "Every single one of these women is risking her life to help us. We have to get them out. You know this. Plus, I have a feeling that Dr. Drew can take care of himself."

He had a point. The doctor appeared resourceful. When she and Jack had run, Dr. Drew had known he'd have to do something with Ezekiel or risk being found out.

"You're right," she said, reluctantly pulling out of his arms.

The door opened and Deirdre came back inside. She hurried over to Sophia and Jack. "We're all set. I've snagged the keys to two of the transport vans. I don't usually drive them, so there might be a few questions, but I don't anticipate any problems. Here." She handed Jack a set of keys and a rectangular plastic card. "Just stay right behind me and if we're stopped, let me do the talking. Use that card to get through the outside gate."

Jack nodded.

Clearly used to taking charge, Deirdre then turned

to face the others. "Everyone listen up. I need you to split into two groups. Half of you will go with me and the other half with Jack. We've got to get moving, right now."

While Sophia watched, amazingly the women quickly divided. All without arguing or debate. Once that was done, they all headed outside.

Even once they were safely inside the large white vans, her nerves made Sophia jumpy. Despite the darkness beyond the outdoor lighting, she kept expecting armed guards to show up at any moment and demand they exit the vehicles.

But nothing happened.

When they reached the iron gates, which were always kept locked, Deirdre inserted her card into the box and the gates swung open. She smiled and gave a nonchalant wave toward the manned guardhouse, put the van in Drive and pulled through. Right behind her, Jack did the same, without incident or question.

"Apparently the guards only come out if there's some sort of problem," he mused. "I admit, I kind of thought they might confront us, but apparently as long as we have a pass card, we're good to go."

Sophia turned around in her seat to watch the gate—and the compound—fade into the distance. Her nerves made her so jumpy, she could hardly sit still.

All of the women in the two rows of seats behind her apparently felt the same. Until now, they'd been absolutely silent. But once the gate could no longer be seen, they began to talk.

Deirdre pulled over to the shoulder, sticking her arm out her window and motioning that Jack should pass her. From this point on, she would be following him.

"Do you think they want to press charges?" Jack

asked her quietly. "Because they can. No one has the right to treat another human being that way. No one."

Cassandra, who'd chosen to ride with them, overheard. "I think we should," she said. "Quite honestly, that man needs to be punished for what he's done to us."

"And what he's done to others, as well," another woman, whom Sophia didn't know, chimed in. "One or two wives attempted to defy him. They disappeared and were never seen again. We all know he killed them and buried their bodies in the forest where they'll never be found."

"Do you have proof?" Jack asked. He frowned when they all began to laugh nervously.

"You don't understand," Cassandra told him. "There is no proof. Ezekiel makes sure of that. Sometimes knowing is enough."

When they reached the outskirts of Landon, Jack drove straight to the Fremont County sheriff's office on Railroad Street.

The brick building had few windows and looked an awful lot like a prison. Or, Sophia thought grimly, like one of the structures inside the compound. As they pulled up and parked, everyone fell silent.

"What is this place?" Cassandra asked.

"This is where we can find local law enforcement," Jack said. "They're the ones who can help you press charges against Ezekiel and his crew."

Cassandra nodded. "And then what?" Her steady gaze and quiet voice told Sophia how Jack answered this next question was important. "What will happen to us after that? What will we do? Where will we go?"

Jack shot Sophia a quick, panicked glance and she

realized he hadn't thought that far ahead. "Jack will help us figure out something," she said. "Won't you?"

He nodded, rapidly regaining his composure. "Yes. We'll figure something out. I live in Texas, so maybe you all can come there with me."

No one reacted. Again, Jack turned to Sophia, his brows raised in obvious question. She sighed. "None of us has any idea what you mean by Texas, but I'm sure that will be fine. We'll do whatever we have to in order to start our new lives."

"You don't learn geography in school?" he asked.

She shook her head. "All of our teachings are centered around the teachings of the *Volumes of Choice* and what it means to be Chosen. The children are also taught math skills and some science, and reading, of course. If Rachel were here, she could give you a lot more details, but…"

Deirdre tapped on the driver's-side window. Jack rolled it down.

"The sheriff's office?" she asked impatiently, rolling her eyes. "Why'd you chose them over the Landon police department?"

"This was the first one we came across. If you'd feel better with the police, then by all means lead the way there."

Eyeing him, she considered. "We'll start with them. Since the compound is in Fremont County, it's probably their jurisdiction anyway." She peered around him, checking on the other wives in the van behind him. "Is everyone all right?"

The choruses of yeses made Deirdre smile. "Okay, let's do this. Everyone out. We're going in."

The receptionist stared as Jack, Sophia and Deidre

entered, followed by all the women in their long dresses. Sophia noticed the receptionist, though she was female, wore men's trousers. She tried not to look at her too long, afraid she might offend her.

Jack introduced himself and asked to speak to the sheriff. Wide-eyed, the woman nodded before she rushed off to the back. She returned a second later with a wiry, older man wearing a uniform. He quickly took in the scene, his eyes narrowing. "Are you people from the cult?" he asked.

"COE is *not* a cult," Deirdre proclaimed, then grimaced sheepishly. "Sorry. I'm guessing to outsiders it must seem that way."

"Yes, ma'am."

"I have a question." Now Sophia found her voice. "What about us looks so different that you could immediately identify us?"

The sheriff—Sheriff Jones, his name tag said—exchanged a quick glance with Jack before facing Sophia. "You're kidding, right?"

"I can assure you, she's not." Jack intervened. "Sophia, it's because of your long dresses. Women outside of your compound don't dress that way."

This was news to Sophia—and all the other women, as well. Deirdre alone nodded agreement, but then Sophia guessed the first wife was the only one who'd ever really been outside the compound.

"What can I help you folks with?" the sheriff asked. He perked up a bit when Deirdre told him they wanted to press charges. His interest quickly changed to righteous outrage when he saw Cassandra's and Enalia's scars and Hallie's missing tongue. "Someone *did* this to you?"

As soon as they answered in the affirmative, he asked them to follow him into the back. Uncertain now, most of the women huddled together like frightened schoolchildren. Sophia gripped Jack's hand hard. Only Deirdre and Cassandra walked with a kind of quiet confidence.

He took them into a room with a long, rectangular table and numerous chairs. "Have a seat, ladies," he said. Then, while they all found chairs, he turned to Jack. "What's your part in all this?"

When Jack explained he was a PI, the sheriff interrupted and asked to see his license. To Sophia's surprise, Jack informed him he'd left it in his hotel room when he'd attended a Narcotics Anonymous meeting. He went on to talk about Thomas abducting him. Sophia was glad to confirm that part of the story.

The sheriff left for a minute and returned with several others who wore uniforms. "My staff," he explained. "They need to hear this, too."

As Jack explained how he'd come to be at COE's compound, the sheriff's staff streamed in. A recording device was set up and Sheriff Jones went from person to person getting their permission to record what they said. Everyone nervously agreed.

"We've got to hurry," Sophia put in, unable to contain her impatience. "I want to go back for Dr. Drew. I truly believe his life may be in danger."

This statement stopped the sheriff dead in his tracks. "Do you mind explaining exactly what you mean?"

"Dr. Drew helped us escape. Jack was shot and the doctor patched up his leg. When Ezekiel came back to check on us, we ran. I know Ezekiel will punish Dr. Drew for helping us."

Jack stepped forward. "Can you just send a deputy out there to do a welfare check?"

"We could," Sheriff Jones drawled. "But the cult won't let us on their land. Since—at least until now—they weren't breaking any laws, we've had no choice but to leave them alone."

"What about now?" Sophia asked. "Surely now you have enough reason to force them to let you in."

The sheriff considered her. "Maybe. But, quite honestly, I'm afraid we'd need more proof. That cult takes a hard line and it could get ugly."

"Why does he keep calling us a cult?" Deirdre muttered. "I don't like it. That word has extremely unpleasant connotations. I know, because I'm one of the few who joined COE willingly, right when it first began. I used to live outside, just like the rest of you people."

More shocking news, at least to the other women. Then, while everyone gaped, Deirdre rolled back her shoulders and lifted her head. "My name from before is Deirdre Sanders. I helped Ezekiel establish COE fifty-five years ago. We both believed in it then. I had no idea he would become the monster that he is now, or that he'd turn something beautiful into a dark and repressive organization."

Sheriff Jones glanced from her to Jack in some sort of wordless communication. It was Jack who spoke what must have been their thoughts out loud. "Deirdre, I believe you're saying you know a lot more than you're letting on, aren't you?"

The older woman sighed. "Unfortunately, yes. But before I divulge anything, you must know that I had no control over what that man and his henchmen chose to do. So I cannot be charged or implicated in any way, correct? Because I was as much a prisoner as these other women."

The sheriff sighed. "I imagine that will be the case."

"Not good enough," Deirdre snapped. "I'll need some sort of guarantee—in writing—before I say another word."

"You really did live outside," Jack commented.

Sophia wondered if that was approval she heard in his voice.

Deirdre nodded. "I know how these things work. Get me an agreement and I'll tell you everything."

Sheriff Jones grimaced and gestured to Jack to follow him. The two men went into an office and shut the door. Watching them go, Sophia thought she had never felt so alone.

All the women huddled together, wearing various expressions of exhaustion, fear or, in a few cases, determination on their faces. Sophia stood apart from them, wishing she could have gone with Jack but understanding why she couldn't.

She bowed her head and clasped her hands together. Events were being set in motion from which there would be no return. Everything about this terrified her. She wanted justice, true. But then what? What would happen to all of them after all this was over? She knew Jack had promised to help her, to be with her, and she couldn't help but hope for a future with him. She loved him, and while she wasn't sure he felt the same way toward her, she knew how easily such a spark could blossom into something more.

But she couldn't just think of herself any longer. In addition to all these women, the wives, there were so many others back home in the compound. If Ezekiel and Thomas were arrested, what would happen to all the other Chosen? Where would they go? What would they do? Would COE even survive?

Chapter 17

As Jack had expected, the sheriff was skeptical. He rounded on Jack the second his office door clicked closed. "You may or may not be aware of this, but here in town that entire group of people is generally regarded as being crazy."

"I understand," Jack replied. "But the branding and torturing women is real. Hell, Ezekiel has like twenty or so wives and apparently mistreats all of them. But there's more."

He went on to tell the other man about the potential child abductions.

The sheriff's eyes widened. "Abductions? As in plural?"

"Yes." Jack scratched the back of his head, wishing he had more than his word. "I don't have proof, not yet. I was working on that when all hell broke loose and I had to get Sophia out."

"And all the other women."

"Right. Except that's not all. There are more of Eze-kiel's wives still inside the compound."

The sheriff eyed him curiously. "So what's your plan after? I mean, assuming we get a warrant and are able to go in and free anyone else who might be in danger. What are you going to do with all those women?"

"Wouldn't social services need to get involved? They could possibly stay at a women's shelter and learn some new skills, things that would prepare them for life out-side the cult."

"Yeah, that would probably work. They'll have to tes-tify, if they decide to press charges against this Ezekiel guy. Once he's locked up, you never know. They might want to go back to the cult."

Surprised, Jack realized he hadn't even considered this. He thought of Sophia. Once she was free from her engagement to Ezekiel, what would she want? Would she choose to return to the only life she knew?

Even thinking about that possibility felt like someone had punched him hard in the chest. He loved her. With all his heart. But he loved her enough that he wouldn't stand in the way of whatever would bring her happiness.

"For right now, we need to see about finding a place for everyone to spend the night. Most likely even the next few days," Sheriff Jones continued. "What about you? Do you have somewhere to go?"

Jack considered. "I left my wallet with my ID, credit cards and cash in the safe of my motel room. I'm sure by now the motel manager has confiscated it. If he didn't steal my identity or go on a shopping spree with those credit cards, there's a chance I might be able to get them back."

"What motel? We have three in town."

Jack named the one he'd used, an inexpensive chain known for clean rooms and no frills.

The sheriff nodded. "I know the manager there. Janis is a good woman. I'll bet when you get your wallet back, the cash is still in it."

Over the course of the next several hours, numerous arrangements were made. The wives—including Sophia—would all be housed in one of the motels, two to a room, for free. It turned out Janis actually was a really good woman, because not only did she agree to put everyone up, but Jack's wallet was, as Sheriff Jones had said, exactly the way he'd left it, cash and all.

Jack hadn't had a chance to talk alone with Sophia. When they finally made it to the motel, he helped everyone get settled. Sophia hung back, apart from all the others. She wouldn't even look at him. His heart ached at how lost she looked, and he wanted to pull her close and comfort her. But every time he tried to get close to her, she moved away.

He figured she was trying to come to grips with the enormity of the change she'd made. He knew if the situation were reversed, he'd need some alone time to think. He couldn't begrudge her that. After all, they had plenty of time to sort out their new relationship. While he knew with rock-bottom certainty how much he loved her, he wouldn't ask her to hitch her star to a failure. And if he couldn't solve the Bartlett family's case, that's exactly what he'd be. A failure. He could barely support himself, never mind a wife.

If only he'd been able to get more information before all hell had broken loose. Still, he had to remain hopeful. Now that the authorities were aware of some of the crimes being committed under Ezekiel's name, perhaps the abduction of children would soon come to light. If he were allowed to review the records on behalf of the Bartlett family, he could discover whether one of these children was theirs.

Once everyone had been settled in their rooms, Janis showed him where he'd be sleeping, a couple doors down the hall from the women's rooms. Though his body felt exhausted, he couldn't sleep. After a few moments of pacing the confines of the ten by twelve space, he gave up. While the motel didn't have a restaurant or a bar, he'd noticed a pub a few doors down. Maybe if he had a drink or two, he'd actually be able to drift off to sleep. Though he'd been addicted once to narcotics, he didn't have a problem with a beer or two. Alcohol had never been his poison.

After checking to make sure he had his room key, he slipped out, moving down the corridor quietly. Just as he reached the glass door that would take him outside, a door opened and closed behind him.

"Jack. Wait," Sophia said.

Heart pounding, Jack took a second to get himself under control before turning. Walking fast, she hurried toward him. Her walk became a jog as she closed the distance. When she reached him, she threw herself into his arms.

Despite his injured leg, he caught her and held on tight. The feel of her, her scent, which even now seemed exotic and floral, made him never want to let her go.

And then she started to cry. Not a noisy, loud weeping, but quietly, though her shoulders shook with her effort to hold it all in.

"It's going to be okay," he said, smoothing her hair and holding on to her with a fierceness that made him feel as if he was the one in need of reassurance. In a way, maybe he was.

"I can't," she murmured, gasping like she couldn't breathe. "I just can't…"

Gently, he steered her back down the hall to his room. Still holding her close with one arm, he fumbled with the key card and managed to unlock his door.

Once inside, he led her over to the edge of the bed and helped her take a seat. As soon as he let go of her, she began furiously wiping at her cheeks with her fingers.

"I'm sorry—" she began.

"Don't apologize," he interrupted, his tone as fierce as the love inside him. "You've been through a lot."

"So have you," she shot back.

Carefully he lowered himself next to her on the bed. The movement earlier had started his leg throbbing again. "It's not the same and you know it. Your entire way of life is about to change. It's completely natural to feel upset."

She sighed. then gave a slow nod. "I'm frightened and worried. Not just for me, but for all the other women. We swore an oath to watch out for each other. I've got to make sure they're going to be all right."

"We'll figure out something," he assured her, even though he had no idea what. When she leaned into him, he put his arm around her slender shoulders. Even though he wanted nothing more than to lower her back onto the bed and make love to her, he wasn't about to take advantage of her when she was at her lowest point.

As she sagged against him, he realized she'd fallen asleep with her head on his shoulder. Carefully he eased himself out from under her, making sure to move her all the way up on the bed.

Snagging an extra blanket from the closet, he carefully covered her. Desire stabbed him again, ever present as always when he was with her. He pushed it away and stood looking down at her for the space of a few heartbeats.

Then he let himself out of the room. Instead of heading to the pub, he turned in the direction of the sheriff's office.

When he arrived, he wasn't surprised to find Sheriff Jones still at work despite the late hour.

After greeting him, the sheriff took him to his office and closed the door. He walked around to the back of his desk and sat. "The FBI is going in to arrest Ezekiel and Thomas," Sheriff Jones said, his gritty tone matching the grim solemnity in his face.

Surprised, Jack dropped into a chair across from the desk. "Now? This late in the day?"

"Yep. I think they should have waited until morning, but they felt like the cult might get tipped off so they rushed through the warrant."

"Why aren't you out there with them?" This made no sense. In Jack's experience with law enforcement, the feds liked to work side by side with the local authorities. Unless… Maybe this was too big of a bust, with too much potential for something going wrong, like what had happened in Waco, when the ATF went to raid the compound and it caught fire. A lot of people died.

A second later the sheriff's answer seemed to confirm that thought. "In this instance, the FBI has asked us to take a back seat. They have to make sure everything goes as planned. We're to sit back and watch, basically. And assist if needed."

"I'm sorry. I can tell you want to be there."

"I do. This is the biggest thing to happen around here in years."

Jack nodded. "I have a personal stake in this. I'd really like to be there myself."

The sheriff reached into his lower desk drawer and pulled out a half-finished bottle of Scotch. "Join me in a drink?"

After considering, Jack declined. "No thanks. I've never been much for the strong stuff. I have an occasional beer now and then, but with my past history as a recovering narcotic addict, I prefer to play it safe."

"Understood." Sheriff Jones poured himself a couple of fingers' worth and took a swig, making a face. "Wish I had ice. Ah, well, some things can't be helped."

The phone lines lit up, ringing all at once. The night-duty operator could be heard struggling to answer them. Eventually she must have placed them all on hold because she appeared in the sheriff's doorway. "It's news media, from all over the state and the country." Her tone contained a hint of panic. "They're wanting comments on the raid at the Children of Eternity compound."

"What?" Sheriff Jones sat straighter. "How do they know about that?" He glared at Jack. "Did you leak something to the press?"

"No," Jack answered. "Not me. And I'm positive none of the women did, either."

"The FBI must have a leak," the sheriff grumbled.

"Sir?" The receptionist again. "Do you want to take any of the calls?"

He swore. "I can't. This is not my investigation. Refer them to the FBI office please."

Turning on her heel, she hurried back to her desk.

"I'll be darned." Sheriff Jones took another deep drink of his Scotch. "Looks like our little town might actually make the national news." He grimaced. "Let's just hope nothing happens out there."

Though Jack somehow doubted Ezekiel would go peacefully, he, too, hoped the FBI team was able to apprehend the COE leader, as well as Thomas, without incident. Thinking of all the people inside the compound he'd come to know and love, Jack didn't want any of them to get hurt.

"Are they going to keep you posted?" Jack asked the sheriff, who by now had finished his drink and had started eyeing the bottle as if contemplating having another.

"I imagine so." As if on cue, the sheriff's cell phone rang. Answering, the older man listened, grunted a few times and thanked the caller before hanging up. "They're in. Looks like they rounded up most of the cultists and are talking to them one-on-one. Also, they're holding and questioning some guy named Thomas who's apparently second in command."

Jack nodded. "That's right. He's the one who knocked me out and brought me there. And from some of the records I saw, he's also the one who grabs the children. Thomas does a lot of Ezekiel's dirty work."

"If only you could prove that."

"I saw the records they have in the database," Jack replied. "If the FBI can seize those, they should be able to get all the proof they need."

"As long as the cult doesn't wipe them clean first."

Jack nodded. "True."

"They can't locate Ezekiel," Sheriff Jones continued. "Right now they're conducting a full-scale search of the compound. If he's in there, he couldn't have gone far, right?"

"It's not totally enclosed. There's not a wall on all sides, just the front and about halfway down on both sides. Beyond that, some fencing. There's a wilderness area on the other side of the fence. He could have run there."

"Are you sure?"

"Definitely. I myself disappeared into the woods quite often. I'm certain they have cameras somewhere nearby, but no one ever stopped me from leaving or coming back."

The sheriff swore softly under his breath. He poured himself a second drink, his movements jerky, as if with anger.

Jack could no longer contain himself. He began to pace, wishing he had a better outlet for his agitation. "I really wish they'd let me go up there. I lived there for a couple weeks. I could help."

"Yeah." Sheriff Jones appeared unmoved. "I could help, too. But as long as the feds are in charge, there's nothing we can do."

"Would you mind calling them back?" Jack asked. "Let me talk to them. I promise I'll keep it short and to the point."

"Why?"

"Because I'm pretty sure with all I know about the compound, I could be of assistance. I just need to point that out to them."

Though the sheriff didn't exactly roll his eyes, his dour expression let Jack know how much he wanted to. Finally he sighed. "What the hell? Okay, I'll give it a shot."

Grumbling under his breath, he dug out his cell phone again and hit redial. Once someone had answered on the other end, he handed the phone to Jack. "Here you go. This is Special Agent Bentrick. Say your piece."

Accepting the phone, Jack began to talk fast, aware he might only have a few seconds to capture the FBI agent's attention. As succinctly as possible, he outlined what his investigation had focused on and what he'd learned.

Bentrick listened silently until Jack wound down. "We'll look into it," the agent said. "Though I tell you what, it would sure save time if we could come and pick you up. We can be there in thirty minutes. Will you be ready?"

After answering in the affirmative, Jack ended the call. When he told Sheriff Jones what had transpired, the older man pushed to his feet. "I'm going with you," the sheriff said. "No ifs, ands or buts about it. Let me go get cleaned up and we'll wait for them outside."

A knock on the door woke Sophia from a delicious dream of sleeping wrapped in Jack's strong arms. She stretched, feeling a bit disoriented since the last thing she remembered she had been doing exactly that.

"Who is it?" Sophia asked, standing on tiptoe to look out the peephole. With all the craziness she'd just been through, she wasn't taking any chances.

The hotel manager stood outside. She appeared to be alone.

"Hi, there," Sophia said, opening the door a crack. "What can I do for you?"

"A woman from the compound is in the motel office. She's asking to see you." Janis appeared bored. "I don't think she's one of the ones you brought here earlier. Says her name is Rachel. That's it. Just Rachel. Do you know her?"

Sophia's breath caught. "Yes," she said. "I do. Is she all right?"

"I think so. I mean, she looks about the same as all the others." Janis shifted her weight from one foot to the other. "I can either send her up or you can come with me to get her."

"I'll go with you and bring her back myself. I don't want to make her wait."

As they walked down the long corridor, Sophia mused out loud. "I can't believe she's here, outside the compound. That's amazing." She struggled to contain her excitement, aware she was failing pretty spectacularly.

Janis glanced sideways at her. "Here we are." She opened a door marked Office and stepped aside to let Sophia precede her. "I put her in the back, where she couldn't be seen by the general public, if you know what I mean."

"Thank you." Sophia swept past the other woman, heading in the direction she pointed. She entered a small office. Rachel sat in one of the faded floral guest chairs. She looked up when Sophia entered.

"Rachel!" Sophia squealed, enveloping her friend in a huge hug. "I'm so happy to see you. How did you find me?"

"Me, too!" Rachel hugged her back. "I'm so glad you're safe. When I escaped on foot, a woman was kind enough to stop and offer me a ride. She brought me here. We didn't know what happened, but you know how gossip flies around the compound. Once we knew that half of Ezekiel's wives had fled, I guessed you'd gone with them."

"I did." Sophia smiled. "I have so much to tell you." She took a deep breath, aware how bizarre her story would sound. "But first, how'd you escape? It's hasn't been that long since we left. I would have thought the compound was on lockdown."

Rachel shook her head. "Actually it was pretty easy

to get out. It's chaos there since you and Jack liberated the wives. Ezekiel and Thomas and their men are saying you and Jack abducted them. The wives who chose to stay are apparently going along with that story, but they've talked to their friends who told other people. Rumors are already swirling. A lot of people know the truth. I knew you'd need somewhere to sleep, and this was the first place I stopped at."

"What about Dr. Drew?" Sophia asked. "Do you have any word on what happened to him?"

"No. He disappeared."

At least he wasn't dead. Taking a seat next to her friend, Sophia filled her in on what had happened, sparing nothing.

By the time she finished, Rachel stared at her, wide-eyed. "You're serious."

Sophia slowly nodded.

"I can't believe such evil has been going on all this time, right in front of everyone, and no one outside of Ezekiel's household knew."

"Oh, some were well aware," Sophia replied. "Thomas, for one. And Dr. Drew. He had to patch up the unfortunate women whom Ezekiel tortured."

"That's terrible." Rachel shook her head. "I'm glad I left."

"What about Phillip?" Sophia had to ask. "Are you still planning to marry him?"

"I don't think so." Eyes shiny with unshed tears, Rachel met her gaze. "When I tried to tell him what I wanted to do, he threatened to turn me in. Because of him, I had to go into hiding like a criminal." She sighed deeply. "That hurts, but learning the truth about COE hurts even more. It's weird how you can believe so strongly in something and then find out it's rotten to the core."

"I know. I'm hoping at least with the wives willing to testify against Ezekiel's torture, law enforcement has enough to arrest him. He needs to pay for what he did."

"Yes, he does. And you know what, I might be able to help with that." A slow smile bloomed across Rachel's face as she reached into her pocket and pulled something out. "A memory stick. We used them in the school to keep a list of all the grades. With all the craziness going on at the compound, I was able to do a little deeper poking around into the children's records. Jack got me started and the little we found made me want to investigate further."

She took a deep breath before continuing. "I found some hidden files. And I think it's proof that several of the kids were abducted as infants—many more when they were small children—and brought into COE. It looks they've been doing that for over twenty years."

Even though she didn't understand a lot of what Rachel meant, still... Sophia inhaled sharply, unwilling to let herself hope. "Is there a list of names?" she asked quietly. "Not just of the newest batch of children, but the ones from a long time ago?"

Rachel nodded. "Yes. And I might as well tell you now, Sophia. You're on it."

Stunned, Sophia didn't know what to say, how to think, what to feel. She'd suspected and even dreamed of such a thing, but not once had she ever truly believed her hope would turn out to be real.

"Come on," Sophia finally said. "Let's go find Jack and get this information to the sheriff."

Hand in hand, they rushed outside from the motel and down the street. When they got to the sheriff's office, Jack and Sheriff Jones were standing outside, waiting, they said, for the FBI to pick them up. Jack appeared thrilled to see Rachel and even more excited when she told him what she'd taken from the compound.

Sophia agreed to wait outside for the FBI while the others went inside to download the information from the memory stick onto the sheriff's computer. "Best to have a backup copy," Sheriff Jones said.

Sophia promised to bring the FBI agents to the sheriff's office as soon as they arrived.

She felt silly standing by herself outside the building, glad no one else seemed to be in town. She liked the quiet.

"There you are," a low voice growled from right behind her.

She froze. Ezekiel. Close. Too close. Instead of turning to face him, she leaped for the sheriff's office door. She might have made it, too, had Ezekiel not swung his cane at her legs, sending her sprawling.

Chapter 18

As Ezekiel lifted the cane to hit her again, Sophia screamed, praying that someone inside would hear her.

"You belong to me." Swinging the cane hard, he laughed.

At the last moment she rolled so that her shoulder took the hit rather than her head. Finding a strength she hadn't known she possessed, she pushed herself up and at him.

Not only was Ezekiel elderly, but he wasn't used to his victims fighting back. He went down with a satisfying thud. Once on the ground, he struggled to get up.

Jack came busting out the door, followed by the sheriff and Rachel. As Jack gathered Sophia into his arms, Sheriff Jones stood Ezekiel up and cuffed him, ignoring the older man's loud protests.

Sophia turned in Jack's arms, wincing at the pain in her legs and shoulder, watching while the sheriff read him his rights and led him inside. After a quick look at Jack and Sophia, Rachel followed the two men, gesturing at Sophia to call for her if she needed her.

Sophia managed a smile, even though she knew she would have some pretty big bruises later.

"Are you okay?" Jack asked, running his hands slowly all over her, his eyes full of concern.

"I think I'll survive," she told him, loving the way he fussed over her. "He got me twice with his cane." She tested out her left leg, then her right, and rolled her shoulder, wincing at the pain. "But I don't think anything is broken."

"I'm glad." He kissed her then. A careful, lingering sort of kiss that contained the hint of something much more powerful to follow later. "I'm sorry I failed you. I should have stayed with you and made sure you were all right."

"You couldn't know." She kissed him this time, loving the taste of him, aware this was the only thing that could banish the pain inflicted by her former fiancé. "Plus, you were excited about the memory stick."

"I am at that." He gazed down at her, his expression serious. "Before we go inside, are you sure you aren't badly hurt? I can take you to get checked out at the ER."

"I'm fine." Smiling up at him, she was struck by how much she wanted her life to be like this forever. Together, with him. She hoped he wanted the same thing, too.

The FBI vehicle pulled up just then. Jack motioned for the two agents to follow him. Once Jack gave them a quick rundown on what was going on, they shut off the engine and did exactly that.

"Did Rachel tell you I was one of the people abducted?" she asked Jack quietly right before they filed into the sheriff's private office.

"No." He bent his head as if to kiss her again, then apparently thought better of it since they had an audience. "We'll make sure and locate your family once this is over."

Her family. Something she'd occasionally longed for growing up, when the lack of a singular close connection had made her ache. The idea that she actually might have a real family out there—a mother and a father, maybe even siblings—filled her with both trepidation and joy.

Once the two FBI agents had viewed the information, they confiscated the memory stick. "Change of plans," one of them announced. "Instead of going out to the compound, we're taking this to the office. Ezekiel can remain in your custody here until we can arrange transfer, after charges are filed."

Though Sheriff Jones appeared disappointed, he nodded. He watched silently as the federal agents took their leave. Only once they'd exited the building did he let out a sigh. "Good thing we made our own copy," he commented, lowering himself into his office chair and peering at his computer.

"I'd like to take a look at the records Rachel found," Jack said. He went around the desk to stand behind the sheriff, gazing over his shoulder at the computer screen. "I need to see if my client's son is listed."

Sophia's shoulder had really started throbbing. She caught Rachel's attention and gestured toward the outside. "Does anyone mind if we go back to the hotel?" she asked.

Immediately, Jack straightened. "Let me walk you."

"That's okay," she protested. "Stay here. Rachel and

I will go together. Since Ezekiel's in custody, there shouldn't be anything to worry about."

Clearly torn, he hesitated.

"Stay." She blew him a kiss. "We'll be fine."

"I'm going to send one of my deputies to escort them," Sheriff Jones interjected. He picked up his desk phone, spoke a few words and a young man wearing a uniform appeared.

With their own armed guard, Sophia and Rachel headed outside.

The records were much more comprehensive than Jack had imagined. When he saw the name Ryan Bartlett appear in a list, he wanted to cheer. Instead he jotted down all of the details. Date of abduction, place and age of child—two. They all matched. This boy—now called Taylor—was not one of the children Jack had met.

The Bartletts' case seemed solved. Even so, he didn't want to notify his clients, not just yet. But he would soon. He imagined that DNA testing would have to be done on a lot of these children as a precaution before matching them up with their families. But with such detailed records available, he felt confident the information would turn out to be accurate.

All of them.

Including Sophia's. As Sheriff Jones scrolled, Jack had him stop when they reached her name. According to the records, Sophia had been abducted twenty-one years ago when she was three. COE seemed to take small children who were between the ages of two and four. Jack tried to keep his professional demeanor, but the enormity and proof hit him like a ton of bricks.

With Sheriff Jones's permission, Jack made detailed

notes about both Ryan Bartlett's information as well as Sophia's. While he couldn't wait to give his clients the happy news, he found his thoughts on Sophia, wondering how she felt knowing she had people out there somewhere. People who still loved her, people who'd welcome her with open arms and laughter and tears.

The FBI phoned an hour later. The sheriff spoke to the agent, saying little on his end. Finally he nodded. "I have men on staff guarding him, but you're completely welcome to send your own, as well. And yes, I can be there in a few minutes."

Once he'd ended the call and placed the phone back in its cradle, he eyed Jack. "They're giving a press conference in thirty minutes and want me to be there. You're welcome to join me. In fact, since you're working an active case, they might even let you make a statement."

"I'd love to, but won't."

"Why not?" Sheriff Jones eyed him.

"Well, even though my business could definitely use the attention, I haven't yet spoken with my clients. I don't want them to find out this way, on the national news."

The sheriff shrugged. "Call them on the way there. Problem solved."

And that was exactly what Jack did. He reached Ted Bartlett, for which he was glad. Through all of this, Ted had been calm and levelheaded while his wife, Janey, had been much more emotional. Yet when Jack gave Ted the news, the other man began to weep. "I can't believe it," he kept repeating. "Thank you. Thank you so much."

"I'm going to be giving a statement in a news conference shortly," Jack told him. "Please let Janey know before then. I don't want her to learn from the news that

Ryan's been found. And we need to make sure he's in safe custody first."

"I will." Ted cleared his throat. "When can we see him? Janey and I will grab the next flight out that way."

He'd expected no less. "Good idea. You might have to wait, though. I'm not sure what the FBI needs to do to process everything. They might want to do DNA tests on the kids to make sure they go back to the right families."

"I'm all for that." Ted's enthusiasm made Jack smile. "I can't believe this is actually happening! I'm going to go call Janey now. I'll text you our flight information."

Once the call had ended, unable to stop grinning, Jack turned to Sheriff Jones. "He's ecstatic."

"Good. You look pretty happy yourself."

As they pulled up at the FBI headquarters in Landon and parked, the sheriff turned in his seat to face him. "This is going to be major news. All these missing kids—some of them grown—reunited with their parents. I'm sure many of them were believed dead. I'm going to give you an opening to say your piece, so seriously prepare something you want to say. Your little private investigation business might just take off after this."

Gratified, Jack thanked the older man. All around him were news vans, some of them local, though many were major affiliates.

"See." Sheriff Jones pointed at the crowd of reporters, several already on-camera. "There you go."

"I'm ready," Jack said. And he was. Shoulders squared, he got out of the vehicle and followed the sheriff inside.

Back at the motel, Sophia was surprised to find Deirdre in her room waiting for her to return. The older woman jumped up from a chair the instant Sophia opened her door.

"There you are. Have you heard anything? Do you have any idea what's going on?"

"Ezekiel escaped and attacked me." Sophia lifted the hem of her dress to show the welt and purpling bruise on her shin. "He got me on the shoulder, too. But he's been arrested now."

Tears filled Deirdre's eyes. "I'm so grateful. I supposed I need to send the women down to press charges?"

"Eventually." Sophia went on to inform Deirdre of the rest. When she finished, Deidre stared, clearly shocked.

"Abducting infants? And children? Why? Why would he do such a thing?"

"That's a good question and one I suspect the authorities will be asking, too."

Deirdre grimaced. "The only possible reason I can think of is he wanted to bring fresh blood into COE. He used to always worry about the bloodlines intermingling too closely." She took a deep breath. "But he's locked up for certain?"

"Yes. And under guard."

"Good." Deirdre twisted her hands together, turning her ring over and over. "I always took pride in the fact that I alone out of all his wives had been given a wedding band instead of a choker. Now, I want to bury it somewhere." She sighed. "What about Thomas?"

"They got him, too. The only one they can't find is Dr. Drew. I'm worried Ezekiel might have killed him since he helped Jack and me escape."

A shadow crossed the first wife's face. "Dr. Drew is a kind man. He used to be one of Ezekiel's best friends. But that changed once Ezekiel decided he was the

Anointed One. His misogynist and sadistic tendencies escalated, especially once he took other wives to abuse. He left the doctor to try to repair the damage he'd done."

Sophia finally dared to ask the question that had been haunting her. "What will happen to all the others?" she asked. "Once Ezekiel and Thomas are gone, how will COE survive?"

"That a good question." Tilting her head, Deirdre considered. "When Ezekiel and I first started it, the Children of Eternity had great intentions. Of course, Thomas and Ezekiel came up with that ridiculous *Volumes of Choice* and everything changed for the worst."

To hear Deidre speak that way over a tenet that Sophia had always been taught was holy felt unsettling, to say the least. But then her actual words sank in. "They *wrote* it? So the *Volumes of Choice* wasn't found in the forest on top of a bluff like it says?"

Shaking her head, Deirdre chuckled. "Nope. They put that in there so everyone would think it was a gift from the heavens."

Tears filled Sophia eyes, stunning her as she realized how so many people had based their entire lives on lies. "They're not used to thinking on their own," Deirdre continued. "They'll need someone to help them find their own way." Her voice grew more animated as she continued. "This is something we could definitely do."

"'We'?" Sophia asked, not comprehending.

"Yes. The wives. Especially me." The last was said calmly, not boastfully. "I more than anyone else know what COE was originally meant to be, what it could become. I can help."

"You don't think one of Ezekiel's sons will try to take over? That's a lot of power up for grabs."

Deirdre's eyes narrowed. "My son is the firstborn.

He's been talking about trying to leave for the last six months. I doubt he'll try anything foolish, but just in case one of the others do, I'll recruit him to help me."

"You truly intend to go back there? It's going to be crazy." And it would. The regular members, people like Sophia's friends and family group, would be in a panic because they wouldn't understand what had happened or why. Those were the ones Sophia wanted to help.

As for the others, those used to more status and power, they'd be engaged in constant battles and jockeying for position. She imagined those had already started. The thought of facing all that insanity made her head hurt.

"Of course." Deirdre eyed her. "Don't you? Now that Ezekiel and Thomas can't hurt us, we can change all of our lives for the better."

Sophia didn't hesitate. "I'm not going back," she said. "I found out I was one of the children abducted and brought into COE. If my parents are still alive, I'd like to meet them. As long as they're open to that," she amended.

"I'm sure they will be." Deirdre's expression softened. "I'm sorry that happened to you."

The door opened. Startled, Sophia jumped. Rachel hurried inside, her expression animated. "Turn on the television," she said, excitement making her voice high. "Some of the others figured out how to do it."

She grabbed a small, black square and pressed the red button marked Power. A few seconds later, they saw Jack and Sheriff Jones and several other law enforcement people.

"Numerous children will be reunited with their parents," Sheriff Jones said. "Please do not contact our office yet, or the FBI. DNA tests will be done to make sure the cult's records are accurate. We will then be contacting the parents of these children."

"When will this occur?" someone asked from the crowd.

"As soon as the tests can be completed," a tall man in a dark suit answered. "We will be gathering samples from both parents and children and will rush these through."

"How did you come to learn that the cult had these children?" someone else asked.

"This man," Sheriff Jones said quickly, speaking before the FBI agent could. "His name is Jack Moreno and he's a private investigator."

Jack stepped forward, explained how he'd been hired, and how he'd been knocked out and woken up inside the cult. "Divine intervention, maybe?" he asked with a rakish grin that made Sophia's heart skip. "I had lots of help from some friends I made inside."

"Those responsible for the abductions have been brought into custody. A hearing will take place tomorrow to determine if bail can be set." The agent took a deep breath. "That's it for now. That concludes our news conference."

Then Jack, Sheriff Jones and the men in dark suits left the room.

When the announcer came on, gushing over the exciting news, Deirdre grabbed the small, black square and turned off the TV.

"Interesting, isn't it?" she asked. "I know the others will have lots of questions. I have answers. Let's go talk with them."

"You go. I'm going to stay here," Sophia said. "I need a shower and a nap."

"I understand." Deirdre turned to Rachel. "You need

to come with me. I want you to hear what I have to say. Everyone, you included, has a decision to make."

On the way back to town, both Jack and Sheriff Jones were quiet, each lost in their own thoughts.

"What do you think will happen to them?" Jack asked. "I got to know a lot of people when I was inside. They're good people."

"Who knows? The compound is registered to a corporation."

"Was COE incorporated?"

"Not that I know of." Sheriff Jones shrugged. "This corporation was formed before the cult came into existence. It's called E&D Development, Inc. Ezekiel and his first wife, Deirdre, are full owners. They must have intended to eventually develop that tract of land. Since my educated guess is that Ezekiel is going away for a long time, I think it all depends on what Deirdre decides to do."

The sheriff dropped Jack off at the motel.

He pushed away his exhaustion and went looking for Sophia. As the elevator doors opened on her floor, he heard women's voices and laughter coming from a room at the end of the hall. Following the sound, he entered the crowded room, searching for Sophia.

"She's not here," Rachel said, materializing at his side. "She wanted a shower and a nap, so she's probably asleep in her room."

"Here," Deidre said, handing him her key card. "I'm planning to sleep here with the others, so you two will have the room to yourself." Then, to Jack's surprise, she winked at him. He grinned and thanked her, turning to go.

Several of the other women noticed him, calling out greetings. He waved and nodded before making a quick exit.

He knocked three times on Sophia's door, trying not to worry when she didn't answer. She might still be in the shower or napping. Finally he used Deirdre's key card to unlock the door. Luckily, Sophia hadn't thought to use the chain.

The dark room meant she'd probably fallen asleep. He thought of where Ezekiel had hit her with his cane and decided against crawling under the covers with her. Instead he went into the bathroom and quietly closed the door before washing up for the night.

When he finished, he removed his shoes and darkened the room before opening the door so he wouldn't wake her. To his surprise, she'd sat up in bed and turned the bedside lamp on.

"Hey," she said softly. "I saw your talk. You did well."

Carefully, he lowered himself to the edge of the bed and kissed her, a quick brush of his mouth against hers. "Thanks. How are you feeling?"

"Sore," she admitted. "But relieved, too. Deirdre's decided she and the others are going back to COE. She's going to try to take over leadership and make the group into what it was supposed to be."

"Really?" But as he thought about it, he realized he wasn't surprised. "What about you?" he asked, trying for nonchalance. "What are you planning to do?"

She didn't speak at first, which scared the hell out of him. When she finally did, her answer wasn't at all what he expected.

"What do you want me to do?" she asked.

"No." The word burst from him. "You can do as you choose now. No one—not even me—has the right to tell you what actions to take. You can make your own decisions, Sophia."

"I'm well aware of that." Fire flashed in her dark eyes. "I'm talking about us, Jack Moreno. It's time for you to tell me the truth. Do you truly care for me, or was that all just to get me to help you leave COE?"

He stared. "I can't believe you just said that. You know how I feel. I've showed you in a thousand different ways."

"Maybe. But, Jack, sometimes a girl needs to hear it, too." Hope shining from her face, she watched him, waiting.

Had he never truly told her? He thought back, trying to remember, before realizing what he had or hadn't done didn't matter. She needed to know now.

"I love you, Sophia." He held her gaze. "With all of my heart. And if you'll have me, I'd like to spend the rest of my life with you by my side." And then he held his breath, eager to hear her response.

"Was that a proposal, Jack?" she asked, a smile playing around the corners of her lips.

"Yes." He bit out the single word, worried because he'd just realized she'd never told him she loved him, either.

"Then my answer is yes, of course." Her smile became a grin so full of love and joy that his breath caught in his chest.

"Good." Though he ached to kiss her, he didn't. Not yet. "Sophia, sometimes a guy needs to hear the words, too."

She laughed then, putting her arms around his neck

and drawing him close, careful to avoid her injured shoulder. "I love you, my Jack. Today and tomorrow and forever and always. And I want to spend the rest of my life with you, as well."

He claimed her lips then, kissing her until they both were breathless.

"Come to bed," she invited him, pulling back the covers just enough for him to see the huge, purple and yellow bruise on her shoulder. "Come to bed and prove it to me."

Regretfully, he shook his head, shifting his body to hide his arousal. "I can't take the chance of hurting you," he told her. "Let me see your leg."

"It looks bad," she admitted, carefully lifting the sheet to reveal another horrible bruise. "There's a lot of swelling. I couldn't get up to go get ice, which is what I need to do."

"Put your dress back on," he ordered. "I'm taking you to the ER to have that looked at."

She didn't move. "I thought you said nobody, including you, could tell me what to do," she teased.

"Okay." He took a deep breath. "Please, Sophia. We need to get that taken care of and make sure there's no serious injury. The quicker we can get you fixed up, the sooner we can make love. And—" he added the last, just in case that wasn't incentive enough "—you can't wear a wedding dress with your shoulder looking like that."

His comments made her laugh. She held out her hand and he helped her up off the bed and into her dress. She winced a couple of times, even gasped when the material of her dress settled around her shoulders. "Let's go," she said. "I've got a wedding to plan."

The hospital doctor insisted on X-rays and then, once he'd ascertained that nothing had been broken, wanted to file a police report. He kept eyeing Jack as if he thought Jack had done this, but a quick call to the sheriff had cleared things up.

When Sophia told the doctor Jack had been shot in the leg, Jack was examined, too. But Dr. Drew had done a fine job of stitching up the wound.

In the end, she was released with a prescription for painkillers and some anti-inflammatories, and was told to rest for at least twenty-four hours.

"I'm glad we're both going to be all right," she told Jack on the way to the car.

"We will," he answered. "As long as I have you by my side."

"In all my entire life, I don't think I've ever been this nervous," Sophia declared four weeks later, smoothing down the seed-pearl-encrusted, formfitting white gown.

Rachel laughed, hugging her carefully before handing her the veil. "You said that when Jack was taking you to meet your parents for the first time," she reminded her. "This little old ceremony can't be nearly as nerve-racking as that."

"Want to bet?"

"Sophia, you have everything you always wanted. You're about to marry a man you love and who loves you back. You found the family you were always missing, and they clearly adore you. You should be celebrating rather than stressing."

Slowly, Sophia nodded. Rachel was right and her words lightened her mood.

"You're right," she admitted. "Instead of worrying about tripping and falling or tearing my dress, I need to focus on what really matters."

A few minutes later a beaming Deirdre knocked on the door. "They're about to begin," she announced. "I'd honestly forgotten how much fun a normal, traditional wedding could be, even if it's not at a church like the Sanctuary."

Deirdre had returned to the compound, along with half of the former residents, to begin the long process of healing. Other children—Theodore, Benjamin and Samantha among them, had also been reunited with their parents, and some adults had begun the wide-eyed process of learning about the outside world. Dr. Drew had been found in hiding and was beginning his own recovery.

Cassandra, Enalia and Hallie entered, giggling like schoolgirls. They grabbed Deirdre and Rachel and hurried away, since the wedding party would enter the room first.

The ceremony was being held in a beautiful, old reception hall that had once been a saloon and now specialized in weddings. Sheriff Jones had booked it, refusing reimbursement.

"Are you ready?" a deep, masculine voice asked. Ralph Edwards, her birth father, waited outside the door. He'd been thrilled when Sophia had asked him to walk her down the aisle.

As long as she lived, she'd never forget how she'd felt inside meeting him and her birth mother, Sharon. They'd all cried, Sophia even more when she'd learned they'd been searching tirelessly for her for over twenty-two years. They'd known she was alive, Sharon had exclaimed, smiling tenderly through her tears. Not once had they even allowed themselves to consider the possibility that she wasn't. She and Sharon even looked alike, a fact that bemused Sophia.

"I'm ready," she said, blinking back tears as she took his arm.

As they walked down a long hallway, music began to play. She lifted her head, taking the measured steps she'd practiced, on her way to begin her new life with the man she loved.

* * * * *

If you loved this suspenseful romance, look out for Karen Whiddon's next book, available Spring 2018!

And be sure to check out Karen's previous books:

THE TEXAN'S RETURN
RUNAWAY COLTON
"Claiming Caleb" in
ROCK-A-BYE RESCUE
TEMPTATION OF DR. COLTON

Available now wherever
Harlequin Romantic Suspense books
and ebooks are sold!

SPECIAL EXCERPT FROM

(H) HARLEQUIN®

ROMANTIC suspense

A murder, a family feud, a missing suspect—and a couple who can't deny their attraction. Despite having exact opposite life goals, Carson Gage and Serena Colton can't resist each other. And when a murderer comes after Serena and her baby, Carson is the only one who can save them!

Read on for a sneak preview of
COLTON BABY RESCUE
by USA TODAY *bestselling author*
Marie Ferrarella, the first story in
THE COLTONS OF RED RIDGE *continuity.*

"Just what is it that you want me to do?"

Serena threw her hands up, angry and exasperated. "I don't know," she cried, walking back around to the front of the building. *"Something!"*

"I am doing something," Carson shot back. "I'm trying to find the person who killed my brother," he reminded Serena.

From what she could see, all he was doing was spinning his wheels, poking around on her ranch. "Well, you're not going to find that person here—and you're not going to find Demi here, either," she told him for what felt like the umpteenth time, knowing that no matter what he said, her cousin was still the person he was looking for.

"If you don't mind, I'd like to check that out for myself," Carson said, dismissing her protest.

"Yes, I do mind," she retorted angrily. "I mind this constant invasion of our privacy that you've taken upon yourself to commit by repeatedly coming here and—"

As she was railing at him, out of the corner of his eye he saw Justice suddenly becoming alert. Rather than the canine fixing his attention on Serena and the loud dressing down she was giving Carson, the German shepherd seemed to be looking toward another one of the barns that contained more of the hands' living quarters.

At this time of day, the quarters should be empty. Even so, he intended to search them on the outside chance that this was where Demi was hiding.

Something had gotten the highly trained canine's attention. Was it Demi? Had she come here in her desperation only to have one of the hands see her and subsequently put in a call to the station? Was she hiding here somewhere?

"What is it, Justice? What do you—?"

He got no further with his question.

The bone-chilling crack of a gun—a rifle by the sound of it—being discharged suddenly shattered the atmosphere. Almost simultaneously, a bullet whizzed by them, so close that he could almost feel it disturb the air.

Find out who's shooting at Carson and Serena in
COLTON BABY RESCUE by Marie Ferrarella,
available January 2018 wherever
Harlequin® Romantic Suspense books and ebooks are sold.

www.Harlequin.com

LOVE
Harlequin
romance?

Join our Harlequin community to share your thoughts and connect with other romance readers!

Be the first to find out about promotions, news, and exclusive content!

Sign up for the Harlequin e-newsletter and download a free book from any series at **www.TryHarlequin.com**

CONNECT WITH US AT:

Harlequin.com/Community

 Facebook.com/HarlequinBooks

Twitter.com/HarlequinBooks

Instagram.com/HarlequinBooks

Pinterest.com/HarlequinBooks

ReaderService.com

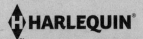

**ROMANCE WHEN
YOU NEED IT**

HSOCIAL2017